SALTWATER CURES

ORCA COVE SERIES BOOK ONE

JEN FLANAGAN

SERENITY ENDEAVORS PRESS

Saltwater Cures

Copyright © 2023 by Jen Flanagan

First Edition: June 2023

This edition was first published in 2023.

Cover design: Haley Tenney

Editor: Kaylin, Happy Ever Author

ISBN: 978-1-961501-00-3 (eBook)

ISBN: 978-1-961501-01-0 (Paperback)

Published by: Serenity Endeavors Press

jenflanaganbooks.com

Acknowledgements

Where do I even begin?

I have so many people to thank with this book. First of all, to my sister and biggest fan, who reads everything I write, almost as fast as I write it and gives great advice. You're literally the best sister a person could ever hope for. My husband, fighting for first place at biggest fan, who also reads everything I write, listens to all my plot thoughts, and has a lot to say about the men in the book. He helps me give them the right 'voice' and gives endless love and support. Finally, to Sydney and Jen, who helped me fix a few description and plot issues.

Also, to everyone in my support group, friends, and family who have encouraged and helped me along the way. I couldn't have done it without you.

To my readers, thanks for sticking with me on my first series outside of Detective Malone. I hope you enjoy this introduction to Orca Cove and the paranormal twist!

CONTENTS

CHAPTER 1

Cold rain pelted down around Nick Ryan as he trudged away from his truck and across the pebbled beach. He pulled the bag he was carrying closer to him, tucking it partially under his open jacket to keep it as dry as possible. It was all he could do in this weather.

Thunder cracked down closer than expected, momentarily drowning out the crashing waves to his right. Raising his head, he searched the sky for lightning, finding it ahead of him, towards his new home. The thought of his fireplace sent a shiver of anticipation through him, anxious to get back into dry clothes.

A body crashed into him, bare arms and legs flailing about to retain balance. Shocked, he dropped the duffel bag, catching the arms of the soaking-wet woman who'd run into him, appearing out of the water.

"What the?" The words were taken from his mouth, the wind carrying the sound far away.

She clutched his arms, her eyes sparked, and her mouth opened in silent laughter. She ran a hand over her face, clearing it of rain.

He looked towards the water and back to her, finally noticing the tan strapless bathing suit she wore. Not a mermaid then, he told himself, chiding his imagination. Although, who would blame him on a night like this? Even on this spring evening, the water had to be forty to fifty degrees. It would be extremely cold without a wetsuit.

"Are you okay?" he tried again, but it was pointless over the howling wind.

Another crack of thunder erupted from the sky above them. Shocked, they tightened their hold on each other's arms as they searched the clouds. The flash of lightning was closer the next time, illuminating the water droplets on her eyelashes and the light blue of her cold lips. A jolt ran through him, a strange connection at the sight of her. Her long hair hung wet, its curly strands plastered to her face. He moved to hold her closer, to try to keep her warm, keenly aware of the mysterious woman wrapped in his embrace.

Breaking their bond, she took an unsteady step back, clutching her arms across her chest. He could see her trembling from the cold. The corner of her mouth kicked up in a playful smirk, then she whirled around and ran up the shoreline, long bare legs kicking up sand and rocks. He had to silently command his feet to stay where they were, the urge to follow was so strong.

She paused only momentarily near the grass line to bend down to gather a blanket, then disappeared into the night.

It took him a minute to recover from the shock, finally remembering his neglected bag at his feet. Panic soaking in, he reclaimed it, holding it tightly to himself, his steps faster as he headed back towards the grass line and the parking lot where his truck waited.

Willa Daniels woke up the next morning exactly where she ended up last night, on the floor in front of her couch, still wrapped in thick blankets. That was strange; she never fell asleep in the living room. She frowned at the fog in her mind. It felt cobwebby and slow. Luckily, the candle on her coffee table had burned out safely at some point in the night. Her mug of tea, almost entirely full, now sat cold.

Shrugging the blankets off, she reached a hand up to her still-damp hair, digging her fingers deep into the curls in an effort to shake them out so they could fully dry. Her strawberry-blonde hair fluffed up haphazardly. She'd try to tame it later.

With a sigh, she bent to pick up her mug with one hand, and rubbed her eye with the other, trying to clear away the last dregs of sleep. That had to be all it was. The cold swim must have zapped her strength. The storm hadn't helped. When the lightning started, they got out as quickly as they could, but it sure seemed like it was striking the water. She shivered involuntarily. They lucked out. But who would have guessed? It rained a lot in Orca Cove, but thunderstorms weren't as frequent.

The water on the Hood Canal was still now, she noticed, looking out the double windows of her living room. Calm and deep blue. Her little one-bedroom condo was right on the coast in a long building, so each unit could overlook the cove. It was beautiful and an easy way to connect to life in the Pacific Northwest. Close to Seattle, but far enough outside the Emerald City for some peace and quiet.

Padding over to her kitchen, she clicked on the electric kettle, dumping out the contents of her mug and giving it a quick wash. She rifled through the many containers of loose-leaf teas on the small bookshelf between her kitchen and living room, selecting echinacea, warming ginger, and astragalus root, just in case her immune system needed it after being exposed to the elements the night before. Her hand hovered over the wakame, a seaweed she had foraged the weekend before, known for its high levels of iron, manganese, and other vitamins. She could probably use the extra energy to clear her brain. She added a generous pinch of ginseng for circulation to round out her tea.

Piling her blankets back onto her couch, she made her way to her bedroom, pulling on a long, embroidered wool cardigan that was practically a blanket with arms. She was still fighting away the chill from last night. She poured the now boiling water over the herbs in her tea infuser and stuffed her feet into a pair of boots, leaving them unlaced as she took her steeping tea out to the back deck.

Leaning against her wood railing, she scanned the coastline for anything washed up on shore from the storm.

A long, dark mass far off to the right caught her eye. At first, it looked like a large tree branch, driftwood not yet bleached by the sun. But the soft roundness of it made her think more of an otter. No, not quite that small. A sea lion maybe. They often made their way on shore for the afternoon sun, but not typically at this time of day.

Shaking her head again to try to clear it, she sat down on her Adirondack chair. She must not have gotten enough sleep last night.

She took a sip of her tea. It tasted especially good this morning. But then again, hot tea always tasted good first thing in the morning.

The ping of her phone sounded from inside. Sliding open her door, she headed back in, sipping more tea.

"You okay this morning?" her friend Nell had texted.

"Yes, a little tired, but taking an easy morning," she answered. That was sweet of her friend. Nell had always had the habit of mothering the rest of them. She sipped her tea, slowly waking up, then texted more. "You doing okay?"

"Yes," the answering text came. "I had a hard time waking up this morning. Didn't even make it past my couch last night."

That was strange. Both of them not making it to bed?

"Weird. Me too. The rug in front of my couch, though, for me."

Three dots appeared to show Nell was texting back. Then they disappeared. Willa waited, drinking her tea. The dots resumed.

"Shelby and Maggie too."

What?

"And Duke?" she texted, asking about the last member of the group that took the memorial dip in the channel the night before.

"No answer yet."

Finishing her tea, she wandered back to the deck, looking out onto the cove. So quiet, so still after last night's storm. Cool, fresh air graced her cheeks.

A dorsal fin broke the glassy surface. Willa cocked her head to watch the water. It was black. Could it be? A black and white back broke the surface, confirming her suspicions. They got an unusual number of orcas in their cove. No one knew why, but it was still always a treat to see one.

The orca's blunt nose rose from the water, and it seemed to acknowledge her. For a moment, it seemed like they were looking right at each other. A shiver ran through her, and she tugged her sweater close around her, her mind now completely awake and running at full speed. Even faster than normal. It was like she had recharged herself. She considered her empty mug. The wakame had seriously rejuvenated her.

Turning back towards the water, the orca was gone. She traced the surface for any signs of it, or other sea life.

A seagull had landed on the dark heap down the beach, picking at it. Discomfort pricked along the back of her neck. Not a sea lion sunning itself then, something dead. Hopefully not a sea lion. The dark shadow formed a plaid pattern. Pieces clicked together in her now clear mind. The meager contents in her stomach tumbled. That wasn't something from the ocean. It was a body.

Spinning off the back deck, she launched herself down the stairs leading to the beach, her boots pulling at her feet as they sank into the sand and pebbles. She cursed at herself for not taking the time to tie them. She raced across the sand until she stood over the body, out of breath but otherwise feeling healthy and full of adrenaline.

The corpse of a middle-aged black man lay on the beach before her. His opened eyes and mouth appeared slightly shocked, as though staring sightlessly into the clouds. She knew better than to touch him, even though she wanted to cover him to protect him from the gulls.

It was then she noticed the dark brownish-red spot staining the front of his flannel shirt jacket, disrupting the blue and green plaid. Willa whirled and heaved into the sand.

"You're sure you didn't touch the body?" the chief of police asked gruffly, his hands on his knees where he leaned over the dead body. She'd known him all her life, having grown up in the cove. "You didn't try to resuscitate him or anything?"

"Warner." Willa cocked her head. "He's obviously beyond saving."

"You tried to put that salve on my razor burn last year." He itched at his freshly shaved neck, still speckled with small red bumps.

"Yeah. And it would have helped." She crossed her arms.

"It's razor burn. It just needs some aftershave."

"I'm glad that's working out for you." She smiled sweetly. There was no sense in trying to help people who weren't ready to be helped.

"I'm just sayin'," he muttered. "Not everything needs-"

"I didn't touch the body." She cut him off. "I waved the gulls away, ran inside, and called you."

"Well, okay then." Straightening, he leaned toward one of his deputy officers. "Ronnie, go get the box of gloves from my truck."

"Yessir." Ronnie ran off.

"Did you see or hear anything strange last night?" Warner regarded her.

"You mean over that storm?" Willa chuckled.

"Yeah, it was quite a doozy. Came out of nowhere too. It's a good thing the body is so far up the shoreline, or it would have gotten pulled into the cove. Were you on the beach last night at all?"

"Yes," she hesitated. "The girls and I, and Duke, were out last night."

"I didn't realize you all were still hanging out." His eyes cast downward. "It's nearly been a year since I've seen you all-"

His voice trailed off.

"Well." She stuffed her hands in the pockets of her sweater. "Exactly. It's been almost a year. And last night was his birthday. It was important."

"I can hardly believe it's been that long. Shame. How's Nell doing?"

"Pretty good. Considering."

"What time was this?"

"Eight, maybe?"

"Walk me through it."

"Like you said, the storm came out of nowhere. We all hurried off the beach.""All?"

"Yes. I was the last off. It was a beautiful storm." She grinned freely. "Wild and unpredictable."

"Did you see anything?"

Willa thought back to the dark stranger she had literally run into the night before. His hair had been nearly as black as the dead man's, with a similar body type, tall and thinly muscular. Had it not been for the darker skin, she'd have thought it was the same person. If she told Warner that he had been on the beach, that he'd been walking from the very direction where they were standing right now, he'd rush off and arrest him on the spot. As soon as he could find him, that was.

11

Sure, she thought the best of people, but she honestly didn't think he murdered this man. Call it a gut feeling, but she was somehow certain. Her brows furrowed. "I saw a lot of waves and rain, Warner."

Huffing, the older policeman turned to meet Ronnie, tugging on his gloves in frustration.

She hadn't lied, exactly.

CHAPTER 2

"How are you?" Willa studied Nell's body language as she walked up the steps to the outdoor bar and tables of The Wild Cafe, its back deck separating them from the main storefront. It was only a few buildings down from her place. It was aptly named; you couldn't get any more wild or fresh. It sat on the water and was next door to Gil's Market and Marina, which had the freshest meats and produce in the area. Nell, the cafe's owner and head chef, got her fish straight from local fishermen. Same-day catch.

"I'm doing okay." Nell frowned, dropping the cloth she was wiping down the tables with. She scrubbed her face with a hand. "Still a little groggy, but okay. Wait! What about you? Did Warner come? What did they find?"

Willa smiled, handing her one of the teas she had tucked into a basket hanging from her arm.

"Nothing yet. Ronnie bagged it after the medical examiner, well, *examined* it."

"How strange." Nell sipped the travel mug, made a face, coughed, then took another, much smaller sip. "A dead body in Orca Cove? What are the odds?"

They both stared out over the water. It was one of the most peaceful little towns along the Hood Canal. Hardly where you'd expect to run across a murder.

"What are we looking for, more people dumb enough to swim in the icy water?" Shelby spoke from behind the two women, causing them to jump. She grinned and slapped Willa on the shoulder, her nearly black mini ponytail bobbing. "Just teasin' ya."

Willa rolled her eyes and reached into her basket to select another mug and handed it to her. "How are you feeling?" She raised a shoulder and dropped it loosely. "Still foggy, but the pot of coffee helped. What's this?"

"Tea. It'll help with that."

Shelby took a sniff, then a sip. Her mouth twisted down in distaste. "That's terrible."

"It's not too bad," Nell said.

"Where's Maggie?" Willa asked, not bothered or surprised by Shelby's dislike of her tea. She pulled out another travel mug, having brought one for the final female in their group, Nell's waitress. There was one more for Duke, just in case, but she didn't see him on the marina or on his big boat docked at its slip near the end.

"I'm here." Maggie walked out the back door of the restaurant, carrying two large glass containers with dispensers full of orange juice and water with lemon and herbs, and set them on the bar counter. She adjusted them in place, then faced the group, the dark circles evident under her bright blue eyes. "What's up?"

"Here." Willa handed her a tea, then paused to put a supportive hand on her shoulder. "That should help."

"Thanks." Her eyes brightened for a moment at the gesture, and she took a hearty sip. She paused, then slowly took another.

"She's too polite to say it sucks," Shelby said, letting out a hearty laugh then, wincing, she put a hand to her head and sat down.

"You know," Nell frowned, peering at the hole in the travel mug as though she could see the tea inside. "I'm actually feeling a lot better."

Maggie took another thoughtful sip.

Shelby considered hers. "Ah, screw it."

She took the lid off hers, upended it, gulped down the contents, and handed the empty mug back to Willa. She launched into a full-body shudder, ending with her tongue hanging out.

"That's one way to do it." Willa tucked the mug back into her basket.

Shelby jogged over to the bar, filled an empty glass with the flavored water, and downed it.

"Did you ever hear back from Duke?" Willa asked Nell.

She shook her head. "And I have no idea why we all passed out last night. It's bizarre."

"Probably we were just zapped from the cold water," Shelby said, rejoining them.

"Cryotherapy is a thing, you know. People use it to help with circulation and healing," Willa said. She'd just been reading up on the treatment, trying to see if it was something she could use. She helped some of the townspeople with salves for arthritis and sore muscles, but was open to anything new that helped.

"Huh. I've never heard about that. Sounds like you've got too much time on your hands alone in that apartment. People get sick from being in the rain all the time."

Maggie watched the interaction silently, still sipping her tea.

"Rain doesn't make people sick. It chills them, making them more susceptible to catching things. It's an immune system thing."

"Same thing." Shelby waved a hand. "Maybe that's what happened."

"To all four of us?"

"Unlikely, yes, but it happened."

"How are you *really* doing?" Willa asked Nell again. She searched her eyes for more than her physical well-being.

Her friend's eyes cast downward. She tilted her head. "I'm doing okay."

Last night would have been her late husband Gary's birthday and almost a year since they lost him. It had taken a significant toll on the group of friends. Instead of banding together in their grief, they all had mourned separately, spending less and less time together as they slowly grew apart.

Their sunset dip had been something Gary did on his birthday every year, just to remember what it felt like to be alive. He had always been so bold and so full of life. It had made his death even harder. Willa had suggested the nighttime dip to honor Gary, but also to bring them back together. He would have wanted it.

"Did they find out who the body was?" Maggie said finally.

"What body?" Shelby stopped. "Who else died?"

Maggie's eyes jumped to Nell, but she just took a deep breath and tucked a longer strand of her blonde pixie cut behind an ear.

"There was a body on the beach this morning." Willa pointed towards her place. Well, it was technically Shelby's building, one of the many properties she owned in town. Willa just rented the unit. From this distance, you could see the yellow tape stretched between stakes in the sand and rock.

"I didn't even notice on my way in."

"Willa found it," Nell said, setting out salt and pepper shakers on the tables.

"Oh, shit. Are you okay?" Shelby broke away from the scene and focused on Willa. "Yeah, I'm fine. And no." She turned to Maggie to answer her original question. "They don't know who it was."

"Whadya know?" Shelby said, stretching. Her arms went up high into the air and her face contorted. "I'm feeling much better. Maybe I will take that run after all."

One side of Willa's mouth kicked up in amusement.

"It coulda been the coffee, though. Mighta just took it a while to kick in." Shelby cut her eyes towards Willa, ribbing her. "Just sayin'."

"I'm going to go down to see if Duke's home." Willa ignored the friendly jab, inwardly glad to hear it. It felt like old times. She picked up Nell's empty mug.

Maggie downed the rest of her tea in Shelby's fashion and hurried to hand it over. "Thanks."

"Let us know if you find out anything," Nell said.

"Will do." She lifted a hand and headed towards the marina, her eyes searching for Duke's tall frame.

Willa made it all the way down the boat ramp without any sign of Duke, but she could see his boat from here and if it was there, he wasn't too far. He made a living being a courier; he met cargo ships in Seattle from overseas and distributed them as instructed. Often those shipments were personal items of high value that another courier then met him at the Port of Seattle to pick up.

Duke was easier to do business with than the large cargo ships. Safety was an issue, too. But then, he'd been on his own most of his life. He'd had to learn to use his brains and brawn to make it. And he'd found a way to make it lucrative and legal. Well, lucrative anyway. No one was sure how legal it all was.

But by this time of the morning, you could normally find him topside working on the large boat, or at the very least relaxing on the large open deck with a cup of coffee.

Crossing over the roped-off entry point, she stepped down the few stairs onto the wooden slats of the deck.

"Duke? It's Willa," she called out. "Hello?"

Approaching the door, she knocked, peering in the window. She knocked again. Still no sign of him. It was a retired Navy fishing trawler, steel, with a cabin below deck that he lived in full-time.

Trailing a hand over the back of a metal chair, she circled the table he kept on the deck and walked towards another, smaller seating area. As old and eclectic as the boat was, it had a certain allure to it, its history nodding at both the adventurous and the mystical.

The seagulls cried overhead, adding to the otherworldliness.

With a scrape of her heel, she spun back to the stairs. Maybe he went into town early. But before she made it another foot, she saw him standing in his open doorway, hands tucked into the pockets of his blue jeans. His flannel shirt appeared tossed on, unbuttoned. He let out a huge yawn.

"Do you need something?" Duke scratched his chin, in need of a good shave. His eyes were red, as though in need of sleep.

"Did you just wake up?" She headed over to inspect him.

"Yeah." He ran a hand through his dark hair, pulling it from where it was tucked behind his ears. It framed his face, falling almost to his chin. He squinted, confused. "What time is it?"

"Nearly ten."

"What?" His eyebrows drew together in surprise. He spun to check the clock on his controls, steadying himself on the door jamb.

"Did you wake up in a strange spot after last night?"

He just cocked his head, still blinking to clear his eyes. "Are you okay, Willa?"

"Yes, thanks." She tried again. "I woke up passed out on the rug in front of my couch."

"That's- odd."

"It is. So did everyone else. Not their rugs, but couches, chairs, wherever they sat down last night."

"Huh." He was quiet for a moment, watching the gulls overhead. "I didn't sit down anywhere when I got home. I went right to bed."

"Oh."

"But I did kinda fall right into it. You talked us into getting into that freezing water late last night. And then it stormed like the devil." He grinned at her as he indicated the water. "Gary woulda liked that. I'd guess we were all exhausted when we got home."

She handed him the final tea from her basket.

"What's this?" He lifted it.

"Tea. It'll help clear the fog."

"The fog?" He paused. "Thanks."

He sipped her brew.

"It's the wakame, some people don't like the seaweed taste," she said preemptively.

"I like anything from the ocean." He tipped the mug in salute. "What else is bothering you?"

"Oh." Willa cast a glance toward the beach. "I found a dead body on the beach this morning."

"A dead body?" he said quietly, watching her.

She nodded. "Just down from my place. I saw it from my back deck. He was shot."

He took a long drink. "Warner find anything?"

"No, and he didn't have an ID on him, either."

"Shit." Duke pushed away from his doorway, walking out onto the deck in his bare feet, and led her to a bench in the corner. "How bad was it?"

"The gulls hadn't gotten to him yet." Willa tried to wave off his concern, but the fact that she had found a dead body was starting to creep up on her. "There wasn't a lot of blood."

"There isn't always." He sat down across from her on another bench. "No one recognized him?"

She shook her head, searching the wood grain in front of her for answers.

"What else did you see?" he asked.

Her eyes shot up to meet his. How did he know? Gulls sounded overhead again, this time as though commanding her to share what she was holding back. She probably could tell Duke. He knew how to keep a secret. Rumor was, he was a smuggler. Or he used to be. No one really knew.

"I know you, Willa." He cracked a side grin. "Maybe not as well as the rest of them, but I know you. And I know people."

They had been friends for a long time. He had only been a couple of years ahead of her in school. And now he was like a brother to her. A slightly estranged brother. But they were working on that.

"There was a man-" she started. Heat crept up the back of her neck, even in the cool morning breeze.

"When?"

"On the beach last night." Her feet stretched out in front of her, and she leaned back. The wooden slats provided support. "After I came out of the water."

"You got out last. I should have checked to make sure you made it off the beach safely."

"I live on the beach. Don't be silly."

"It was a raging storm. We were all soaking wet and freezing. I shouldn't have been in such a hurry to get back home."

She raised her shoulder. "I was fine. Nothing happened. I ran into him."

"Literally?""Literally." A soft breath blew out followed by a smile at the memory.

It had been so cold, but the wind was whipping up all around her and she felt so alive. It was intoxicating. Then she ran into *him*. She could nearly feel the electric current that zinged through them when their gazes locked under the lightning-lit sky. It was magical, the stuff of dreams.

"Woah, you've got it bad." Duke chuckled.

"But that was it. I ran away after that."

"And you have no idea who he was."

"None at all. He's just a mysterious stranger I ran into on the beach. He's tall, with dark hair, like Shelby's. Ice-blue eyes."

"And you found a body the next morning. Same area?"

How did he know? "Yes."

"And you didn't tell Warner about the man."

"No."

"Well, this just got interesting." He rubbed his chin. "And that tea is amazing. I'm gonna need more of that."

She laughed. "Stop by the yoga studio later today. I'll mix up a jar of it for you."

"Done."

"You're not going to tell Warner, are you?""No, but I will be looking into your mysterious stranger. Get a feel for him myself. See if I can get a read on him other than tall, dark, and handsome." He winked at her.

"I didn't say handsome."

He blew out air in a snort. "When's your yoga class?"

"You going to join? You do look creaky." It was her turn to tease. Then her face went white. "Oh no! I've got to run. I'm going to be late."

She jumped from her seat, forgetting her basket, and leaped over the rope back onto the dock, her long legs eating the distance.

"Great class, Willa." A woman stopped next to Willa an hour later, her electric purple leggings and hot pink 80s tunic top identifying her as Izzy, the local boutique shop owner. "You tried to murder me yet again, but I prevailed!"

"Thanks, Izzy, but I still feel bad for being late." Willa knelt to spray and wipe down her yoga mat. "You could have people waiting on you."

"You were ten minutes late at most," the mid-fifties woman reassured, rolling up her mat. The colorful bangles lining each arm sent a pleasant jangle throughout the studio.

Most of her morning classes were older women who didn't have a work schedule to work around, but Izzy did. She closed up shop on Tuesdays and Fridays to get a class in at her lunch hour.

"Get over yourself. Pissed-off customers can get over themselves too," Izzy continued, winking at her to let her know she was kidding. "Besides, if they're shopping at my store, they've come to expect the unusual."

It was true, her shop was just as wild and eclectic as the eccentric owner, spanning tastes and decades. It was a blast.

"Yeah, we didn't mind the wait. We just gossiped and talked about the body on the beach," another older woman replied.

They had descended upon Willa when she arrived, out of breath, hoping for any juicy tidbit. She hadn't had much to share, much to their disappointment.

"But I probably should head back." Izzy leaned forward conspiratorially. "It's one of my regulars' birthday tomorrow and her husband will have forgotten until she calls at lunch to find out what they're doing tonight."

"I don't know how you remember everyone's birthday, Izzy." Willa shook her head. "You could give him a heads up."

"Nah, it's more fun seeing him panic." Izzy cackled, bending to grab her water bottle. She waved. "See you ladies later!"

Willa stood, rolling up her own mat. "I'm sorry I didn't bring your salve in today, Loris. I didn't have time this morning."

She'd told her the day before she was out, so that meant Mary, an elderly woman who lived further in town, was out too. She'd never tell Willa when she was out, but she seemed relieved when she showed up with another jar. Mary was hard to read. "That's alright, dear! Your morning was busy, what with all that business on the beach. Besides, I'm doing much better after class." The woman in black bent her knees and went up and down a few times. "Loosened me right up!"

"Well, I'll get it mixed up and bring it by your house later."

"That would be lovely. I'll get to see you twice today, then." She patted Willa on her back and made her way out.

CHAPTER 3

E ggs sizzled in the skillet Nick dropped them in.
Grease from the bacon already in the skillet bubbled
up and over their edges, curling them and forming round
pockets of hot air.

Watching the food cook, he leaned on the counter and
sent a paranoid glance towards his detached workshop
across the yard. It was safe there, tucked behind a wall, he
reassured himself.

The workshop was the first thing he built when he
bought the place. At that time, he hadn't known he'd have
the need for a hidden stash spot. But habits were hard to
break, he thought, pulling thick slices of toast from his
toaster oven and shaking his cast iron pan to slide two
perfectly cooked sunny-side-up eggs over them. A crack of

salt and pepper and they were ready. It was a late breakfast. He'd slept in longer than normal.

But then again, was it ever too late for eggs?

With a sigh, he sat down at his kitchen bar to eat. He wasn't happy with how he left things with Jimmy last night. Scraping his knife and fork across his plate, he took a bite. But he'd get over it. He'd have to. It was all he could do at the moment.

After cleaning up, he headed back outside and across his lawn to his workshop. Flicking the lights on at the breaker, he reviewed his space. It was almost as large as the main cabin, but he easily spent more time here than he did in the primitive living space.

A few more orders had come in for charcuterie boards and handcrafted boxes. He'd need to package them up and mail them out, then build his supply back up. The charcuterie boards were selling better than the boxes. Maybe six more of those; he set some lumber aside. He'd also been interested in trying his hand at epoxy. One of those waterfall tables would be fun to build; his lip kicked out in thought. It might sell well online, too.

He tucked his hands in the pockets of his flannel jacket. The workshop was finished nicer than the cabin, too. He had added insulation in between the stud walls and the metal siding, then closed them up with sheets of OSB, polyed them to a shiny-smooth surface, and hand-cut trim boards to finish the area out.

He had left a set of trim boards loosely attached. It was never a bad idea to have a place to conceal things. Last night, all he had to do was gently coerce them back out with a pry bar. Then, he unscrewed the panel of OSB from the wall. It was a perfect hiding spot. His eyes scanned over the trim boards; they were smooth. He had worried he hadn't gotten everything put back together well at the late hour last night, but they didn't appear different than the rest, not obvious in any way. And it was a dark corner he used for scrap lumber. He nodded, setting his mind at ease. The bag was safe. For now. Hopefully, it wouldn't have to be there long.

He'd bought the old hunting cabin as-is. The trim boards in there were rough-cut lumber. He scratched his head, considering. He still had some scrap lumber from the workshop and he could probably just plane and refinish some of the existing trim boards in the cabin. Between the two, he should have enough. Already half into the trim job in his head, he pulled his pry bar and his hammer off the wall where they hung and headed into the cabin to see how much wood he could salvage. The post office didn't close until five. The orders could wait.

There was no line at the post office when he got there a few hours later. It had been difficult pulling himself away from the pile of baseboards currently in his workshop to refinish, but it was better than getting here during the rush hour. Too many people. He was getting so he enjoyed not having to deal with them on a daily basis. Those eight-to-fivers, in a hurry to get home on a Friday night. Nick was relieved not to be one of those people anymore. No way could he do that again.

Which was why he was standing in line, mailing what he had sold online. He had to keep his customers happy and keep money coming in. He'd saved up a nice little nest egg, and life was cheaper out here on the Hood Canal than in Seattle, but still, money was a necessity.

At least now work was on his terms.

Bracing his packages on one hip, he pulled the door open and noticed a man jog across the street and up the ramp to the post office. He paused to hold it open for him before continuing inside.

"That's either a lot of care packages or Christmas is coming early for someone," the man laughed, tossing his slightly too long brown hair. He tucked an errant end behind one ear.

Another overly friendly resident of Orca Cove. Nick bit back a sigh and pasted on a polite face. "Just some orders I'm mailing out."

"Orders?" The man leaned in, interested. "Do you make stuff?"

He nodded, edging forward towards the rat maze of the post office line. When the man's attention stayed on him, he reluctantly added, "I'm a woodworker."

It still felt odd saying that. But good, too.

"No shit. That's cool!" The man bobbed his head, following him through the maze of ropes. "You must be new in town. I don't think I've seen you around before."

He hesitated. The man sounded like he was hedging for information. He didn't have a package or letter in his hand, and he hadn't gone to check the post office boxes for mail.

"Sorry, I'm not trying to be weird." The man chuckled, tugging on the open edges of the flannel shirt he wore tossed over a t-shirt. "It's just a small town, you know?"

Maybe not poking around, then. Maybe he was just awkward? Nick dipped his head in a polite nod, sliding the boxes onto the counter. "I'd like to mail these."

He kept an eye on the man, though, who walked up to the other counter.

"Hey, Tracy." He pulled out his wallet. "I just need a book of stamps."

"Sure thing, Duke." She opened a drawer to hand him a small slip.

"That'll be thirty-eight sixty-seven," the older gentleman in front of him said, smoothing mailing labels over the boxes. He stacked them behind himself.

Nick paid the man and headed out.

The man in need of a haircut jogged, following him out. "I'm Duke."

Sighing aloud this time, he stopped. He should attempt to be polite, right? He lived here now. He stuck out his hand. "Nick."

"Nice to meet ya, man." He eased closer.

"Nice to meet you, too." He cast a glance around, seeing the market across the street. "Sorry, but I'm running late. I need to stop in and get some groceries before it gets too late. Stew takes a while to cook."

"Oh, no worries." Duke stepped away, bobbing his head. "I get ya."

He made it to the sidewalk before the wave of guilt hit him. Duke was just being friendly. Wasn't that why he was here? To get away from the meth heads and assholes of the city?

His foot hesitated on the curb and he turned halfway. "Maybe I'll run into you again sometime."

"Looking forward to it!" Duke raised a hand. "Have a good one."

He needed to quit being so paranoid. This wasn't Seattle. He'd left that life and all it entailed behind him.

There was a break in traffic, so he picked up his pace to cross the street, angling past the waterfront cafe to the market with the big fish painted on the wood siding. Gil's Market and Marina.

This place was busy no matter what time of day he stopped by, he'd learned. He slowed, picking up a basket near the door as he scanned the room. He hadn't lied, exactly; he needed a few things. And stew sounded good.

When would he quit thinking people always had ulterior motives? Would that fade with time? He found the produce; his hands slid over the tomatoes. Maybe chili tonight instead.

Mounding a small pile of tomatoes in his basket, he walked over to the onions. His bright blue gaze searched the patrons and he found himself looking for the woman from the water. He hadn't seen her around before last night. Then again, he hadn't spent that much time in town.

As if of their own accord, his eyes found the marina through the large window at the back of the market where the fishermen brought in their morning catch. The water beyond the boat ramps was calm and nearly half the boats were still out for the day. Nick scanned the gentle waves, knowing that the woman he had run into wasn't going to be out there in the blue water. But still, he had to check.

Shaking it off, he grabbed a couple of onions and then garlic, tossing them in with the tomatoes. There was no way she was a mermaid. They didn't exist. But if they did, he'd believe in a heartbeat that she could be one. Chiding himself, he found the cold cases, absently considering bison and elk before taking a pound of beef wrapped in butcher paper off the shelf.

When he first moved into the tiny cabin, he'd stocked up on canned goods, worried about the winter, but he'd made it through just fine with very little snow to show for it. He still had several cans of beans on his pantry shelves.

"Nick, right?" a voice spoke at his elbow.

Turning, he saw a young man he'd met on one of his first trips to the shop.

"Right." He shook the offered hand. "Emiliano?"

"Right." The younger guy smiled broadly, giving him a friendly slap on his opposite shoulder.

"Glad to see you again, Nick." An older man, Emiliano's father, joined him, standing shoulder to shoulder with his son. The two could have been brothers if not for the age difference. Both almost the same height, with the same tan from spending mornings out on the marina buying fish off the fishermen, and the same friendly smile spread from ear to ear. Gil's Market was theirs. He tapped his chest. "Hugo Gil."

"I remembered your name too, Hugo." He couldn't help but smile at the friendly duo.

"You made it through the winter." The corners of his eyes crinkled in mirth, and a little from his advanced age.

Nick had the grace to laugh at the jab. He had moved in late fall, just finishing his workshop before winter. He'd stocked up on everything from water to paper towels, and the pantry of canned beans. "It was touch-and-go there for a day or two, but I made it out alive. I learned a few necessary skills to get through the winters in Orca Cove."

"What's that?" Hugo's gray eyes brightened even more.

"The farmer's market moves indoors through the winter," he said seriously.

Both men let out a hearty laugh. Hugo rubbed his midsection, still trim for his age. "You can get fresh produce here too, throughout the winter."

"It's certainly not what I thought it would be." He regarded the stocked shelves of the market. Nearly everything was local. The place wasn't fancy, but it had a rustic appeal that worked for the little town. "But I like it."

"Well, we're glad to have you." Hugo gave him a clap on his shoulder before moving on.

Emiliano watched him leave. "Let me know if you ever want to set up a stand to sell a few smaller items."

"Here?" He hadn't considered it. Wait. "How did you know?"

The store owner's son smiled again. "I looked you up online."

"Really?" That was quick.

"I have a knack for computers."

The place had a few displays set up with local souvenirs and other craft items. One of his handcrafted tables or a stack of boards would work well alongside the hand-knitted sweaters and leather aprons.

"Let me think about it, okay?"

"Of course." Hugo moved to leave.

"Thanks."

Emiliano nodded once before ducking back behind the checkout lines at the back of the store.

Nick wasn't used to the kindness of strangers. Here, he just kept running into it. Deep down in his stomach, he had that familiar feeling.

Doubt. Discomfort. Could Emiliano be trying to make a profit off his sales?

Or maybe the townspeople were genuinely that nice.

Taking his purchases, he got in line to pay. It was time to get back home. He could probably whip out a few more charcuterie boards before the chili was done simmering.

Nick pushed out the door of the market and back into the warming afternoon. Where had he parked? Remembering that he'd left his truck at the post office, he walked across the lot and scanned the road for traffic before crossing.

"Psst," a strange voice sounded from the bushes ahead. "Over here."

He squinted, but the day was unusually sunny, and he raised his hand to shield his eyes from the sun's glare on the concrete.

A woman hurried over to him, grabbed his arm, and tugged. Her hair was wild with curls. Long strawberry-blonde hair cascaded down her back, whipping around her as she scanned to the right and the left, as though on the lookout. It wasn't until he saw her eyes that he recognized her from the night before. It was her, the mermaid, the woman from the beach. And her eyes were green.

He was so shocked, he let her half drag him to the bushes next to the sidewalk.

"Hi," he managed to squeak.

She blew out a nervous laugh, then noticing her hands still wrapped around his arm, dropped it. "Hi."

Just as quickly, she stood up straight, frantically looking up and down the street again, pulling him down by the bush.

"What's going on?" he frowned, trying to keep the laughter from escaping his lips.

"Shh." She pressed her hands against his mouth, her eyes flying to his, wide with surprise. A tingle passed from her hands to his lips where she touched them.

"Shit." He stumbled back a step. What the hell was that? It was like last night's electric shock, only not as strong.

She dropped her hand, her mouth hanging open. So, she'd felt it too. His skin still tingled from her fingers. The intoxicating scent of lavender lingered too. He leaned forward to catch another whiff.

A car backfired, spurring her back into action. She set her jaw and took a firm hold of his wrist. "Come on."

It didn't make sense to argue with the strange woman. He was too curious about what was going on between them.

She led him across the lawn and through another to a parking lot in front of a set of small condos. Sending one more glance over her shoulder, she flew to a doorway, twisted the knob, and sailed inside, tugging him along.

Once behind the closed door, she dropped her hold on him again. The tingle remained on his wrist. What in the world?

"Did you feel that?" he asked, raising his hand. It was already starting to fade.

"Yes," she flexed her hand.

"What is it?"

She shook her head. "I don't know."

He tilted his head; his eyebrow rose.

"I swear." She raised her hands. "It's as much of a surprise to me as it is to you."

"It's never happened to you before?" he questioned her, watching her reaction. She seemed genuine.

"No. You?"

He shook his head, taking in his surroundings. Everywhere he could see there were soft textures. Loads of blankets and pillows overflowed a pair of couches in an open living room. A long, fluffy rug sat in between them. He could see the water from the cove through the large sliding glass door and windows on the back wall. The whole place was decorated in natural colors such as oatmeal, blush, and blue-green. And it smelled herbal, like lavender. It had to be her apartment.

He indicated her door. "What was going on out there?"

She tugged at her bottom lip. "Chief Warner is looking for you."

His eyebrows went up and he took a reflexive step back. "For me? Why?"

"Because word on the street is you're the newest resident, and our tourism hasn't picked up for the season yet." She raised her arm as she explained. "It's barely spring, not quite warm enough yet."

"What does that have to do with me?"

"Well, this morning I found a body on the beach." She winced.

"A body?" He froze, eyes wide. He grabbed her arm. "Whose?"

She leaned away from him. "I don't know. Some guy was shot."

It couldn't be. They'd been too careful. *Please don't let it have been Jimmy.* "What did he look like?"

Her shoulders pulled up and in. "He wore a blue button-down shirt. Bl-black pants. Close-cropped hair."

"Was he black?" His eyes bored into hers like ice daggers.

"Yes." She whispered the word.

The world around Nick pitched and he could feel his face go cold.

"Jimmy." His name was a breath on his lips.

He barely heard her asking if he was alright before he went down with a thud on one knee, his face in his hands.

CHAPTER 4

Willa wrung out the wet washcloth over her bathroom sink. Catching sight of herself in the mirror, she ran a still wet hand over her curls, trying to tame them. Gathering them together, she pulled her hair to one side and took a deep breath.

She had a man sitting in her living room.

Oh, she'd had men in her place before, but it was always because they needed a salve or a tea, or something like that. Dating hadn't been all that common for her in Orca Cove. She knew everyone and she suspected they thought she was a little too much of a peace-and-love hippie for their self-sufficient outdoorsy tastes.

Seattle and Olympia were decidedly more holistic, but she'd never felt as at home there as she did here, watching the orcas in the cove or standing deep in the forest under the canopy of trees.

She cast a glance over her shoulder. How did he know the man? Jimmy, she corrected herself. And how did he die? Giving the poor washcloth a final squeeze, she blinked to focus herself and went to get some answers.

The man in question was still where she had left him, in the center of her overstuffed couch. But now he was staring off into the waves.

"I thought you came from the sea," he said, as though in a dream.

She chuckled softly, coming to stand near him. Her gaze found the gentle waves as well. "I did. But I was only in there for ten minutes, max. It was too cold."

"It's so peaceful." His eyebrows went up a touch, catching sight of something. "Is that...?"

"An orca, yes." She had just spotted her too.

She'd named her Cora. She didn't know for sure it was a she, of course, but she liked to think so. She'd seen an infant orca and its mother out in the cove the year before. This year, there was often an orca with a smaller one, so she suspected they were the same mother and child. "Is it the first you've seen here?"

He nodded.

"Keep an eye on the water. We get them frequently. Only one or two at a time, but two to three times a week at least.""This far from the strait?" He angled himself to peer up at her.

The Strait of Juan De Fuca stretched north of the Puget Sound, just north of Washington. It was a known foraging area of resident orcas and the number one place in North America to see the wild mammals.

"I know, but the water is deep here."

"Strange though." He squinted at the waves. "What would bring them this far? Maybe an unlikely food source or something?"

"Something," she said. "No one really knows why."

That made him frown. He stood suddenly. "I'm Nick Ryan."

They were close, so when he stood he bumped into her. Taking a step back, she smiled, shaking his offered hand. "Willa Daniels."

Remembering what she had been doing, she reached up to his forehead with the wet washcloth, pressing it to his forehead with both hands.

"I'm okay." He reached to take it from her, bumping her awkwardly again. Soft electricity hummed between them at their touches.

He stopped. She dropped her hand.

His gaze found hers, questioning. She honestly didn't know why it kept happening. The temperature between them rose as the tension in the room increased.

"I'll make some tea," she said, stepping back and out of the buzzing atmosphere.

Busying herself, she made a tea similar to the one she'd made that morning. She hoped it would have the same effect on him as it'd had on the rest of them, clearing his mind and helping him focus.

"What is all of that?" he asked, following her to her loose-leaf shelves. He scanned the herbs contained in the various mismatched glass jars.

"Just herbs." She flicked on her electric tea kettle, almost finished selecting herbs for him. A simple blend of chamomile and lemon balm for her. She could use their calming energies. She turned to face him. "So, how do you know him?"

His eyes dropped, searching her floor for answers. She gave him time.

"We worked together," he said finally, dropping down onto a barstool at her kitchen counter, lost in his thoughts. He paused, his eyebrows furrowing. "Why're you keeping me from Chief Warner?"

"Because I don't want him to know we met on the beach last night."

"You didn't tell him you saw me?" he said, surprised. "But why?" "Because you didn't do it." She poured the hot water into their mugs, confident in her assessment of him. People didn't always believe her, but she'd learned to trust her gut about things like this.

"How do you know that?"

"Did you kill that man?"

"Uh, no." He pulled back and away. "Not directly?"

He said it like a question. One that could mean anything.

"Did you have anything to do with why he was killed?"

He just remained silent.

"Do you know who killed him?" she tried again.

"I'm not sure." He studied the mug that she had set down in front of him.

It didn't seem like he was going to say anything more on the subject. Yet.

"Then you'll need to get your thoughts together before you talk to Chief Warner. When he finds you, he's going to question you and he's going to think you killed that friend of yours."

"How are you so sure that I didn't do it?" He raised his gaze to hers again, searching for answers. His fingers clenched around the steaming tea. "You know we knew each other. You know I was at the scene of the crime. How do you know I didn't have anything to do with it?"

She paused, watching his reactions. Guilt was evident in his flushed face and the emotions coming off him. A little anger was there, but so was sadness. Sure, she'd been wrong over the years, people weren't as good as she'd like to believe. But there was something about the man.

Oh, how she hoped she was doing the right thing and it wasn't just her ovaries getting the best of her.

"You'll probably think I'm crazy, but I tend to trust people." She'd start with that. A sip of tea helped calm her nerves. "Warner will bulldoze in and want to arrest you. He's a good guy, ultimately. He just wants to protect us. And...you're an outsider."

"I live here now.""You're *new*," she corrected. "Mr. Pemberley moved here six years ago and he's still considered an outsider."

He frowned, finally taking a sip of the tea. Stopping, he examined it curiously and tried it again.

"I just wanted to prepare you before Warner finds you. Figure out what you want to say. I thought you might react badly to being arrested by the local law enforcement."

She tried for a half-hearted smile, but the questioning expression he gave her halted it. Maybe she shouldn't have gotten involved. And now she had a strange man in her residence.

Was she just being reckless?

After a few long moments, he raised his head, scratching at his dark five o'clock shadow. "I appreciate the heads up."

"So, you knew this Jimmy?" she gently prodded. "He was a friend of yours?"

He shut back down, his eyes looking for somewhere to land. Lifting them, he found the sea. Walking to the window, he gestured with his mug. "What were you doing in that water, anyway?"

"Gary." She gave him a lopsided smile. At his curious expression, she continued. "He used to say..." She halted, emotions welling up within her. She took a calming breath. "He used to say it was good for the constitution. He went into the water, without a suit, mind you, every year. But not last year."

He waited patiently, his demeanor changing, softening. "What happened last year?"

"We lost him." It was her turn to shut down. It shouldn't still be raw, but it was. Gary had meant a lot to all of them. He took care of them, their little band, since high school. Plus Maggie, she had come along later and was quickly adopted into the crew.

"I'm sorry."

A tear slipped down her cheek. "It's okay. I'm okay. It wouldn't be as hard if we didn't all love him. We did it in his memory."

"That's a beautiful gesture." He lifted a hand as though he was going to reach out to her, but then lowered it.

"And then it rained." Her mouth slid into a sudden easy smile. "He would have loved that."

Leaning against the wall, he stuck the hand in his front jeans pocket. "He sounds like a good guy."

"The best."

"What was Jimmy like?" she tried again. She'd shared hers.

"I don't think I'm ready to talk about that yet." He swirled his mug. "By the way, what's in this?"

"Herbs. Wakame."

"The seaweed?"

She nodded.

"It's not bad. What's it for?" He lifted it to finish the brew.

"Stamina. Clearing the heart. The lungs."

"I feel...clearer."

"It's a powerful plant."

"Are you an herbalist?"

"I am."

"You're full of mysteries, Willa Daniels."

"I'll take that as a compliment."

"Please do."

He walked into her kitchen to set the empty mug in her sink. She watched him carefully, curious if he would share about his friendship with Jimmy and what had happened last night.

It was obvious he didn't know until now the man had been murdered. He'd been too shocked. Too emotional.

Nick frowned at the small crock of money she had sitting on the counter under her shelf of herbs and salves.

"It's for my products." She waved a hand. "I leave it out in case people need to stop by and get something they need."

"When you're not here?" His eyes widened, meeting hers. "Really?"

She shrugged. "I'm not here all the time."

"What if they don't pay?" he questioned her. "Or they take money?"

"Then they must need it. I'm happy to share." Not everyone understood it, but it was how she chose to live.

"Well, okay." He studied her for a moment, not saying anything, then nodded. "Thank you for the tea, and for the heads up about the chief. If he's trying to find me, I'd better go see him myself."

Her heart swelled. She knew he'd do the right thing.

"But I may wait until tomorrow. I need a little time to process this news." His face grew hard with emotion. "Jimmy's family. He had a little boy."

"I understand." She did. None of her friends wanted to talk about the painful truth when Gary died. They still didn't. But they would have to deal with the pain of it eventually. And Nick would have to when he talked to Warner.

He glanced at the door, taking a step towards it. "Thanks for the hospitality. I'd better be going."

"Anytime."

His work boot scraped the wood floor. "Can I give you some advice?"

She nodded.

"I used to be like you. I used to want to trust people. But they tend to disappoint."

Considering his words, she tilted her head. "I don't think you will."

His eyes caught hers. "I honestly hope I don't."

But then he frowned and walked out her door, leaving her more confused than when he entered it.

The door to her yoga studio opened with a click. Willa tucked her keys back in her pocket and dumped her bag on her little desk. She wasn't much for locks, but her landlord had complained too many times about the studio, so it stayed locked when she wasn't in it.

When she remembered.

She'd mixed up the tea for Duke and the arthritis salve for Loris that afternoon, adding a few extra to her shelves. The menthol and birch scents were still on her skin. She'd added helichrysum and German chamomile to the salve like normal, but also brown algae puree from her foraging earlier in the week.

She'd been doing a little research lately on plants and herbs in the Pacific Northwest that she could harvest locally. Seaweed and mud packs were being trialed with success for use post-knee surgery, so it didn't hurt to see if it helped the cove's residents. Loris and Mary would have to keep the new salve in the fridge, but the cold might help the inflammation as well.

Loris had talked her into a game of cards and a glass of lemonade when she dropped the salve off for both of them. She'd stop by Mary's house later that day to check in on her. Willa couldn't help but smile at the reaction the cantankerous seventy-year-old woman would have when Loris brought over something new to try on her hip. Mary had a good soul, she could tell, but she sure liked to hide it. Well.

A shadow crossed her desk. Lifting her head, she saw Duke filling her doorway, basket in hand. Of course, she'd left it in her rush to class earlier today. Mentally chiding herself, she motioned him in. She was always forgetting something somewhere.

"You left this."

"Thanks." She took the proffered basket, setting it behind the desk.

"I met your man." Duke leaned against the wall near her desk, one foot propped up casually.

"He is *not* my man." She rolled her eyes at his proclamation and tried to ignore the flutter the thought sent through her. No sense in getting excited about something that might never happen. If it did, well, it did. She'd been disappointed more times than she could count. She was a little...different. Not everyone liked that. And she was no longer willing to be someone she wasn't. Pulling a mason jar out of her bag, she handed it to her friend. "Tea."

"Thanks." He lifted it. "What do I owe you?"

She lifted her shoulder. "Don't worry about it."

He shook his head, pulled a twenty out of his wallet, and walked around her to tuck it in between the travel mugs in her basket.

"That's too much," she protested, but he only scooted the basket further under her desk with a boot.

"It's not. You provide a service, and you should be making more for what you do."

"I have what I need." She always had. She took care of the townspeople, and they took care of her. Loris and Izzy brought her cookies or dinner on a regular basis.

"This tea is incredible." He raised it to study the loose-leaf herbs and gave it a light shake. "It'd be good for anything from fighting off an oncoming cold to not getting enough sleep. Or even a bad hangover."

"It's not for hangovers." She paused. "Although, it would probably work for that too."

He raised an eyebrow and gave her a shameless grin. "Priceless."

"I rarely drink alcohol."

"You have to have *some* flaws."

She folded her arms across her chest. "I can have fun too. I talked you all into almost freezing water."

"It was forty-five degrees."

"I said *almost*."

"You could call it Fog Lifter." Duke brought them out of their elementary school banter and back to business. "I could help you turn a profit."

"I'm not selling it by the basket." As far as she knew, he only sold large-quantity goods and specialty, hard-to-find items.

Tossing the jar in the air, he caught it. "You wouldn't have to make that much. It's easier to overprice if supply is low. But you wouldn't be able to pass it around like candy in town."

"You know I don't work like that." She was able to pay her bills. Sometimes it got a little close, but it always worked out. "It brings me more happiness to help. And make it affordable to those who need it."

"Well, I need it."

"And you have it."

He tilted his head in thanks. "Let me know if you change your mind."

"You said you met my man-" Stuttering to a halt, she wrinkled up her face and slapped a hand over the red that creeped up her cheeks. "I meant Nick."

Mischievousness glittered in his eyes. "He's super cute, isn't he?""Ha ha."

"He genuinely seems like a nice guy." He dropped the act.

"I told you so." It was still good to hear it from Duke. No one read people like he did.

"He's a bit of a loner, though. Doesn't trust much." He considered his words carefully. "He's got a big secret he's keeping close to the vest."

"I know."

He raised a brow in question.

"I don't know what it is, exactly." She waved her hands in explanation. "I ran into him again today."

"Again? Please tell me not *literally* again."

"No," she widened her eyes. "Worse. I pulled him behind a bush."Duke bit back a smile, but Willa raised a slender finger in warning. She was already feeling like a crushing schoolgirl. She certainly didn't need his teasing.

Finally, he settled on, "Please elaborate."

"Warner was looking for him. I overheard Ronnie at the cafe when I stopped in for lunch. He's heard people talking about the new guy in town with no past."

"That kind of secrecy doesn't go over well in a town this small." His lips pressed flat. "I should know. If I hadn't grown up here and everybody didn't already know my sordid history, I'd have to find another place to live. Or never be accepted."

It was true. Orca Cove was a great place to live, but it also had its challenges. Everybody knew everybody's dirty little secrets. Well, to some extent.

"Anyway, I warned him." She bit her bottom lip. It had felt right, and also it hadn't. "I know I shouldn't have."

He nodded. "You did what you thought was right. You always do."

"I try. And you were right about him. He's got secrets. I heard a little about them." She wasn't sure what all to share with Duke. She wanted to share the weight of them but didn't want to betray her newfound friendship. "I'd rather not share."

"A man like that would be grateful for it." He tucked his hands in his front pockets and leaned back, assessing her. "But don't let him put you in a bad position either. Trust your gut."

"I'm trying." She really was. It was challenging at the moment though. Murder wasn't a trivial thing. Willa embraced her friend. "Thanks, Duke."

"Anytime." He ruffled her curls.

"Hey!" She raised a hand to pat them back down.

"Be careful, Flower Child."

Duke hadn't called her that since they were kids. What a blast from the past. She grinned widely up at him, appreciating the brotherly familiarity. "With what?"

"Nick. I said he's a good guy. He seems honorable, but he's nothing like you." He lifted a strand of her hair from where it obviously had been sticking out from the rest and set it in place. "He's guarded where you're open and cool where you're warm. It's not a bad thing. I see a lot of my younger self in him."

"He's probably a couple of years older than you."

"You know what I mean. I've come a long way." He smoothed down the front of his flannel shirt as though it was a suit jacket.

"We all travel on different paths."

"I know." He took her long, slender hands in his wide, rough ones. "Just be careful. I don't want you to lose your spark."

He was acting so much like Gary that she had to bite down the emotion that flooded her. Gary always took the time for them, giving them advice and being there for them. It appeared that Duke was picking up the torch. Or trying it out at least.

"I won't," she promised.

Before she could say anything else, the front door banged open. Loris stood slack-jawed in the doorway, one hand still on the door, the other holding the new container of salve.

"Are you okay, Loris?"

"This, uh. I, uh," she stammered. Then, she bobbed up and down on the balls of her feet. Then, bending her knees in a squat. "I went over to Mary's."

Willa crossed to the door, taking the salve from her, and handed it to Duke, who was watching curiously. "You took Mary's salve to her?"

"Yes." She resumed her bouncing. Tears bubbled up in her eyes. "No pain."

"What?" Willa checked to see if Duke was following any better than her. Then it clicked; she had used the salve. "You mean in your knees?"

She shook her head, a teardrop falling over and making its way down her cheek. "Anywhere. No pain anywhere."

Shock flooded Willa's body. That was it. She'd done it. She'd finally found a mix of plants from Mother Nature to heal her friends. Or at least keep the pain away. Tears pricked her eyes in return. "Really?"

Loris took hold of her arms. "Mary too."

It was great news, all she'd been working towards. But why her salve? All she'd added was the brown algae. People had already been studying it. If it was a miracle cure for arthritis and other topical pains, it would have been shared widely in the medical and herbal community by now. It just didn't make sense.

What in the world would have made her salve different?

CHAPTER 5

There! It finally fit. After five cuts on three different boards, he'd figured out an odd angle of wood to replace a rotten trim board outside of the cabin's bedroom. The floor had sloped from the foundation settling over the years and it was far from square.

Pushing up from the floor, Nick stood to examine his handiwork. He barely registered the burning smell from the kitchen. When he did, he cursed and raced back into the kitchen, flipped off the oven, and opened it to billowing smoke. Coughing, he used a towel to fan the air, dispersing the smoke out the opened window over his sink.

After the smoke cleared, he reached in with the towel to remove the cast iron pan of cornbread covered in a layer of black char. Exhaling, he tossed the towel in frustration to the counter and turned off the stovetop. The chili had simmered long enough. Luckily that was still edible. He'd stow his tools for the night and eat dinner.

But before he flipped the switch off in his workshop, he paused, taking the time to run a hand over the wall in front of his hiding space. Everything still appeared to be in place. It was a secure spot, and not visible to the naked eye. Why was he so worried about it?

Probably because Jimmy gave his life trying to protect it. That was why.

Visions of Jimmy tossing little Luke up in the air played in his mind again. They hadn't been the best of friends. They'd had issues like any coworkers did. Hell, it had taken them a year of working together to even get along, but he'd grown to respect the man. They didn't always have to agree because, bottom line, Jimmy was fair. And Nick had trusted him with his life.

His fist hit the wall board with a hard bang. His head fell forward to rest against the wood.

He'd protect this with his life as well. It was the only way to honor the sacrifice Jimmy made.

It'd better be worth it.

Pushing away from the wall, he switched the lights out and locked the door behind him.

Back in his kitchen, Nick cut a big hunk of cornbread out of the pan, flipping it onto a cutting board to see if any of it was salvageable. If he cut the top and bottom off, some of the middle seemed alright. Cutting a few pieces, he had enough to stack on top of his chili. It was better than nothing.

Standing in his kitchen, he leaned against the countertop and dug into the chili, taking big spoonfuls up to his hungry mouth. He'd built up quite an appetite with work today, but damn, the chili was good.

Life sure was different here in his little cabin on the edge of the woods. He didn't mind the work to keep it up and make it more livable. The labor felt good. He was building things. He wouldn't call it art exactly, but it felt like he was creating something beautiful. And after all the years of death, it felt like a breath of fresh air.

But it was quiet.

He missed the guys, his friends from the job, and sometimes he even missed the job itself. He was trying not to, though. He'd left that life behind.

He had one task left, though, it seemed.

Scraping the last of the chili into his mouth, he considered his next move.

The weight of his phone sat heavy in his work vest. Jimmy was gone now. He couldn't ask for his advice. And it wasn't like there was anyone else he could trust with this. He itched to call one of the other guys, but this was too big. Especially now.

Instead, his mind went to his not-so-distant past. He pulled his phone out and scrolled through the news for articles on Larry Dupree. Maybe there'd been some progress. But no, he found nothing.

Willa's enchanting smile appeared in his mind, uninvited. The one that spread through her whole body and made her shine. He'd never met anyone that open or kind.

Oddly enough, he felt the urge to talk to her. She was the only one in town that knew about Jimmy. And she'd even tried to protect Nick, a complete stranger. Normally he'd say that kind of blind faith in someone was just naive, but instead...he felt grateful and, um, indebted. Yep, that was the feeling. It wasn't anything else. Besides, he'd sworn off women, at least temporarily while he got his life in order out here and the business with Larry straightened out.

He sagged against the counter. Tomorrow he'd have to go into the station and find this Chief Warner. He'd introduce himself and let him know he'd heard about the body. He'd have to tell him he knew Jimmy and that he'd seen him before he was killed. In fact, he was likely the last to have seen him alive. It would look bad. Really bad.

But it was better than waiting until the chief found him and started asking questions. Especially if he found out Nick knew about his death and hadn't come forward. The truth would come out sooner or later; they'd eventually identify his body even without Nick's help. And that would make things worse.

No, he'd be honest about seeing him. He'd let the chief know they used to work together, but he wasn't going to tell him why Jimmy had come, or anything about the bag. That had to be protected and the chief didn't need to know.

For tonight, he'd grieve the loss of his coworker and friend. For himself, Patty, and Luke. Setting his dish in the sink to take care of later, he moved to the cabinet and pulled out a bottle of Jameson and a glass.

The Orca Cove police station was up the hill from the marina, towards the tiny residential streets downtown. It was much smaller than those he was used to in Seattle. Once he shared what he knew with the chief, he'd be marked as more of an outsider than ever before. It would take even longer for the place to feel like home. Not that the townspeople hadn't been welcoming, but there was a difference between welcomed and included. And once he was marked as a potential threat, it would stick with him.

But it was unavoidable.

Straightening, he swung out of his truck.

He passed an older man sitting on the curb on his way to the door.

"Roy, come back here," the man said, waving his arms.

Nick stopped. "Name's Nick, not Roy."

"Not you." He wheeled and pointed to the air. "Roy."

"Ah, okay then." He continued to the door. It would seem this town was just like any other. There were always people in need of help. He tipped his head to the man before walking inside.

It was quiet inside the beige station. A female police officer sat at the front desk.

"Can I help you, sir?" the young woman asked.

"Yes, I'd like to see Chief Warner, please."

"He's at home today, it being a Saturday and all." She gave him a polite smile. "Can I help you?"

"Unfortunately, I think he'll want to come in for this." He stuffed his hands in his pockets. "I knew the man that was found on the beach."

The police officer's eyes grew wide. "Oh! Yes. I think you're right. Let me...uh-"

She trailed off, deciding what to do.

There was no way they were used to this sort of crime in Orca Cove.

"Could you call him, please?"

"Yes! I'll do that. Would you mind taking a seat?" She glanced at the seating area and then back at him. "On second thought, if you don't mind, I think I should put you in a room to wait for the chief."

He bit back a sigh. She was going to put him in an interrogation room. Of course, she was. It was the right thing to do. Straightening his shoulders, he walked through the door and followed her down a hallway and into a small room with a table.

This was going to be fun.

"I'll be right back." She left, shutting the door behind her, most likely locking it as well.

Taking a seat at the table, he scooted the chair back, lacing his hands across his lap. This was going to take a while.

Thirty minutes later, the door swung open and a man in his mid-sixties with a clenched jaw and gray hair marched through. Not as long as he'd guessed.

"I'm Chief Warner." He circled the table, taking in everything from Nick's clothes to his boots and posture.

Sitting up in the chair, Nick stretched his neck from being still so long. Moving slowly, he stood, extending his hand. "I'm Nick, Nicholas, Ryan. Originally from Seattle."

Ignoring the offered hand, the chief nodded to the waiting officer, apparent irritation on his face that she hadn't gotten his name when he arrived.

She rushed off. She'd be bringing in a file on him in the next ten to fifteen minutes.

"So, I hear you have a name for our John Doe.""I do."
He met Warner's gaze. "It's James Haddish. Jimmy."

"You were friends with him." Warner gestured for
him to return to his seat, waiting until he did so before
sitting himself.

"I was. He came from Seattle to see me Thursday
night. We met on the beach, before the storm. Then he
went home, or so I thought. I was probably the last one
to see him alive."

"Son, I don't have to tell you that this doesn't look
good."

"I'm aware." Oh, boy, was he aware.

"You're going to need to tell me everything you can.
What you were doing on the beach, how you know Mr.
Haddish, how long you've known him...the nature of
your relationship. Everything."

He was playing good cop right now to see what information he could get. Nick nodded. He would be
finding out in about ten minutes anyway.

"I met Jimmy about ten years ago in the police acade-
my." He watched the older man's eyes flash momentarily,
giving away his surprise. And there went his anonymity

and semblance of security. He'd have to be more careful from here on out. "We were partners on the force."

"Seattle Police Department?"

He nodded again. "That's correct. We didn't get along right off the bat, but we learned to work together. He was a good man and a fair one. I respected him."

He had to stop. Emotion bubbled to the surface again. Sadness. Frustration. Anger.

"Someone will need to call the SPD. Let them know to notify Patty, his wife. It should be them. She's going to be a wreck," he continued.

"We'll take care of that once we let the coroner know. What were you two doing on the beach?"

He shrugged. "Just catching up. He wanted me to come back to the force."

"You two argued about it?"

"No, it wasn't like that." He'd expected this type of questioning. It was what he would have done. "We talked about his son, Luke. He just started kindergarten. He's doing well. Driving his teachers crazy...but doing well."

"What time?"

"We met at eight."

"That's late."

He nodded.

"Sounds like you didn't want to be seen."

"I can see how it would look like that."

"You didn't meet at your place, or at Wild's. As an officer, you have to know how that sounds."

"I do." He wasn't wrong.

"Why'd you pick the beach?" he pressed when Nick didn't elaborate.

"We don't have a nice beach at home. All we have is the marina for the Sound. Jimmy wanted to see it."

"In the dark?"

"It was the earliest he could get away from the job."

"Couldn't wait till he had a day off?"

"He didn't want to miss out on time with Luke. He was already in bed." He knew it was thin, but it was all he was giving him.

"Okay," Warner said finally, leaning back in his chair. Nick could see the wheels spinning in his mind as he searched for the best line of questioning. "So, you two caught up on the beach...at night. It was chilly. Then, it started pouring rain."

"Correct. That's why we ended it so early. We were going to get dinner, but he was worried about getting home in the storm," he lied easily.

"He could have waited it out."

"He could have. Didn't want to."

"Where's his car?"

Crap. He knew the chief would get to that one eventually.

"He brought a boat."

The chief remained silent for a minute, just watching him. "He decided to take the boat back in the storm? Up the canal?"

"Like I said, he was anxious to get home." He set his jaw. It wasn't entirely untrue. Jimmy didn't want to risk being followed, so he'd rented a boat from someone at the Port of Seattle.

"Son, I'm trying to help you."

"You're trying to figure out what happened on the beach and how Jimmy was murdered," he corrected. "And I get it. It sounds bad. But that's what happened."

"You don't know what happened to him after you left?"

"I left; how would I know?" He spread his fingers.

"Do you know anyone who would want Jimmy dead?"

"Several people. We're police officers- *were*," he caught himself. "We were police officers."

Nick had chosen to leave. Jimmy's choice had been taken from him.

"People he put away?"

"Plus an ex or two," he cracked a smile.

"But you don't know who would have been coming after him Thursday night?"

"I do not."

There was a knock on the door, then the young officer poked her head in, handing the file to her boss. He took it, gave her a raised eyebrow and opened it in front of Nick. There was a Post-it note on the top page. He read it, then flipped through the pages, reading as quickly as he could. Nick waited.

Finally, he flipped the folder shut and folded his hands over it. "Nicholas Ryan. It appears that you are who you say you are. You've got quite the reputation on the force, detective. Not a single mention of misconduct. Quite a few arrests and raids under your belt. Even got a medal for one of those. You should be proud of that."

"Not a detective anymore." He shifted in his seat. "I was just doing my job, Chief."

"Why would someone leave a promising career like that?"

"I needed a change of pace."

"You could have transferred to a smaller town." He gestured around him. "Like this one. We'd have been happy to have someone with your qualifications in the cove."

"That's kind of you to say, Chief, but openings in places like this don't come that often. And besides, I was done. I didn't want to transfer, I wanted out."

"You have a bad call?"

"Something like that." It was all he was going to say on the matter. He didn't have to explain himself.

"It says here you live just outside town, on the way to Liberty Village."

He nodded.

"You bought Hostettler's old cabin."

"I guess so."

"He died last spring."

"Sorry to hear."

"The place needed some T.L.C."

"It did. I've been working on it."

The chief nodded, still watching him. "Well, I don't have enough to hold you."

"You could." He knew full well he could hold him twenty-four hours without a reason.

"Do I need to?"

"No. I haven't done anything."

"Well, then." He stood. "I don't have to tell you not to leave town, right?"

His nostrils flared. Damn, he hadn't thought of that. "But, what about Patty?"

"It's best you leave that to the SPD."

He clenched his fist. He hadn't expected to give her the news, not now that he wasn't an officer, but he should at least be there for her and Luke. They'd need the support.

But the chief was right. It would be best if he stayed out of Seattle for a while. There was a reason he'd left.

"Will you let me know when she's told?" he said, finally. "I'd like to call and offer my condolences afterwards."

The older man nodded. "Of course."

He stood, ushering Nick out of the room.

On the way out, the officer at the desk gave him a clipboard to fill out his personal details. They already had his address, but he added his cell phone number and checked the rest of it.

Finished, he stepped back out into the clean air, breathing a sigh of relief. He hadn't been sure he'd make it back out today, not knowing if the chief would hold him.

But what to do with the day now? If he went home, he could get nearly an entire day in the shop. It was just beginning to drizzle.

He could see the marina at the bottom of the hill and the cove beyond it. Sure enough, he saw a black dorsal fin. Willa's townhouse was also visible from this vantage. He imagined her in her living room watching the orca.

Snorting at his foolishness, he unlocked his truck door. He could grab breakfast at the cafe. He'd only eaten at The Wild Cafe once before, but it was good. The morning was warming up, enough to sit outside even. The light rain likely wouldn't last long, and if it did, they had umbrellas.

He tried not to think that he might run into a certain strawberry-blonde-haired herbalist, but he failed.

They'd only met twice, but each time was strange. Not in a bad way. But he probably hadn't left a very good impression on her.

Starting his truck, he headed down the hill.

CHAPTER 6

"Mary? Are you home?" Willa tried again. It had been too late to stop by the night before after yoga class, even though she was anxious to after Loris's news about the salve. So, as soon as her Saturday morning class wrapped, she headed right over.

"Where else would she be?" Loris, having tagged along, balanced on her tiptoes. She peered through the window, trying to see past the dark curtains.

"Maybe she just doesn't want visitors right now." Willa stepped off the porch, giving the woman space.

"She never wants visitors, but it's too early for her to be out." Loris huffed, her hands on her hips. "Mary, answer the door! Willa just wants to ask how you're doing. She did make the salve, after all. And isn't asking payment for it."

Loris' exclamation turned Willa's stomach. She gave it to them freely. A true gift didn't come with conditions.

"I think we should leave." She put a hand on Loris' arm, stopping her from going around to another window. "She could be in the bath or sleeping in. I'll try again tomorrow."

The flick of the bolt lock precluded the door opening precisely six inches.

"I'll pay for the salve if that's what you want," a gruff voice bit out from inside the tiny house.

"No need." Willa held up her hands, trying to put her at ease. "I just wanted to see how you're doing. And see if it is working as well as Loris said."

"Makes sense." Mary cut her eyes to the other woman. "She can be a bit dramatic."

Willa had to bite her lip to keep from laughing. There was a reason the kids called her Mary, Mary, Quite Contrary. At least they had when Willa was in school. Mary had seemed old to Willa even then, but thinking back on it, she couldn't have been that old. She'd always been a recluse, and...not overly friendly.

"I don't know what you did differently, but the salve works well," Mary said, her voice pitched lower and softer. "My hands hurt less now."

"How much less?"The hard lines on her face softened. "Almost none."

"Really?" Willa stood there stunned. "How long did it last?""Pretty much all afternoon. I went to bed early because I was able to rest."

That was incredible, even for herbs.

"And this morning?"

She flexed her hand. "It hurt a little this morning, but less so. I rubbed the salve in and it worked within ten minutes."

"Can I stop by tomorrow?" She needed more data. "I'd like to see how long it lasts this time and how often you need to re-apply it."

Mary considered the two of them on her doorstep and finally made a sharp nod. "Fine. But tell me what you put in it. You didn't put any of that CBC oil in it, did you?"

The corner of her mouth curled up. "No, ma'am. I know you're opposed to trying it, although a lot of people have had good luck with it. I used brown algae, right from the

Hood Canal. It's been very helpful in recovery for knee surgeries."

The woman harrumphed. "I don't need that CBC stuff. I have your algae balm, now. I don't need anything else." "You've never used it before, and you've told me that you don't have any allergies that you know of, but it's always good to keep an eye out on anything new that you use."

"I'm fine. And I'll see you tomorrow." Mary narrowed her eyes. "And Loris, keep your face outta my window!"

The door slammed shut. It was the most information she'd gotten from her. At least she'd been invited back the following day. If you could call that an invitation.

Loris quickly hopped off the front porch, her mouth wide in a grimace.

"You too, Loris." Willa waved at her lower half. "Be careful."

"I will, but I feel fantastic! I think I'll take a walk."

"After yoga? Just take it easy, okay?" It wasn't like she could stop the rambunctious woman. "If the salve is numbing the pain, you could still hurt yourself."

"Is it supposed to do that?""No, it's more about reducing inflammation. But still... It's new and this is the first time you've used it."

Loris waved a hand. "I'll be fine."

"Just take it slow." Willa followed her down Mary's walkway. It was lined with flowers, but they hadn't been pruned for spring yet. The woman had been paying Loris' grandson Tommy to mow her lawn, but she still got out to tend her own garden.

Willa dialed Duke's number.

"Did you visit Mary?" he answered.

"Hi to you too."

"Hello." She could hear the smile in his voice.

"It helped her all afternoon, Duke!" She held the phone tightly in her excitement.

When she left the yoga studio the night before, Duke had been anxious to hear about Mary. The older woman had been a sort of surrogate grandma to him.

"Well done, Willa. You still insisting on not going commercial?"

"Yep."

"Think about everyone you could help."

"I don't think that's for me."

"Yay for being your friend, then."

"Funny."

"Brown algae, huh? That's common, right? It's everywhere."

"Maybe I found a potent batch."

"Maybe." He paused. "Do herbal remedies usually work that quickly with one application?"

"Sometimes, yes. Tinctures, teas, menthol, they all work right away."

"That well?"

"Sometimes. Not always." It was true, most herbs took the edge off while supporting or strengthening other parts of the body system or energies. Valerian root worked on the spot. "Maybe it was a fluke. The algae gave both of them exactly what they were needing."

"You've done it, Willa." He sounded proud.

"Hopefully. We'll have to see. I still want to watch it," she said, checking her watch. Oh no, not again! "Later. I have to get back to the studio. I have a yoga class about to start."

Scribbling furiously in a notebook, Willa pulled another card out of her recipe box to study the properties of sea lettuce. That was interesting. It was high in lutein, good for eye health. She'd heard from Loris that Mary was having trouble seeing. Might be glaucoma or cataracts. How Loris got any information out of the woman was beyond her. Old age might have made her grouchy, but most of it was probably caused by aches and pains that came as she aged.

If Willa could help alleviate some of that, she would.

Making another note, she flipped her notebook closed and pulled on her boots. Then she grabbed her foraging knife, her license for harvesting seaweed to tuck into her pocket, and a couple of glass jars in case she found something else interesting. Her wicker baskets were still drying on her back porch. Taking two large ones, she went down the steps onto the beach.

Of their own accord, her eyes found the spot where she had seen the body the day before. The stakes and police tape were still there. Who knew what Warner thought could still be found after a day or two in the sand, but he'd probably leave it for a few days until he found out more. Nick's information would help.

She smiled.

He was a good man, like she suspected. The thought warmed her. It was nice when people proved to be who she thought they were. They didn't always. But he had or, well, he would when he went to see the chief of police. It was well into the afternoon now; he probably already had. She resisted the urge to cross her fingers.

Skirting the crime scene, she walked the pebbled coastline, the tiny rocks shifting with each step. She found not two but three orcas out in the cove. Two days in a row. That was unusual. There had to be a big school of fish in the cove or something.

At the end of the pebble beach section of the shore, she slowed, carefully stepping on the big boulders that lined that portion of the coastline. They were covered in algae and mussels. Spotting the sea lettuce, she stepped slowly down onto a rock closer to the water, trying not to slip. Waves lapped over the rocks and onto her boots.

Squatting, she set the baskets down and cut the sea lettuce. Only the tops, though. She left the part that was attached to the rock so it could regrow quicker. Working her way down a few rocks, she laid the greens in her baskets. Nell might like some for the restaurant. Just in case, she took a bit more. She'd dry it so it would last a while.

Unscrewing the lid from a mason jar, she lowered it into a small pool in a low spot between the rocks, letting water slide into the jar. Capping it, she set it gently in a basket and stood.

Her foot slipped and she caught herself, but she'd neglected to set her foraging knife in the basket. The blade pressed against her hand, fingers still curled around it. She gasped at the biting pain. Steadying herself, she dropped the knife to see blood pool in a single line across her palm. Boy, did it sting.

It was her left hand too, the one she wrote with. That was going to be fun.

Gingerly, she picked up the knife, pausing to rinse it in the water. After a moment's hesitation, she dropped her injured hand into a fresh pool and let a wave wash over it, wincing. The water was cold, and the salt tingled and stung even more, but would help clean the wound and start the healing process. Pretty much everything from the ocean was healing.

Saltwater cures all wounds, as the saying went. She knew that saying nodded to relaxing and enjoying time on the beach or in the water, but there was more truth to those words than most knew.

Shaking off her hand, she wiped the back of it against her jeans and tossed the knife in the basket this time before trying to stand again and making her way back to the shore.

Before she went back inside, though, she went around the building to the side yard, searching through the grass and weeds. Finally finding what she was looking for, she bent, dropped a basket on the ground to tear off a few leaves of broadleaf plantain with her good hand, and stuffed them in her mouth. By the time she got back to the steps to her back deck, the bleeding had stopped, but her palm still stung.

Setting the baskets on her deck, she toed off her boots and went inside to her kitchen. Spitting out the chewed poultice, she pressed it against the cuts. The stinging was slowing, but the tingling remained. Hopefully not nerve damage. It didn't seem too bad. She'd thought the cuts were deeper. Oh, well. She wasn't going to argue with a more *minor* wound.

Digging into a drawer in her kitchen, she found a clean strip of cotton and wrapped it around her hand, using her teeth to tie it and pull it tight. Now that the wound was dressed, she went back to her deck to spread out the baskets and let the sea lettuce dry. She brought in her jars, cleaned her knife, and stored it.

Sighing, she considered her hand. It would make work a little harder, but she got to it anyway.

"I would have come by after work to pick it up," Shelby said when Willa delivered the white willow bark tincture later that afternoon.

It hadn't been easy to strain the headache-relieving extract and keep the alcohol from her wound, but she'd gotten it done. Shelby lifted the blue glass bottle from Willa to examine it. She tucked it into her purse and pulled out a twenty.

She worked hard and often got tension headaches. Willa didn't think she'd even consider valerian root given its bitter taste. White willow bark or meadowsweet would be better. Or even skullcap if this one didn't work. Either way, it felt good helping her friend again.

It was her love language.

"That's too much." Willa frowned, taking a step back from her friend's desk at Siren's Song Cabins, a small, rustic resort east of the beach. It sat just beyond the edge of the downtown area. The place was pretty but was as structured and efficient as its owner.

"It is *not*," she said, rounding her desk to tuck the money into Willa's jeans pocket. "Especially with the delivery."

"It's no bother, I've been at the house most of the day. I thought it'd be good to take a walk. Besides, you didn't even ask for it."

The tingling in her hand increased and she gave it a shake.

"Did you cut yourself?" Shelby changed the subject, noticing the bandage.

"Yes, but it's not that bad." She opened and closed her hand. "It really doesn't hurt much. It feels like it's healing."

"Itchy?" She gave her a sideways glance, watching her carefully.

"Kind of."

Except it just happened. It was a little early for healing.

"I'm just about to close up here. I can walk out with you." She flicked off her lamp and grabbed her messenger bag.

"Sure." She followed Shelby out, waiting as she said goodnight to the receptionist on duty. "It's a full moon tonight."

Shelby peered up at the sky under the timber awning. The drizzle had stopped, and dusk revealed the moon, visible where it hung over the white-tipped mountains in the distance. "Beautiful."

"It sure is."

"Sometimes I forget how lucky we are to live in a place like this." She took a deep breath and headed down the path to the parking lot, pausing for Willa. She lived further in town and drove in to work. "You hear anything from Warner yet?"

She shook her head. "Not yet. You?"

"I ran into Izzy at lunch. She said that the new guy was at the station today, but she doesn't know what happened."

Good vibes hummed in her chest.

"Huh," she grunted softly, falling in step next to Shelby.

"What do you know?" She stopped, her eyes narrowing to slits.

"What do you mean?" Willa kept walking a few feet, then stopped and turned to face her friend.

"You're smiling."

"Oh." Her face fell. "I just ran into him a few days ago. He seems pretty nice."

"Ah." She resumed her walk. "Pretty nice means you think he's cute."

"I didn't say that. But yes. He is cute. His name is Nick." Shelby chuckled.

"It's not like we're dating or anything."

She stopped again. "Oh, you have it bad. You really *do* like this guy."

Willa shifted from foot to foot. "I, uh. I don't know him that well.""Willa Daniels. In all the time I've known you, you've always made up your mind about people too quickly. And you rarely change it."

"Maybe because I get a good read on them right away." Shelby snorted.

"You also tend to be too trusting."

"I choose to see the best in people. That's not a bad thing."

Shelby just raised an eyebrow.

"Anyway." Willa kicked an invisible rock. She didn't want to bring up the past. "I might like him a little. What I do know of him."

What was so bad about liking someone? And why did she feel like she was on the playground with Shelby at seven years old again, being teased about a cute boy?

They reached Shelby's old Chevy.

"Good for you, Willa," she said, unlocking the door. "Just be careful, okay?"

"I'll try."

Why was everyone saying that to her?

"Do you want a ride into town?"

"Nah, I'll walk, but thanks. Don't forget to let me know how the tincture works. I can try another herb if this one doesn't help."

"Will do. Thanks."

She hugged her friend, then headed back down the drive towards the sidewalk. Shelby honked as she passed.

When she got back to her house, it was nearly dinnertime. She debated walking to Wild. It was a nice night for sitting outside, but she didn't feel like company.

Deciding a nice bath was in order before reheating some leftovers for dinner, she fixed a nice cup of chamomile and lavender tea and filled the tub. She shook in sea salt that she'd infused with lavender.

Stepping into the warm water, she realized she'd nearly forgotten about the bandage on her hand. Easing the knot open, she unwound the fabric, slowing to gather the poultice gingerly in the strip and not letting it fall in the water.

She pulled it away to find the wound almost entirely healed.

Standing there, half into her bath, Willa's mind tumbled through the possibilities.

First Loris, then Mary, now this?

Did it have to do with the mysterious tingling she felt when she touched Nick?

She had no idea. But one thing she knew for certain, something strange was happening in Orca Cove.

CHAPTER 7

Nick swirled his morning coffee in his favorite chipped mug. The sun was just coming up over the horizon. He squinted to find it through the overcast sky. He'd already been in the workshop this morning but had trouble getting into the groove.

It was unfortunate, really, since it was the one thing that he had to connect with to find peace. It had always worked, and now that he finally had time to enjoy it, he was coming up blank. He rubbed his eyes. Maybe he just needed more sleep.

He was still confused about the night on the beach. Why hadn't the shooter come after him as well? If he'd seen Nick, he would have followed. Surely, he was after the bag. He must have been following Haddish from Seattle. Whoever it was wouldn't have backed off just because Nick ran into Willa. He would have just taken them both out.

Absently, his hand traveled to the belt holster he wore now that his solitude was broken. After he handed in his duty weapon when he left the job, he had bought the exact same model for personal protection. He'd hoped to never need it. But if Larry's guys were looking for the bag, they'd eventually find him.

His mind kept going back to Jimmy's boy, Luke. His world was probably upside down by now, never to be like it once was. His and others, as Nick knew well.

That and a certain lavender-scented, wild-haired woman. She had kept him up too. And what was going on between them? It still had him perplexed.

He'd eaten a late breakfast again the day before at the cafe. It was good, no doubt the freshest salmon and eggs he'd ever had. Which was saying something with Seattle's foodie scene. It was a wonder Nell was way out here in Orca Cove. She could easily have a restaurant in the Emerald City.

Now that he knew more about the chef, he appreciated her even more. She had to be Gary's widow that Willa had talked about, part of her crew. She and the waitress. He couldn't remember her name, but she had a heart-shaped face with short blonde hair that wasn't easy to forget. And she was easily the sweetest person he'd ever met.

But that wasn't what impressed him the most. He'd been a little out of sorts when he arrived at the cafe, but Nell had been so comforting when she came through and introduced herself, he'd actually felt welcomed by them.

It felt good. Like he belonged.

He'd missed any sight of his new friend though.

Tossing back the rest of his coffee, he inspected the wood-paneled kitchen. He'd better do something about that. Wood planks would look a lot better. They would lighten the place up as well. And the light fixture was downright awful, too small and yellowed with age. He didn't know where to go to find a new one in a town this small, though. He hadn't seen anything like it at Gil's.

A thought rumbled in the back of his mind. Maybe he could ask a certain someone where to find things to spruce up the cabin. It could use a woman's touch...and they could talk about the connection they shared, maybe figure something out about it.

Before he could talk himself out of it, he headed for his truck.

Turning into town, he decided to try The Wild Cafe first. He hadn't had breakfast and he could get those scrambled eggs again. If he didn't see any sign of her there, he'd try her place next.

Before he could cross the parking lot to the door, he saw the guy who'd been sitting outside the police station the day before. He was bent over, laughing excitedly.

"Good morning." Nick nodded to the older gentleman.

"Hee hee." He leaned backward, his hands on his lower back, still laughing. "That Roy. Did you see him?"

Looking around, he didn't see anyone. "Uh, no. I must have missed him."

The man wiped a tear from his face, still chuckling. "I've never seen him eat his breakfast that fast. I thought he was going to fall over the fish the way he tripped over it."

"The fish?" Frowning, Nick checked the pavement and found wet residue a few feet away from them. Maybe the man wasn't challenged. Maybe he had a dog nearby. But yesterday, he had pointed at the sky like he'd seen a ghost. It didn't track.

The man pointed up again. This time, Nick was able to follow his gesture to Gil's Market next door and the large pelican that sat on the roof.

Finally, it clicked. Apparently, *that* was Roy.

"Ah, well, he certainly seems happy," he said. A pet pelican. This town was getting stranger and stranger.

"He sure is." The man shook his head, the smile plastered to his face. "What a hoot."

Nodding, Nick continued around him towards the building and another cup of coffee.

The cafe appeared to have been built by the same person who built Gil's, with the same weathered cedar planks on the outside. But inside, where the Market and Marina was lined in stained OSB with a huge mural on one wall, the restaurant was drywalled with live-edge beams and tree trunk supports running throughout the place. He loved the atmosphere.

Hoping he would run into Willa and be able to forgo an awkward conversation at her place, he pushed through the doors of the cafe and scanned the room.

He didn't see any immediate sight of her but found a table near the window after reading a sign that said to seat himself. It was busier than yesterday, but also earlier. He recognized the lady from the post office and raised a hand in greeting at the blonde server who had just sped into the dining room.

"Morning," she said, balancing several plates piled high with pancakes.

"Morning," he said, casually reading through the menu, even though he knew what he was going to order.

"Want coffee? I can grab it on my way back out," she asked from two tables away.

He nodded.

"I could use a refill." A man sitting at a table with two other men all dressed in camo and fishing vests raised his mug.

"I'll bring the pot," she cheerfully replied, disappearing through the kitchen doors.

A minute later, she whirled back in with two trays. How she managed both, he'd never know.

Depositing the order, she combined trays and refilled their coffee before appearing at Nick's table with a mug and poured coffee.

"Are you the only server this morning?" Nick asked.

"No, Barnaby's helping out this morning." She flashed him a sweet smile. "Glad to see you back, Nick."

Inwardly he cringed; he hadn't remembered her name. "Nell's the owner, but I can't remember..."

"Maggie," she came to his aid. "No sweat, you'll get there. Being new is hard."

"It's not so bad."

"What can I get you?"

"The salmon and eggs again, please. It was so good yesterday. I had to have it again."

"I'll let Nell know. It's her recipe." She tucked a strand of short hair behind an ear.

"Is she cooking today?"

"Yeah, she's got help back there, but she runs the show pretty much every day."

Absently, he scanned the cafe, but there was still no sight of Willa or her mane of curls.

"She's in the back."

"Willa?" His head whipped back to Maggie.

"No, Nell." She chuckled. "Are you looking for Willa?"

"Uh." He paused, not knowing how to answer. "Kind of."

"I haven't seen her today, but you never know. She may come in." Maggie tucked her order pad into her apron. "Can I get you anything else?"

"No, that's all, thanks."

"I'll get this right out for you."

Once she left, he ran his hands over his face. He felt like a kid with a crush. When was the last time he had gotten this twisted up about someone? It had been a while. Memories flashed in his mind and he frowned. The last time hadn't worked out so well for him.

Scooping the last bite of salmon and eggs into his mouth, Nick leaned back in his chair. Man, was that delicious. He'd had salmon in Seattle, but it didn't taste as good as it did here. Maybe it was how Nell prepared it. Either way, he was a customer for life.

He picked up his coffee cup, recently topped off by Maggie. As soon as he took a sip, the bell over the door jingled and Willa rushed in, making a beeline for the kitchen door. She disappeared through it.

Curious, he kept watch on the door.

A few minutes later, she came back out, talking to someone behind her. Nell followed her out.

"I know, but Carlos isn't here. This afternoon when he gets in, I'll have more time," Nell said, a kitchen towel in her hand. She glanced back towards the kitchen. "I'm sorry."

"That's okay." Willa sidestepped a customer walking past. "I'll see if Duke can meet with us then. Can we meet here?"

"Of course." Nell sounded relieved. "We can meet out back, it'll be warm by then."

"Great, see you later." Willa took a step before she noticed Nick sitting at the booth, watching her.

He dropped his gaze, not wanting her to think he had been eavesdropping, even though he obviously had been.

"Hi." He gave her a flash of a smile, hoping she wouldn't think he was being rude.

"Oh, hi." She took another step towards him, brushing a chunk of hair back behind her shoulder. She looked flustered.

"Everything okay?" His eyes flicked to the kitchen door and back.

"Yeah." She bobbed her head. "Just making plans for later with my friends."

"Ah." He nodded, as though he hadn't noticed how unsettled she appeared. "Do you want to sit down? I was actually going to come by and see you after breakfast."

"You were?" The pinched corners of her light green eyes eased. She slid into a chair across from him. "What for?"

"Well," he awkwardly brushed at his hair. "I, uh, need to get some supplies to fix up the cabin. I thought you might know the best places to go."

"Gil's has some nice lamps and stuff." She glanced off to the left, her mouth twisted up on one side. "But you've probably already been there. What about Izzy's Boutique? She's got some cute tables and stuff."

"That's cool. I've never been there before." He nodded, even though the likeliness that he'd buy a table he could build was low. "I need fixtures like a new light and maybe a new sink and faucet for my kitchen."

"Oh!" She brightened. "There's a cool salvage and resale place in Liberty Valley, not far from here. It's just up the road a bit."

"I'm out that direction."

"Hostettler's old cabin?"

"So it would seem." He smiled. Did everyone know where he lived? "Did you know him?"

"Who, Hostettler?" He nodded.

"No, he was from California. He used the cabin for fishing. Came up a few times a year." She toyed with a sugar packet.

"Can I get you a cup of coffee?" Nick asked, lifting his head and looking for Maggie.

"No, I'm good, thanks." She flashed him a smile. "How's the cabin coming along?"

"I honestly haven't done much with it yet." He held up his hands. "I was focused on the workshop. I just started working on the cabin."

"Yikes." Her eyebrows went up. "I heard that place was in bad shape." "It's not too bad." He laughed. "I took out the old carpet, curtains, and furniture. The cabinets are in decent shape. They need a little refinishing, that's all."

"Is that what you do?" She tilted her head. "Cabinetry?"

"Some. Woodworking mainly. I make a lot of boxes and charcuterie boards."

"Do you like doing that?" she asked, staring into his eyes. "I mean, is that what you want to create?"

"Sometimes. Truthfully? I like making tables and furniture. Live-edge. River tables. That sort of thing. Custom furniture to meet a need. Or even to match a theme. It's fun to figure out a new design."

It was so easy to talk to her. It just spilled out.

"Art, then," she said simply.

He let out a laugh. "I wouldn't call it art."

"Why not?" She cocked her head.

He didn't know how to answer that. "It's not something you put on a wall."

"It's not something you'd find at a furniture store."

"Well, no. It's design *and* function."

"Art."

He scratched the stubble on his chin. "I guess you could call it that."

She just smiled.

It made him uncomfortable to think of what he built as art, though. It made it sound fancy. He didn't feel fancy. He just liked making well-built things with his hands that highlighted beautiful pieces of wood.

"So." He pulled out his wallet. Willa was coming back here this afternoon to meet her friends. So maybe she was free now. They could talk more on the road. "I don't suppose you could show me how to get to that store, could you? If you're free."

"Oh." She flicked a glance towards the kitchen door, then back at him. A blush grew on her cheeks. "I, uh...I'm free right now. I don't have any classes today."

"Classes?"

"I teach yoga at a studio up the street." She lifted her chin in the direction of her studio.

"Yoga." He tried to keep his mind on topic, but the thought of her stretching and her apparent level of flexibility scattered every thought.

"Yes, have you ever tried it?"

"Tried it," he repeated, trying to force the blood back into his brain. "Tried what?"Her face flashed into a smile. "Yoga."

"Oh! Yes, of course. Uh, no. Not really." He shook his head to clear it. "I've stretched, though. Does that count?"

She let out a twinkling laugh that went straight to his heart. Man, did he like the sound of it. It was so light and happy. "Sure, it counts. If you ever want to try the other benefits of yoga, though, stop by my studio and take a class. I think you'd like it."

"I'm not that flexible, though." It was an understatement. After standing at his workbench for a couple of hours, his lower back got tight like a rubber band.

"Then you're perfect for the class." She interlaced her fingers in front of her.

"How's that?"

"It'll improve your flexibility and mobility. You're probably super tight because you're not used to moving outside your normal range of motion."

"Oh, sure. That makes sense." It did, actually. Maybe there was something to it. "I'll think about it."

Thirty minutes later, they stood inside Days Gone By, an architectural salvage store that made all of Nick's dreams come true. Well, the ones involving vintage craftsmanship and hardwood design. Barely able to contain himself, he found an old hutch with a spalted maple inlay. He ran his hands over the dovetailed drawers.

"You really like vintage furniture." She grinned, watching him caress the piece.

"They don't make furniture like this anymore." He opened a cabinet door to see that the woodworker had affixed the face panels with tiny metal brackets instead of just gluing and screwing them in. "The attention to detail is stunning."

"Tell me what I'm missing." She squatted down to inspect it.

"See this?" He pointed at the dovetailed edges. "This is to replace nails. It's held together by its own tension. They probably used a hide glue given of the age of the piece, but no nails."

"Like a puzzle."

"Exactly." He moved to the door. "This panel was cut from the same wood and book matched. That means it was one piece cut in half and flipped open like a book, so the design matches on both sides. See the wood grain?"

She reached out a hand to trace the lines in the wood. "It has a lot of detail."

"Yes, that's knotty alder. Very pretty."

"Is this how you make your furniture?"

"When I get the chance." He tore his gaze off the cabinet door to cast her a smile, finding her watching him with interest. "It doesn't sell as fast, so I only work on a piece at a time."

"Do you sell online?"

"I do, but with the shipping cost, furniture doesn't move as quickly. Also, I'm still new. I have to build a name for myself."

"You can try some of the craft fairs that come into this area. This summer, when we get more tourists, it'll get busy. We have lots of seasonal festivals."

"I'll have to try that." Finally tearing himself away from the hutch, he searched the space for light fixtures, seeing some in the back. He pointed. "Lighting is over there."

"Have you always been interested in woodworking?" She strolled along beside him.

"Sort of." He glanced at her. It was a personal conversation. As much as he liked talking to her, he wasn't sure if he was ready to share that yet, or why he had left the force. If they kept the conversation on wood, though, it was safe. "My grandpa was a carpenter. He worked exclusively with hand tools. His joints were incredible. I used to spend time with him in the summers. He taught me some stuff."

"You obviously kept it up if you've made a living out of it."

"I did." Not at first, though. It had taken him a while.

He stopped to inspect a pedestal sink that would work in his bathroom. Better than the old water-stained one currently there.

"Is he still around? Your grandpa?" She ran a hand over a nearby sink.

"Uh, no." He cleared his throat. "He passed away a few years ago."

She turned to him. "I'm sorry to hear that."

He shrugged it off. "It's okay. He lived a long life. A happy one at that."

His grandpa had been more full of life than anyone he'd ever met. If Nick could find half as much joy as his grandpa had fitting two pieces of wood together or enjoying pie that his late grandma had made, then he'd count that as a success. He hoped to find it.

"That's all that matters, in the end."

"I'm trying to learn that." He gave her a half smile, then resumed his examination of the porcelain sinks in front of them. "Okay. Which one do you like best?"

She stood back, propping one elbow on a hand, the other fist held against her chin as she scrutinized them both. She wrinkled her nose as she considered them. It was adorable. Finally, she pointed to one with wrought iron framing. "If you get that one, you could put a basket underneath it for towels and stuff. The other one doesn't have any space for that, so unless you have a cabinet nearby, you might need that feature. The wrought iron one looks older too, like it has a story."

"I have a cabinet, but I like the wrought iron too." He liked the fact that she admired the history of the piece. Maybe they weren't that different after all.

CHAPTER 8

Willa watched Nick tap the steering wheel on the ride back from the store. He'd done that a few times today when he was thinking hard on something.

"Everything okay?" she asked.

He blinked, obviously deep in thought. "Yes, sorry. I drifted away for a minute there."

"No worries. I do that all the time." Especially when she was deep in thought about a new product.

"I've been thinking." He glanced over at her and gripped the steering wheel. "About our connection."

"Yes?" She bit her lip, not liking that she had no clue what was going on between them. Shouldn't she? She knew all about this sort of metaphysical stuff.

"Do you think it was the electricity from the lightning that night? Do you think it created some sort of field around us that's still there, but not strong enough to notice otherwise? And our proximity increases it enough to feel?" He pinched the bridge of his nose. "No, that's dumb. It would have neutralized when we grounded, or the first time we touched anything metal."

"It's not dumb." She reached out to touch his forearm. "Maybe it's not normal electricity."

The tingling sprang up between them and she pulled her hand back. What *was* that? Maybe it had to do with whatever was going on with the salve...and her hand. She flipped over her hand to study the pink line that ran across her palm. It had nearly faded away entirely.

"Maybe not, but what else could it be?"

"Some kind of energy?" Everything that was happening was related to healing in some fashion. "Do you have any injuries? Do you feel different in any other way?"

He jerked back his head at her question and cast a glance her way. "No, why?"

She shrugged. "I'm experiencing it in other ways."

"With other people?" His voice rose an octave. That was weird.

"No. With the salve I made. With healing." She was worried about sharing her healing hand. Sometimes people got scared when they heard things they couldn't explain. It made them uncomfortable, which could evolve into anger. Fear and anger were tightly intertwined in some people. "Anything healing on you after we touched? Maybe wherever it's tingling?" He seemed relieved about her answer, but the frown stayed on his face. His jaw stayed set. "I don't have anything in need of healing."

It was a vague answer and made her think he was offended by the question. She wasn't implying there was anything wrong with him.

She checked the clock on his dash, anxious to get back to the cafe and see if she could learn more about what was going on with her. But it wasn't even eleven o'clock yet. She wouldn't get to discuss it with her friends until that afternoon.

She had some time to kill. "I'd love to see what you've done with the cabin so far. And see your workshop."

The tension left his shoulders. He glanced over at her. "That...would be nice."

"Maybe over time we'll figure out what's going on between us."

"Maybe." His eyes slid back out over the road.

They weren't that far from the cabin. She might not have ever been there, but she knew where it was. It was in a great location, just within the town limits at the foot of the mountain, tucked into the woods.

It wasn't long before he put on his blinker and turned onto a gravel road. Trees lined the drive, casting speckled shade over the windshield. It looked like a fairy tale.

The road curved and a small log cabin came into view. The exterior seemed to be in good shape, with a brand-new metal roof. Across the small yard sat a metal building of roughly the same size. It had the same metal roof, probably added at the same time.

Opening the truck door, she hopped down and gazed up at the large sugar maple in the front yard. Its huge, dinner-plate-sized leaves swayed in the breeze. Caught up in the magnificence of it, she spun under its branches, letting the filtered light fall on her face. Her arms went out and she took a large breath of fresh air.

It felt like one of those magic places you stumbled upon when you weren't expecting it, not even realizing you're unbalanced or out of sorts until you hit it and then it feels like everything is right in the world.

This place was like that.

Walking to the tree trunk, she placed her palms on the bark, feeling the tree's energy. It was a living thing, like her houseplants, but on a much larger scale. She wished she lived closer to the woods like this, not that she didn't like her little place on the water.

She stopped, realizing she was being watched. The urge to apologize bubbled up in her throat. But no, she was done with being sorry for who she was. It was on him if he judged her. Instead, she gave him a shy smile, hoping he'd accept her.

The way he looked back at her gave her hope.

"It's just gorgeous," she said finally.

Stepping under the canopy of the tree, he walked in close to her, his proximity making her breath catch. What was he doing? He stared up through the leaves, finding her vantage. A smile spread over his face. "It really is."

"You know..." She gazed up at him through her eyelashes, flashing him a teasing smile. "When I was younger, I got teased for being a tree hugger. Even though I never actually hugged them."

He tilted his head, listening. "Is that so?"

"It is."

"I mean, are you sure you didn't hug them?" He cracked a smile, letting her know he was teasing too.

She caught her lower lip between her teeth and pretended to think back. "I can't be sure. It's possible."

The sounds of their laughter meshed perfectly with the rustle of the leaves shifting against each other. It was music to her ears.

"I can't wait to see it all put together," Willa said, sliding out of the seat of his truck a couple of hours later when he brought her back to the cafe to meet with her friends.

He'd let her roam the property for a good half hour before they even got to the tiny cabin. It was small, but it worked for him. Utterly cozy. She loved everything about it. It would be perfect when he finished renovating it.

"I'll have you over after I get things fixed up," he promised. "You can help me with the final touches."

"I'll probably take you to Izzy's for that." The woman had the best selection of homewares in the area. "But you might not find a style that you like. It's a bit vintage and eclectic."

"Sounds perfect."

Happy, she moved to go.

"Hang on." His demeanor changed. He was checking something behind her.

It was Solomon coming up from the marina, his long, skinny legs walking toe out. He spent so much time on the water, he walked wide to keep his balance on land. Confused, Willa found Nick coming around the truck to her. "It's just Solomon."

He watched the man carefully, standing close to her. "You know him?"

"Yeah." She smiled, raising her hand in greeting to the older fisherman. "He's a friend."

"Is he-" He paused. "Okay?"

She shook her head, not understanding what he meant. Did Nick think he was a threat? "Yes, of course."

Nick nodded, his body relaxing a little. "He was talking to a pelican earlier today."

That was strange, but not completely out of the ordinary. Solomon spent a lot of time by himself.

"Hi, Solomon," she said when he got close enough to see her.

"Afternoon, Willa," he answered, his weathered face smiling wide.

"How's it going?" Nick asked.

"Good." He placed his hands on his back and peered up toward the sky. "I haven't seen Roy since I came back ashore, though."

"Who's Roy?" she asked.

"I got a pelican!" His eyes twinkled. "He chose me, you see."

"He did?" She wasn't sure what to say. Maybe he needed a friend. "That's cool. I'll keep a lookout for him."

"You should!" He pointed a finger. "You'll recognize him because the black tips of his wings are darker than most. He's real funny."

She couldn't help but smile. She hadn't seen Solomon this happy in ages. "I'll do that."

Nick seemed confused, but no longer on edge. It was sweet, him being there in case she needed him.

On impulse, she reached up and hugged Nick. He was only a little taller than her, but she still had to rise to her toes to reach him. He smelled like cedar and fir.

He seemed surprised but hugged her back.

Tingles erupted on her cheek and chest where she had pressed against him, spreading down her arms. She saw him blink in shock. He must have felt it too. Giving him a smile, she backed away. "Sorry, I'm a hugger."

"It's okay," he stuttered out.

It was nearly time to meet her friends, so although she wanted to, she couldn't linger. She wanted to spend the afternoon hearing more about how he crafted wood together and the art he wanted to create.

But she had to figure out what was going on.

"What are you trying to say?" Nell set down the sugar packets she'd been reorganizing and faced her.

"Um." Willa fidgeted. "Maybe we should wait for Duke." "That could take all day." Shelby checked her watch, her foot bobbing. "He's not the most reliable."

"He said he'd come." Standing at the edge of the cafe's outdoor patio, she peered down at the marina. With relief, she saw Duke's tall frame on the pier heading toward the shore. "He's coming!"

Maggie was quieter than usual, sitting next to Shelby. She was still in her server apron and watched them all with wide eyes.

"You're okay, though, right?" Nell grabbed Willa, searching her face for answers.

That day over a year ago popped back up in Willa's mind. They'd all sat out here, where they so often gathered. Gary told them he was dying.

Shit. It had never even occurred to her that Nell would think she was bringing them similar news.

"Oh, no! I'm fine." The words bubbled out of her mouth. She gripped Nell's forearms to emphasize it. "I'm so sorry, Nell. I didn't even think."

Tears formed in her friend's eyes, threatening to spill over, but she lifted her head, blinking them away. She sniffed and nodded. "It's okay. I'm okay. It was just too similar. I was afraid."

Overcome with emotion for her friend, Willa pulled her in for a big hug. She couldn't begin to know what Nell was feeling, but she felt bad she'd dredged it up.

"So, we're hugging. Hope it's not bad news," Duke said, joining them on the deck.

"No!" Willa pulled away to address them all. "No bad news. At least, I don't think so.""What is going on?" Nell held out her hands.

"I made some new salve," she started into her tale. "Kinda like Biofreeze for joint pain and arthritis, for Loris and Mary. Both of them are almost entirely pain-free now."

Nell frowned. Duke's eyes shifted from one person to the next.

"I checked back in on Mary again this morning. She only has to apply it twice a day to find relief. It lasts around six to eight hours."

She'd left Mary some of the dried sea lettuce this morning to try for her eyes as well. She could sprinkle some in her food once a day. Hopefully, it'd be just as effective.

"The white willow bark you gave me helped too," Shelby said, rubbing the back of her neck. "I had another tension headache last night after I got home and went ahead and tried it. It helped right away."

"How much did you take?" Willa asked her.

"I only took half the dose you suggested." She pursed her lips. "I was worried it was going to make me feel weird or something."

"And?"

"And nothing." She shrugged. "Nearly instant relief."

"See!" Willa spun to the rest of them. "That's not normal."

"Your potions are working for once?" Shelby raised an eyebrow.

"Hey, they work! Nettle has helped Nell's allergies many seasons."

"It's true," Nell spoke up.

Shelby grinned.

"They don't normally work *that well*, or that quickly, though, do they?" Duke pushed off the corner of the bar where he'd been leaning and moved closer, his movements fluid.

Willa shook her head. "Shelby should have had to take the full dose to get relief, and technically white willow bark isn't the best for tension headaches, valerian root is."

"Then why'd you give it to me?" Shelby asked.

"I wasn't sure they were tension headaches. And I didn't think you could handle the taste of the valerian root."

Shelby scoffed. "I could handle it. I just may not *want* to."

Willa rolled her eyes. "The point is...my products are more effective than before. Also, this happened."

She lifted her hand for them all to see the light pink line across her palm.

"I cut this yesterday morning."

Shelby stood up and took Willa's hand in hers. "I thought you said yesterday it wasn't that bad."

"It wasn't. I didn't need stitches, probably. But it bled across the entire two-inch cut."

"Maybe it wasn't that deep." Nell moved closer to see for herself.

Maggie's mouth dropped open.

"And it itched?" Shelby leaned in.

"Yes, but not in the way healing skin does. I would say it tingled. There's more to it than that, but it all began Friday morning, the day after Gary's birthday and our swim in the cove."

Duke spoke finally. "What else?"

Willa's eyes dropped. She wasn't sure what to share. She didn't know why she had a connection with Nick. Maybe it was because he had been on the beach at the same time?

Maybe it was the electricity in the air? Or an otherworldly connection they shared? She had no idea. But she was here to share with her friends. If they were going to be close again, she had to trust them.

"I met Nick that night. On the beach." Duke raised his eyebrows at her declaration. He obviously already knew but must have been surprised she was letting the rest of them in on it. "Ran into him, technically. Maybe whatever energy I picked up from the water or from that storm was still on my skin and passed between us. When I touch him, it tingles the same way."

"Still?" Duke asked, interested.

She nodded.

"For him too?"

"Yes."

"Well, damn." Shelby grinned at her. "That sounds fun."

A blush spread up Willa's neck like red tentacles of heat winding up and into her hair, setting it on fire.

"I think something happened to me in the water." Willa tried to focus on what was happening.

"What was in the salve?" Shelby asked, digging into the details.

"Brown algae," she answered.

"Did you make it after Thursday night?"

"Yes, I made it Friday."

"How did you cut your hand?" Duke asked.

"With my foraging knife. I slipped on the rocks with it in my hand."

"Ouch." Maggie frowned.

"Did your hand touch the water?" Shelby asked.

It was a strange question. She thought back and remembered rinsing her hand in the icy waves. "Yes, but I think it's like a healing energy I have."

"What about the white willow bark?" Shelby cut her off. "When did you make it?"

"Saturday, the day after. Well, I mixed it six weeks ago but strained and bottled it Saturday. Still within that window."

"White willow bark doesn't come from the ocean."

"No." Willa shook her head. "It's a tree bark, but it's local. I get it from an herbal shop in Olympia."

She was drawn to local herbs, things she could get foraging in her backyard or from shops in Olympia or Aberdeen. They were businesses she knew only sold sustainably harvested herbs.

"Did you put anything else in it?" Shelby's gaze was intense.

"Uh, no. Just a neutral alcohol to pull out the constituents." But wait. "That's not entirely true. I used a rough moonshine I picked up from a farmers market last summer. It has a higher percentage of alcohol to water, so I had to add a little water to balance out my percentages."

"What water did you use?"

Where was she going with this?

"I boiled off some ocean water, distilling it.""How?" Duke asked.

"It's very similar to how I make hydrosol, with a large pot and an upside-down lid to catch the steam in a bowl."

"When did you collect the ocean water?" Shelby's voice rose an octave.

"Saturday, when I cut myself." She blew out, not following her line of questioning. "I was harvesting sea lettuce for Mary's eyesight, and some for Nell too. I thought she might like it for the cafe."

"Then it's the water," Shelby said suddenly, as though it explained everything.

"But apart from when I touch Nick, it's always about healing." She was still no closer to figuring out why they had a connection. She studied her hands. "I thought maybe it was my hands. There are lots of old stories about healing with hands.""Maybe that's how you're using it," Maggie said quietly. She smiled her vibrant smile at Willa. "You're a healer."

It warmed Willa's heart to be identified as her deepest desire. Healing people or bringing them as much relief as possible was her purpose in life. She just knew it.

"I think it's a combination of both," Shelby said. "She's got some sort of healing energy, but it's being transmitted using things from the ocean."

"Why are we taking it this seriously?" Nell said, shaking her head. She glanced from one friend to the next, reading the room. Her face went wide in a grimace. "I'm sorry, Willa. I don't mean to be rude, but you're very- holistic. You often try to find connections between us and the earth. I don't think you're wrong, exactly. It's worked out well for you, but not everything is magical like that."

"Magic is a word often applied to things science hasn't explained yet," Duke spoke up.

"And why isn't it just the plants? Herbalism is a thing. It works," Nell countered. "Like she said, I've been using nettle for years."

"Her hand." Duke gestured, challenging her to explain it away too.

"Maybe it wasn't that deep." Nell's eyes hopped between them. "I don't get it. What am I missing?"

Shelby's mouth twisted to the side. "I can tell where water is."

"What do you mean, you can tell where it is?" Nell's brows drew together.

"Well, you know how I could get lost in my own living room?" She let out a laugh. "It's always been an issue for me. I have no spatial awareness. A few days ago, just post-swim, I was driving down near Lacey to meet a guy about a business opportunity, and I knew which way to go because I could *feel* how close I was to Puget Sound. That's when I realized it. I started paying attention and realized I just know where water is."

"You can feel the water out there?" Duke indicated toward the cove with his head.

Shelby nodded.

"I can even feel other water, like lakes or rivers. But it feels different, less active. And there's less of an itch." Her eyes sparkled. "I can even kinda tell which direction it's running."

"Are you serious?" Nell breathed out in amazement.

Maggie's mouth formed an O.

"It seems I'm not the only one who got something that night." Shelby cocked her head, watching Duke. "What've you got?"

Willa was shocked. She'd thought it was only her, but this was way better! She had been gifted something from the water and she wasn't the only one.

A slow smile spread over Duke's face. "I can make the water move."

"What?" Shelby hollered. "That's no fair. That's way cooler than mine!"

Duke just blinked, pleased with himself. He let out a cocky snort.

"How'd you figure that one out?" Willa asked, desperate for more information.

"I didn't think much about it initially, but I finally realized some of my trips were going faster than normal. And I wasn't hitting any of the normal slowdowns on windy days. It was like the waves were going in the direction I wanted them to, every time. So, finally, I just tried to-" He squinted his eyes and raised his hands. "Push them. It worked."

"Well, damn." Shelby sat on a bench with a thud. She stared off at the water.

Duke chuckled and patted her on the back. "Maybe yours will get cooler with time."

She peered up at him, curling her lip, but it only made him laugh harder.

"How'd you get Mary Mary Quite Contrary to give you feedback?" she said suddenly, addressing Willa.

Nell listened in as well, obviously curious. Mary was Gary's great-aunt or something and Will knew Nell had tried to help the woman over the years to no avail.

"Maybe she was just in too much pain before," Willa wondered out loud. "I mean, she still wasn't overly friendly, but she answered my questions. I think she was grateful for the relief."

"She's always been like that," Duke said quietly.

"This is amazing, everyone," Willa said, excitement bubbling up within her. Her hands formed little fists. "We've been given gifts. From the earth!"

"Calm down, Flower Child," Shelby huffed, using Duke's old moniker for her. "Remember the part where Duke talked about science? Just because we don't understand how it happened doesn't make it mystical."

But it didn't douse Willa's enthusiasm. She'd known, trusted all these years, that everything they ever truly needed was available to them. They'd just finally tapped into a part of it. She was elated.

"Apparently not everybody got gifts," Nell mumbled, staring at her hands. "Nothing's changed with me. I'm just the same old Nell."

Gary's death had taken a larger toll on her than the rest of them. Of course, it had. She'd lost her partner, the love of her life. She had been pushing herself too hard lately and was looking older and more tired.

"Maybe it's for the best," she went on sadly. "What would I do with a superhero ability?"

"Give it time." Willa put a hand on her shoulder. "Maybe you just haven't figured it out yet."

All eyes shifted to Maggie, who still hadn't said much.

She leaned back from all the stares, her shoulders raised and her hands twisted around each other. In a voice nearly inaudible, she whispered, "I can kinda sorta make it rain."

CHAPTER 9

"**A**ny sign of anyone familiar?" Isaac asked, his voice menacing through the tinny speaker of the phone.

It had been three days and still...Palmer hadn't found Haddish's bag. He was starting to get worried. His name was technically Reginald Palmer, but Reginald didn't sound as strong, so he went by his last name.

"Nothing at all." He toed a loose rock in the pavement outside the general store downtown. The morning traffic had died down and he wasn't sure where to check next. "I didn't see who he was meeting. It could be anywhere."

"You'd better think of something. Mr. Dupree doesn't tolerate failure."

Palmer's eyes narrowed at the blatant threat. Then a wave of embarrassment hit him. He'd done nothing but fail since he arrived in the tiny hick town on the Hood Canal. On Dupree's orders, he'd been watching James Haddish and thought he'd finally gotten him when he saw him with that duffel bag.

"Any idea what was in the bag?" Isaac pressed harder.

"I really don't." He threw up one hand. "But it was obviously something important. I watched him move it from the station to his cop car, and then to his personal car before renting a boat in the port. Look, he put the boss in the big house. If there's something he's trying to keep hidden, I'm going to find it."

"Well, you'd better hurry. Mr. Dupree isn't exactly comfortable at the moment, as you well know."

"I know!" He rubbed his head, then ran his hand down his face. He couldn't blame him, really. Being cooped up in the big house would do that to you.

He needed something to pin on the cops. Whatever was in the bag might be just that. If he could prove that Haddish was dirty, then maybe the evidence the SPD had found on Larry Dupree would be dismissed.

If he'd only been a few minutes faster, he might have had him.

By the time he'd caught up with the lousy cop, it had started to rain. He hadn't even realized Haddish didn't have the bag with him when he shot the man. The rain had made it hard to see.

Failure number two.

He'd seen footsteps, though, so he knew Haddish had met someone on that stretch of beach that night. If that wasn't suspicious, he didn't know what was. Maybe he could still redeem himself.

"I'll find out something tonight," he snapped into the phone. "Someone has to know who was on the beach that night."

"You'd better. And be quick," Isaac's voice shifted from razors to rancid honey. "Or else he'll send me. That won't be good for you or that town."

Nick skimmed the shelves at Gil's, adding a bottle of wine and a couple of wine glasses to his cart. Maybe when he got the cabin done, he could invite Willa over and they could celebrate with dinner.

He studied the bottle. She was into herbs and yoga. Maybe she didn't even drink wine.

He frowned and put the wine back on the shelf. Turning, he could see the outdoor bar behind the cafe. Willa and her friends were gesturing wildly.

They seemed stressed, like there was a problem. His eyes shot to the door. If he went over there now, what would he even say? He knew she was meeting with them, and it was obviously important, but she hadn't shared anything about it on their shopping trip or at his place. It must be personal.

It wasn't his business, he tried to convince himself.

Sighing, he went back to the wine. Maybe he'd take a bottle for himself. Men could drink wine by themselves, right?

"They're always like that," a voice spoke up behind him.

It was Emiliano, leaning over a low shelf of canned vegetables.

"Who?"

He nodded towards The Wild Cafe. "At least, they always were growing up. Passionate, I'd say. Boy, did they get into arguments, especially Duke."

"Really?" He studied Duke through the windowpane.

"You wouldn't know it to see him now, but he used to get into it with practically everyone. Or conversely, he'd be silent as the night. There was no in-between with him. When we were young anyway. Still, it's good to see them back together, getting along and arguing."

The store owner's eyes stayed trained on the group, almost wistfully.

"Were you in the group?" Nick asked. "You grew up with them, right?"

"Nah," Emiliano waved a hand in the air. "I was too young. I never made it into the club."

"I'm sorry." It was never easy to be left out of the main group, especially in as small a town as this one was. Nick had never been the right age himself to have a friend group in his neighborhood, so he'd found friends where he could, eventually following in his dad's footsteps to law enforcement. He already knew several officers through his dad.

"It all worked out for the best. I didn't have a ton of free time anyway."

"Did you work here in high school?"

"Absolutely. My mom left when I was young, so I've always been in the market helping out."

"I'm sorry."

"That's okay. I was young. I got over that years ago."

"Still. That's hard for a kid."

"Nah, it was great." Emiliano beamed at him. "I knew everyone in town. I was running the register at ten."

"Sounds nice, having that exposure," he said politely, but in reality it sounded lonely. He would know. It sounded a lot like his past. Lots of interactions with people, but no deep friendships.

"What were they like back then?" he went on, tipping his head towards the wall. What he really wanted to know was about the one that was no longer with them. "What was Gary like?"

"He was the glue that held them all together," Emiliano said, slipping into memories.

Not wanting to intrude further, Nick grabbed a bottle of dark red wine, hoping it wouldn't be too sweet. He left the glasses in his cart; he didn't have any at home anyway. He had literally walked away from everything in his old life.

"I think I'll take a bottle after all." He nodded at the other man, moving away.

"Have a nice day." He lifted a hand in farewell.

Checking out, Nick's thoughts went back to meeting Duke. It had been the morning after Jimmy was shot on the beach and he ran into Willa. Pieces clicked together, like it was a case he'd been analyzing. His first instinct about the man that day was that he was asking questions, trying to get answers out of him, but he'd dismissed them as him being paranoid.

Maybe he'd been right to be.

The timing would suggest that Willa had shared their meeting with Duke. She told Nick she hadn't told the chief about him, but she didn't say she hadn't told *anyone*.

Duke must have intentionally sought him out to see what kind of a man he was. He didn't linger too much on what that meant Willa thought of him. She may not even know he'd done it.

Taking his bags, he could still see Willa and her friends. Their movements were less frantic now and they were gathered closer. Duke stood around the women protectively, his body language open as he kept his attention on all four of them. Definitely not the same version of Duke Nick had run into at the post office.

He pushed out the door. Discomfort bubbled up within him. He wasn't the trusting sort, and it didn't sit well with him that the man had hidden his intentions and put on a show like he didn't know who Nick was. He'd had enough deception for a lifetime. Frowning, he cast them one more glance before heading to his truck.

Still, Duke had done it for Willa. Might Nick have done something similar for someone he cared for?

Willa's motivations were still a mystery to him. He hadn't expected her to share something like that with others. Then again, he'd only just met her.

He shook his head, not liking the feelings he was experiencing. Hadn't he sworn off women for a while?

Remembering what she'd said about the cove, he tossed a glance behind him, finding the water behind the marina. Sure enough, two dorsal fins grazed the water. No, there was a third one off to the right. It crested the surface, the blunt black and white face emerging from the water. He stopped in his tracks halfway across the lot. It looked like the orca was watching Willa and her friends.

A cool wind whipped up from the water, breaking his trance. One of the two orcas to the left jumped into the air, its long, patterned belly exposed above the waves. Awe and wonder filled him. He'd seen orcas before, but for some reason it seemed more majestic out here, far from the skyscrapers and highways in the city.

The way the light hit the animal, even at this distance, he could see a terrible scar running along the length of its body. It was probably from the boats in the Puget Sound. The water was much safer here, less densely populated.

He liked it here with the clean air, and even felt friendly towards some of the more neighborly townspeople. The ones that still treated him as a tourist didn't bother him. He didn't trust easily either. He was more than happy to live quietly alongside them.

Unlocking his truck, unease pricked his senses. An outsider stood at the end of the parking lot watching him. And he recognized the face.

It was everything he'd been afraid of.

His right hand immediately went to the concealed weapon he carried once again in his belt holster. He hated carrying it. He'd seen too much death and violence in his lifetime, but he'd been expecting this day ever since learning about Jimmy's death. Someone wanted the bag and if they were willing to kill for it, they wouldn't just give up because they had missed the hand-off on the beach.

They must know how valuable the bag was. Jimmy had been continuing to gather evidence against Dupree. If Dupree managed to get away with everything else lodged against him, this would put him away for good.

Palmer, Nick's mind tumbled, landing on his name. Reginald Palmer.

Recognition lit the man's eyes. They narrowed. His chin rose and his chest puffed out. The heavy leather jacket he wore might mark him as an outsider, but it also effectively concealed a shoulder holster. If Nick hadn't known where to look, he wouldn't have seen it.

Palmer would be able to clear a fast draw, but he was still a few car lengths away, with various vehicles between them. Nick's hand was already wrapped about his replacement pistol.

Before either of them could react, a cop car pulled into the lot and parked between them. Palmer's eyes broke from Nick's to follow the car. The driver's side door opened and Warner stepped out, slamming it behind him, his gaze firmly fixed on Palmer.

Hands on hips, he took in his appearance and rotated, his hand hovering near his weapon, to see Nick at the other end of the encounter. Palmer turned to walk away.

"I'd like to have a word with you," the chief said, moving between the vehicles toward Palmer.

Nick stayed where he was, waiting. His hand remained ready.

Palmer stopped, waited a beat and spun to face the aging man. "Yes?"

"I hear you've been poking around, talking to people. Asking questions." Warner's gravelly voice carried over the small lot to where Nick was standing. His hands were still on his hips, ready for action.

"That's not illegal."

"No, but you're going into shops, walking up to people on the street, getting into their business. Did you think that wouldn't be noticed?"

Palmer shrugged. "I'm a curious person. Still, not illegal."

"What are you doing in town?"

"Just passing through."

"This morning, you asked Izzy about people who live here, people who are new. What are you trying to find?"

147

A wolfish smile crept up the burly man's face, not reaching his eyes. They remained dead as they changed focus, finding Nick's. "I'm not trying to find anything anymore."

"You'll be on your way, then." The chief lifted his chin.

Dipping his head, Palmer gave his back to them both and stepped over the curb, heading along the sidewalk toward town.

Letting out a large exhale, Warner rounded back to Nick, his boots crunching on the gravel. "What the hell was that about? Who was that man?"

Nick's hands went up in front of him. "I didn't know he was here until now. His name is Reginald Palmer, hired hitman for Larry Dupree. I think you've found your shooter."

A muscle ticked in the side of Warner's jaw. "Do you have any proof?"

"Of course not."

"Why is he here?" "I suspect he followed Jimmy here. We put Dupree in jail, it was our last big bust."

"So, he's come for revenge?"

"Something like that." Nick sighed, running a hand through his hair. He didn't know the chief that well, or how he'd react if he knew about the bag. It was better if he didn't get involved.

"And you just brought this drama into the cove."

Nick's head dropped. Warner was right. It was his job to protect others and here he'd put them in harm's way. His original plan was to stay in his cabin and keep to himself. Why had he deviated from that? Visions of long, curly, reddish-blonde hair went through his mind, wild and lifted in the breeze outside his cabin. Oh, yeah.

Now she was in danger as well. He'd fix that.

"I'll take care of it."

"Like hell you will." Warner's hands formed fists. "He'll leave town and that'll be the end of that."

He wouldn't be leaving without the bag, but Nick didn't want Warner to get in the middle of it. "I hope so."

"If he doesn't, I'll run him out." Warner pressed the radio on his shoulder. "I'm calling a briefing in thirty minutes. Everyone, meet at the station."

Releasing the button, he raised a finger towards Nick and went on, "I've got to make a few calls. Go straight home. I might be calling with questions."

"Yes, Chief." He gave him a nod, lifting the latch of his truck door. He needed to get home and fortify his place anyway. He'd bought the place under an LLC. His name was connected to it, but only if someone pulled the records on the LLC. There were a lot of properties in the area, and technically, he lived just on the edge of town. If Palmer focused on Orca Cove, he might not even find him.

That would protect him, but not the rest of the town. The best thing he could do was stay remote, get back on course, and keep to himself.

"And Nick," Warner said when he lifted a leg to step into the truck, "stay home tonight."

"Not a problem, Chief." He got in and shut the door.

Not a problem at all.

CHAPTER 10

That night, Willa stood at the railing on her back deck overlooking the water. Three orcas played in the fading light. A shiver ran down the center of her back and she pulled her cardigan tighter across her chest and hugged her arms.

The reality of what had happened to her and her friends was still sinking in. It still felt like a dream. She'd always believed in something more, something bigger than herself. She knew the universe had a plan and that nature had answers that could heal and help, but this...this was way more than she'd ever dared to believe.

Why had it happened? What did it all mean?

That had been the theme of the conversation this afternoon, but for her it was simple. She knew what to do with her newfound powers. She was meant to heal people. And heal people she most certainly would.

Struck with clarity, she hurried back into her apartment, snagging her notebook from her desk, and plopping down on the rug in front of her TV. Using the coffee table to write, she tucked a foot underneath herself and started scribbling.

Now that she knew that her powers only worked with items from the ocean, she could harvest more ocean water to distill for all her other herbal applications.

The lemon balm she kept on her front porch for anxiety and depression, imagine how well that would work with some ocean water in a tincture! It would be like Shelby's white willow bark. She made notes. Maybe she could water the plant with distilled water from the ocean. Would that imbue the plant itself with additional strength?

Pickled sea asparagus for Sandy who was recovering from surgery, lavender and chamomile sleep spray for Izzy who had trouble sleeping, St. John's wort for Solomon's nerve pain. She couldn't keep her mind from coming up with more ways to use it, more ways to help others.

Her pen hovered over the notebook. She hadn't gotten around to checking in on Mary today. She'd gotten too caught up this morning with Nick. Pleasant bubbles of joy drifted up through her and her mouth curved into a smile. They'd had such a nice time shopping. And that cabin! She loved being near the ocean, but being surrounded by trees like that? With their leaves dancing in the breeze... Heaven.

It was easily one of the most peaceful places she'd ever been.

She'd go check in on Mary in the morning, right after she brought in more jars of ocean water.

Pushing up off the floor, she carried her notebook back to the table and clicked on her electric tea kettle. Her hands were drifting over her various dried teas when her phone pinged.

It was Nell, but this time it was the group text they used to use. The last time they'd used it was her suggesting the nighttime dip in the water and their varied responses.

"Sorry about my attitude earlier," Nell texted. "I'm happy for all of you. The cafe is closed and there's loads of leftover food. Who's up for a late meal?"

Willa let her eyes close for a minute. Nell hadn't invited them over for a late meal of cafe leftovers since Gary passed away.

Sniffing, she texted back, "I'll be there in ten."

Luckily, she hadn't eaten yet, distracted with everything.

Duke simply texted, "In."

Shelby sent a thumbs up emoji.

Maggie would still be there after cleaning up.

Maybe those days weren't behind them after all.

A sign was propped up in front of the door to the cafe, reading "Closed for private event." Willa practically skipped around the corner to the back. propped up against the locked front She could already hear 80s music coming from the outdoor speaker.

Maggie met her at the top of the stairs to the back deck.

"Can you believe it?" Her eyes twinkled from the Edison bulbs strung over them. "It feels like old times."

Willa hugged her friend. "It certainly does. How're you feeling?"

"Me?" She pulled back. "Oh, I'm fine. Better than fine. I can make it rain, remember?"

"How could I forget?" She laughed. At least she knew why Maggie had been so quiet lately. "Can you tell if it's going to rain too?"

"I think so." She pressed her lips together, staring off over Willa's shoulder. "I think I can feel the water in the air. And it's not accumulating."

"So, no rain tonight?"

"No, definitely not. It would need to come together more." She raised her hands in front of her and wiggled her fingers. "And get excited."

"Then you *can* tell!" Willa gripped her shoulders in support.

"I guess I can!" She bounced excitedly. "How cool is that?"

"Very cool."

Grinning, they walked arm in arm to where Shelby sat at a table. Nell was leaning over it, arranging the plates of food. Duke hadn't arrived yet.

The outdoor patio heaters were lit, adding a little warmth to the chilly evening.

"There're some stuffed salmon pinwheels left over. The scallops wouldn't have been good tomorrow, so I went ahead and sauteed them in a lemon garlic butter and added a little angel hair pasta." Nell tossed a towel over her shoulder and pointed to another dish. "Those are some roasted potatoes that were already prepped and leftover garlic green beans. I know it's a mess of little dishes, but I think it's enough."

"It's perfect." Willa laid a hand on her shoulder, stopping the woman. "We're lucky to have it."

Nell huffed and tucked a strand of wavy brown hair behind an ear. "Well, thanks. It's been too long."

"We might all have needed a little time." Willa dropped her head, then remembered the mason jar she carried and handed it to Nell. "Dried sea lettuce. It's bright and briny. A little goes a long way, but it's loaded with potassium, iron, and magnesium. Also, vitamin A and B12! All sorts of good stuff."

"Is this what you gathered for Mary?" Nell unscrewed the lid and gave it a sniff.

"Yes, it's also high in lutein. This little baby reduces free radical damage to the eyes."

Snagging a dark green curly bit, Nell tossed it in her mouth and closed her eyes. They popped back open quickly. "It tastes like nori, but it's bitter and more intense. Delicious!"

Shaking a little more into her hand, she set the jar down and ran the palm of one hand over the other, crumbling the dried seaweed. Then, she scattered it over the scallop pasta.

"What's that going to taste like?" Shelby eyed the dish.

"It's going to be beautiful. You'll see." Nell wiped her hands on her towel. "Thanks, Willa." "Anytime." She found a seat across from Shelby.

"You're not starting without me, are you?" Duke's voice carried over the lighthearted, happy beat of the music.

"Of course not." Nell looked up. "I just got the food set. I need to grab some wine."

"Leave it." He lifted his hands; a bottle was in each. "I got a couple of cases out of my last trip."

Nell took one of the bottles he offered and examined it, letting out a low whistle. "These aren't cheap. You got these from a job, as in trade?"

Duke just shrugged. Ducking behind the outdoor bar, he flipped a wine opener up in the air and caught it, giving them all a mischievous grin.

"I had a wine key in my apron." Maggie laughed at him.

"You're off duty." Ripping off the foil, he screwed in the metal opener and wiggled it out. "Who wants some?"

Willa checked the table.

"Sorry, I don't have kombucha. We're out," Nell apologized.

"That's alright, I'll have a glass." She smiled. She didn't drink often, but it was a special occasion.

Shelby snorted. "Kombucha."

"What? There's alcohol in it." Willa set her chin.

"Like point-five percent." Shelby rolled her eyes. "That's considered non-alcoholic in beer."

"That's commercial kombucha. Home brews can be two to three percent!"

"That's still only like half a beer."

"And it's good for healthy gut flora."

"Ah, gut flora. Right." Shelby winked at her to let her know she was teasing.

"Oh." Willa threw her napkin at her.

"Come on, children," Duke shook his head and made a playful tsk sound. He split a bottle between the five of them. "Let's try and behave for once."

Everyone lifted their glasses.

An hour later, even though she'd only had one glass of wine, Willa felt almost euphoric. Brushing her hair back over her shoulders, she opened her knit cardigan, letting more cool air onto her chest. The patio had grown warm and laughter had drowned out the music.

Nell got up and adjusted the flames on the heaters when "Don't You" by Simple Minds started playing. Her eyes lit up and she started to sway dance on her way back. By the time it got to the chorus, everyone had stood and they all joined in, singing along with the music.

Willa laughed in glee as they all hopped around the deck, voices raised in joy.

At the last chord, Duke pumped his fist in the air and they all collapsed into their chairs, giggling.

A cozy feeling had taken its rightful place back in Willa's heart. It felt so big it could burst. Maybe they were finding a new normal. But as good as they felt, there was one person she wished was with them.

A new friend, one she wanted to share her news with. But since her new abilities were connected to theirs, she wasn't sure if she could tell him without giving away their secrets too. She'd have to see how they felt about it.

But that was a conversation for another day.

The sun came through Willa's windows, casting sunshine on her face. Stretching, she kicked her covers off and hopped up, bounding out of bed. Pushing her window open, she stuck out a hand to see how cold it was. Chilly, but not cold. Perfect.

From her window, she caught sight of a dorsal fin cruising the waters. Without thinking, she raised her hand, still out the window. "Morning, Cora!"

Stepping onto the yoga mat she kept in the corner of her room, she stretched up high into the air, then bent over and stepped back into a downward facing dog, bending her knees as she melted into the position. Rolling forward into a plank, she held it for several breaths, warming her body. Dropping into a chaturanga, she moved through the rest of her vinyasa smoothly, then repeated it twice. Ending in the standing position, she brought her arms down in front of her to center her thoughts on the day in front of her.

It was going to be another good day. She just knew it.

After getting ready for the morning, she made a quick trip out to the rocks to gather more sea water. Leaving the jars on her counter, she poured hot water over some chicory and dried mushrooms and headed out.

"Good morning, Mary," she called out, knocking on the woman's door.

She heard a scuffle, then watched the door crack open a few inches. Mary's face came into view, her eyebrow raised questioningly. "Morning."

"Hi. I just wanted to check on you. See how you were doing."

"I'm doing fine. More than fine." She opened the door wider but kept her hand on the edge of it. Her eyes narrowed. "What'd you give me, girl? Mary Jane? That CBC stuff? You tell me right now!"

Surprised, Willa stepped back, nearly falling off the stairs to Mary's front door. She caught herself on the railing. "No, of course not!"

Mary stepped out onto the threshold and wagged a finger at her. "My eyes haven't been this clear in years and my body isn't hurting. That's not normal at my age. Tell me what you did to me!"

It was Willa's turn to frown. "Isn't that a good thing?"

Why was she complaining about feeling good?

"Not if you gave me contraband drugs!" Mary's chin rose high in indignation.

"I most certainly did not!" Willa took considerable care to ensure she was accounting for people's allergies, other medications, and personal wishes. Then again, she could imagine how it had felt for Mary if her symptoms magically disappeared. The water was making her products unusually effective. She softened her tone. "I would never give you anything you made clear you didn't want to use. I don't work that way. That sea lettuce is high in lutein, which is great for the eyes. You can look it up."

Mary's chin dropped a notch and her voice quieted. "Really? Then why hasn't my doctor given it to me?"

"There haven't been a lot of studies about it." Willa chewed her lip. How to explain without sounding like a hater of western medicine? She wasn't, exactly. It definitely had its place, but there were other options to try too. "Full studies are expensive, especially to test safe levels for people with different ailments. And there's not a lot of money to gain from selling natural treatments. Not when you can get them free by foraging."

Mary's eyes resumed their narrowed slits. "Greedy moneygrubbers."

Willa raised her hands. Maybe she'd gone too far. "Testing is expensive. Who's going to pay for it?"

"You're using it."

"I am, but I also know your medical condition well. And I start with small amounts and see how people do. I'm certified as an herbalist, you know. I'm not just playing around with it, testing willy-nilly."

"That's good." Her finger rose again. "You be careful with people. They can be very fragile."

That surprised her. "Very true, Mary. I'm very honored so many people trust me."

She nodded, satisfied. "Now, go away. I have things to do."

Willa bit back a smile. "Can I ask how much you took? For my testing documentation?"

"Oh, yes, of course. For science. I added a healthy pinch, just like you suggested, to my morning oatmeal yesterday. It tasted terrible, by the way." Mary's face twisted down and she stuck out her tongue. "I took it in a little water this morning. Still bad, but easier to get down. I think it started helping in a few hours. My eyes itched a little, but

I didn't notice my vision getting worse again until the end of the day."

"Things got clearer?" Willa's heart raced. She'd never get tired hearing how someone got better.

"Well, I didn't need as much light to see, and then the itching went away and I noticed things weren't as blurry. I didn't have to grab my cheaters as often."

"How long did it last?" The itching again. Like her tingle. It had to be connected to the water's energy.

"This morning my vision wasn't as bad as it was yesterday morning, but I took it anyway. My eyes itched again, but not as much. It cleared up within an hour. Yes, I think I can see fairly clearly now." Mary blinked, staring off in the distance, down her drive. "Those plants look terrible. When did they get so bad?"

Willa checked. They seemed the same as they had the other day when she was there. Daffodils were poking their sunny yellow heads up from last winter's dead leaves. It was late for bulbs. It'd been a long winter, but now that it was warming, they'd come out in full force.

She wouldn't mind getting her hands into the dirt. It would be nice. "Do you need help pruning them back for spring?"

"No!" Mary shocked her with the force of her refusal. "I tend my own garden. I don't need you mucking about in my business."

"I'm sorry to intrude." She couldn't understand the change in her attitude. She'd thought the woman was getting nicer since she wasn't hurting as much. She took a step down off her porch. Maybe Mary thought she was suggesting she couldn't manage on her own. Either way, Willa knew how to set boundaries. "I'll stop by in a week or so with more. Stop using it if you have any problems."

Without waiting, she twirled and left, trying not to take the older woman's anger personally. It wasn't about her. She'd done what she could. Besides, she had a yoga class to teach. And for once, she wasn't late.

She checked her phone for the time. Well, almost.

CHAPTER 11

That should do it, Nick thought, wiping his hands on his jeans. He straightened to peer up through the tree branches above him. Walking backward, he inspected his handiwork from another angle. He nodded. If anyone was right up on it, they'd be able to see the platform and half wall he'd built, but not at a distance.

If he needed it, he could keep an eye out here, or have a place to wait things out should they go south. It was just a precaution.

Picking up his tools, he headed back in to finish installing the sink they'd picked up. He'd only gotten as far as tearing the old sink out before he thought of the tree stand. Parts sat all over his bathroom floor. The room was a lot larger without the curved porcelain build-out and cabinet taking up space.

He'd hauled it out to a small garden shed until he figured out what to do with it. Maybe he could take the old sink to the salvage store to exchange for credit. Kneeling, he checked a board behind the old sink. Rotten. He'd have to replace that first, and maybe put a fresh coat of paint on the walls.

He wished he could have Willa over again and get her thoughts on colors. He was terrible at that. She'd seen the vision he had for the old place, smiling when she touched the cleaned-up beadboard in the kitchen and commented on the old mantel. The thick black walnut slab was one of the reasons he'd bought the place. It was live-edge and had a beautiful grain.

But solitude was good for him, especially now. And it still bothered him that she'd talked to Duke about him. She'd kept their meeting from the chief, arguably a dishonest thing to do, but then told the town troublemaker. It didn't add up. And he was tired of sifting through lies.

White would be fine for the bathroom.

Letting out a low grumble, he stood. He didn't want to run back into town, not with Palmer running around trying to find him. The paint would have to wait.

Making a quick walkthrough of his cabin, he re-checked all his weapon stashes. He had knives and a few long sections of heavy pipe tucked behind doors and under furniture. A shotgun he'd bought for hunting leaned up against the kitchen door, but he'd take that back to the bedroom with him at night.

It was the best he could do.

Pulling his tape measure from his pocket, he headed back into the bathroom to measure the board that needed replacing. He was jotting it down in a notepad when his phone rang.

It was the Orca Cove Police Department.

"Hello?"

"Detective Ryan?" Chief Warner answered.

"Just Nick Ryan now, Chief," he reminded him, yet again.

"You still holed up at home?"

"I am."

"Good." He huffed. "I talked to your boy Palmer again. Found him after I left you. He's out of town for certain."

"Was he staying in town?"

"No, in some hotel."

That was something, at least. "And you're sure he's gone?"

"That's right. Ronnie followed him out of town."

He was in a hotel nearby, most likely. "I appreciate you letting me know. I'll probably still lay low for a bit."

"Not a bad idea."

The chief hadn't hung up, though. He wanted something else. "What is it, Chief?"

Warner cleared his throat. "Autopsy report came back. Confirmed cause of death was a bullet wound to the chest. Two shots. Ballistics report said it was a .380. Ryan, I have to ask."

"I carry a nine millimeter Glock 19," he answered. He'd known the question would come up eventually.

"Of course." The chief chuckled at his unimaginative choice for off-duty carry. "Anything else registered to you?"

"Remington 870 twelve-gauge. I bought it to hunt duck when I came out here."

"Have you?"

"Haven't had the chance yet."

He grunted. "Ballistics connected the bullet to several other shootings in the Seattle area."

That made sense. He'd already told him it was Palmer. It had to have been. "And?"

"And they were crime scenes associated with shady dealings, thought to be connected to Larry Dupree."

"Palmer," he said anyway.

"Your theory is solid. I notified SPD he's been hanging around. They're being cooperative, but it's one of their own. They'll want to investigate, too."

Not surprising. They were a tight-knit group. It was personal.

"He's got a bone to pick with you? This Reginald Palmer?"

"Jimmy and I put his boss away."

"How long ago?"

"About nine months ago," he told him, even though he'd already know that.

"That's a long time to hold a grudge."

"Dupree's trial is coming up. Maybe he's trying to discredit us. Get the case thrown out."

"Is that what you think?"

He didn't have to think; he already knew. Palmer was looking for the bag hidden in his workshop. "It's a possibility. Or he could be trying to pick off any usable witness."

"Were there many witnesses at the bust?"

"Several."

"Personal, then."

"I think so too."

Silence filled the line. Maybe Warner was thinking about his next steps. But it had gone on too long.

"What else, Chief?"

"Patty Haddish was notified yesterday by the SPD."

His throat tightened. The bastard. "Thanks for letting me know."

"I don't have to tell you to take care of yourself. But Detective, you call me if you have any problems." His voice rose. "You hear me? You're not going to go vigilante on me."

It was an oxymoron, calling him a detective in one breath and a vigilante in the next, but he thought it best not to push his luck.

"Of course, Chief," he lied. He wasn't going to endanger anyone else.

The chief finally ended the call.

Nick sat on the edge of his couch, the weight of the last few days finally feeling like too much to bear. He might not have gotten as close to his old partner as others had, but Haddish had been one of them. It still stung. He wished he'd let Haddish in earlier, but he'd been too hot-tempered and ready to take on the world, even the low-lifes like Larry Dupree.

He ran both of his hands over his face, scrubbing hard. The clear morning had gone gray, and rain misted against the windows outside, gathering to roll down the glass in satisfying trails.

He felt like that. Like things were slipping away. He'd come here to get away from all of this and now he was dealing with it all over again.

And he'd brought danger with him.

That knowledge had a bitter taste. His face turned down in disgust.

He could beat himself up later; right now he needed to offer condolences. Picking up the phone, he dialed his old partner's widow.

Reaching up, Nick was gently twisting tight a nut on the new bathroom sink drain when he heard a knock at his front door. Jerking upright, he hit his head on the wrought iron legs under the sink. Blinking back tears, he stumbled to his feet. Drawing his weapon, he held it down as he walked quietly to the living room.

A little white Fiat was parked behind his truck. He remembered seeing it in front of Willa's apartment. Frowning, he holstered his pistol. He could see light, curly hairs in the arched window at the top of his door.

Willa.

Unlocking the door, he swung it open.

"Oh, hi!" she said, startled either by the abrupt door opening or by his expression. A rug was rolled up and tucked under one arm.

"Good afternoon." He scanned the driveway, making sure she hadn't been followed.

"Can I come in?" she asked when he didn't move. "I brought you something."

Instinctively, he stepped back to let her pass, shutting the door behind her.

"You didn't have to do that." He wasn't used to people giving him things. It made his stomach twist uncomfortably.

Grinning widely, she hurried into his kitchen, unrolling the rug and toeing it in place in front of the sink. It was denim, red, and charcoal and appeared hand-woven, like a rag rug. He loved it immediately. "That'll look great when you get that stainless steel farmhouse sink in place."

"I didn't get that one, I just got the one for the bathroom."

"Yes, but you were eyeballing it." She sent him a grin over her shoulder. "You'll end up getting it."

"Maybe." He shuffled his feet, sticking his hands deep into his pockets. "I just got the other sink installed."

"You did?" Her eyes lit up and she hurried past him down the hall to inspect his handiwork. "Oh, Nick. This is amazing! I love the wrought iron in here."

"Me too." He leaned against the door jamb, watching her kneel to peek under the sink.

Standing, she touched the scalloped medicine cabinet they'd picked up to go with the sink. "I can't believe you got all of this done in one day."

"Well, I took the day off from my other work, but I wanted to see how these would look in here."

"It's so beautiful." She ran her hand over the white porcelain of the sink. "What a difference!"

"It needs paint," he said without thinking. He wasn't going to ask for her help with anything else, but at that moment he couldn't exactly remember why.

Standing, she put her hands on her hips, her vibrant green eyes traveling over the rest of the bathroom. "You could go with gray, it'd be safe and work with the wrought iron, but it might be kind of cool. But you know what would be awesome? A light turquoise. Can you see it against the white sink and clawfoot tub...and the black pipe and iron?"

He tilted his head, seeing the bathroom as she was seeing it. It brightened up the room immediately. The wooden floors and baseboards would look great with that color. "I could add a fluffy gray rug in here, too."

"Ooh! And if you have anything you use regularly, you can put it in little blue bottles." She raised her hand to gesture to the space over the clawfoot tub. "And add floating wood shelves there. I can make you some lavender bath Epsom salts. I even have some extra blue mason jars that would be perfect for that."

She twisted around, smiling up at him, closer than he'd expected. He could smell the herbal lavender drifting from her hair. It curled to settle down in his gut. All other thoughts fled his mind. Without thinking, his hand curled around her elbow, electricity dancing between them. Her smile dropped a notch, warming. She leaned forward against him, her bright green eyes enrapturing him.

This close, he could see faint freckles across the bridge of her nose. Slowly, he raised his other hand, wanting to touch her. He hesitated, curling his hand to brush her cheek with the back of it. Tingles buzzed between them and she smiled, her eyes closing for a few moments before opening again to enrapture him further.

Who was this woman? Once again, he felt like he had a magical mermaid in his arms, just emerging from the ocean. He could almost feel the breeze of the ocean on his face. His hand tightened on her elbow, and he dropped his lips to hers.

Sparks of electricity exploded between them. Willa slid her hands up his chest and deepened the kiss. Nick grew heady, lost in the sensations and vibrations building between them.

A ringing noise broke through the fog.

Shaking his head, he realized it was a phone.

"Oh, I think that's me," Willa said, her voice wispy and dreamy. She checked the phone in her back pocket. "It's just Duke. I can call him back later."

Duke. The guy she'd spilled all her secrets to. His eyebrows dropped and he blinked. What was he thinking? She wasn't who he thought she was. He stepped back, banging into the door jamb.

"Are you okay?" She raised her hand.

"Yeah, I'm fine," he said gruffly, backing into the hall, ignoring the hurt expression that passed over her face. He hadn't meant to confuse her, but she had her friends to lean on. She could go complain to them later. He was sure they'd listen. "If you need to get that, it's fine. I'm behind on work anyway."

She cast a glance back into the bathroom, then found his gaze again, hurt and confusion filling her eyes. "Oh, okay."

She followed him back out to the living room.

"Thanks for the rug." He put distance between them. She was safer that way anyway. He didn't have to trust her to want to keep her out of harm's way. She was still a good person, just not who he needed in his life. He needed someone who would respect his need for privacy.

"I got it from Izzy's Boutique." She cast a glance towards the door.

He hadn't exactly told her that he needed privacy, but he'd thought she recognized his need for it. They had connected so well. Either way, she was from an entirely different world than him.

She was at one with nature and open with other people. He protected people like her.

"Just let me know how much it was and I'll pay you back." He took a step towards the door.

"It was a gift." She faced him. "I'm sorry. I'm not sure what I did wrong, but I'm sorry if I offended you in some way."

"No, it's not like that." He ran a hand over his hair. "I don't think I'm ready for any of this."

Especially not with a killer on the loose.

She worried her bottom lip, then dipped her head in a short nod. "Okay. I'd better be going then."

Moving past him, she opened the door and left. He made fists with his hands to keep from touching her or asking her to stay. Gripping the door, he watched her walk to her car, but shut it before she could look back. He was afraid he'd lose his resolve and ask her to stay.

He flicked the lock and leaned against the door, his forehead connecting with the smooth wood. It was better this way. His heart was safe and so was she.

CHAPTER 12

Willa's eyes filled with tears as she backed out of Nick's driveway. What on earth had gone wrong? She beat a frustrated hand against the steering wheel of her car. Everything had been going well. Better than well, it had felt fantastic. The shame of embarrassment burned up the back of her neck, turning her ears red.

It had been a long time since she felt that, regret over something she'd done. She lived her life intentionally and had thought they were on the same page. They had to have been. He'd been the one to initiate the kiss. She was sure of it. What, then, had happened?

She searched through her memory of the last thirty minutes. Maybe she'd been too excited or too presumptuous in bringing him the rug. No. She wasn't going to spiral down that rabbit hole. Taking a long, deep breath, she centered herself.

Spotting the entrance for the Bigleaf Maple Trail in the Orca Cove State Park, she took a right off the highway before town, turning into the deep woods. They always helped her find herself. Parking, she left her car behind, crunching her feet into the carpet of pine needles and dried leaves on the trail, letting the canopy of the trees cover her and guard against the rampage of emotions she was battling.

His emotions had changed when her phone rang. Had he thought her rude? No, she'd just checked to make sure it wasn't Mary or one of her older clients needing her. Or Nell, but no, she hadn't called her in a state of need in a long time.

"What, then?" she wondered aloud, trudging forward, one step at a time driving her further into the woods. Then she stopped suddenly. Was it because it was a guy? She'd told him about her friend Duke before. She'd told him about all of her friends. Maybe he was surprised he'd be calling her directly like that. It might have indicated something closer than friendship to him.

If that was the case, she could explain their relationship. That could do it. But if he was the jealous type, she'd have to leave it be. She wasn't sacrificing her friendships for the hope of a relationship, no matter how it made her stomach flutter when he studied her with those piercing, ice-blue eyes and perfectly groomed stubble beard. Not to mention his gently tousled, almost black hair.

Letting her shoulders relax, she resumed her hike, letting the calmness of the forest descend upon her. Foot after foot, she pressed further into the arms of the forest. She couldn't control his emotions. She'd let it go and see where it ended up.

Feeling better about her situation, she took the short loop of the trail and ended up back at her car in less than an hour. Satisfied, she drove back to town. The cafe was closed today, and she didn't have another yoga class until six, after the younger crowd got off work.

Driving up the hill to the residential area, she took a right and found Maggie's neighborhood. She lived on a street full of smaller two-bedroom houses. It was a cute, cozy place. She parked behind Maggie's car in the driveway.

"Willa!" Maggie pulled her into a hug when she answered the door, a happy smile on her perpetually sweet face. Her blonde pixie cut was sticking up more than normal and she had flour on her oversized sweatshirt. "What brings you here?"

"I thought I'd check in on you, see how you were doing with...everything. I almost said your newfound powers, doesn't that sound strange? Amazing, but still so strange."

Maggie pulled her into her house, brushing the flour off. "Sorry, I didn't see that. Oof, I got it on you too."

She tried to brush flour off Willa's canvas jacket, but she waved her off. "It's fine. Are you busy? Have I caught you at a bad time?"

"Of course not. I'm just trying to learn to bake."

She led the way to her kitchen, where the counter was covered in flour and a ball of dough sat in the center, covered in even more flour. A large bag of flour sat open on the counter and her sink was stacked full of bowls and wooden spoons.

"Bake?"

Maggie blushed. "Nell's just so busy at the cafe. She gets so stressed with all the bills and stuff. You know."

"Yeah." Willa sat at the kitchen table. Gary had handled all of that. He'd helped her open the place so that she could do what she did best, cook. "That makes sense."

"So, I thought I could help out a little. If I could learn to do some of the baking, she could focus on dinner and creating new meals." She plunked down in the chair across from Willa, eyeing the mess.

Nell already had help prepping in the kitchen and during the dinner rush, but she still managed everything. "That's really nice of you, Maggie."

"It's a nice thought." She ran a floured hand through her short hair, causing it to stick up even more. "But so far, it's not going anywhere."

"New skills take time. I remember when we were kids, Nell used to make these griddled sandwiches for us. They were turkey with tomatoes, pesto, and provolone cheese. But back then, she got her bread and pesto from Gil's. She wouldn't dream of serving jarred pesto or bagged bread now.""Definitely not." Maggie laughed. "So, what you're saying is that I eat better now than you did back then."

"Not exactly." Willa shook her head, smiling. "I'm saying when you're starting anything new, you've got a learning curve. You can start with something simple and build from there. She used to use jarred marinara too."

"The horror!" Maggie faked shock, clapping her cheeks with her hands, adding more flour to her face. "Are you sure we're talking about Nell Wilder here?"

"Back then she was still Nell Fitzgibbons. And yes, definitely. Even Nell had a learning curve. She didn't make her pasta back then." Maggie hadn't gone to school with them in the cove. She'd moved to town with her sister when she was eighteen and her sister was seventeen. They'd left some kind of bad situation in Seattle. She didn't talk about it much. All Willa knew was that she'd come to their small town, enrolled her sister in her senior year of high school and showed up at the cafe asking for a job.

That was thirteen years ago. It felt like a lifetime ago.

Nell and Gary hired her, barely more than kids themselves at that time, and she became family to them and their little crew. Sometimes it was hard to remember that Maggie wasn't with them all from the beginning.

"You keep using words, but they're not making sense." Maggie shook her head.

Willa laughed, enjoying the lighthearted mood. "What're you making over there?"

"You mean, what am I *murdering* over there? It's supposed to be pie crust."

She took in the pile of flour and mass of overworked dough. She didn't know that much about baking, but she did know it was a tricky, delicate thing. You didn't want to add too much flour. She coughed to cover a wince.

Maybe trying a less ambitious recipe would be better.

"Why don't you start with something like cookies? I love a good chocolate chip cookie."

"Chocolate chip is the hardest, Nell always says. Everyone is particular about those babies." She caught her bottom lip between her teeth. "But maybe a sugar cookie. Or shortbread."

Cookies had to be easier than pie crust from scratch. "That sounds great. Anything I can have with my tea is a win."

Maggie brightened. "I'll make you some!"

"That'd be amazing."

"I can't believe I even have the energy after last night, though." Maggie shook her head.

"What do you mean?" It hadn't been that late when they all broke apart and headed home.

She put a hand to her head. "I had *way* too much to drink. I think we all did. We all walked home, even Shelby."

She had seen them all walk home, but figured they were just playing it safe. They'd only had two bottles between the four of them. Willa herself only had one glass, but that still didn't amount to an overabundance of wine for the others.

"I was surprised I didn't feel sick this morning," Maggie went on.

"I don't remember you having that much." Willa frowned.

"Maybe it wasn't that much, but I sure felt heady and giggly."

"I think we all did. It was the first time we've all gotten together like that in a long time. We needed to let loose a little."

"True, and we had the music going." She spun a finger in the air.

"Yeah, we did." Willa smiled at the memory of their sudden dance party. "It was a good night."

"It really was."

"And you have control over the weather! How incredible."

"And you with the healing."

"Yeah, it's unreal. But I've always been into healing. Shelby and Duke both have good uses for their abilities. What is your connection with the weather?"

"Not the weather exactly." Maggie's mouth pursed in thought. "Just rain."

"And knowing if it's going to." Willa raised a finger.

"True."

"But why the rain?"

"I don't know exactly. It seems kinda random to me, not that I'm complaining."

"Huh, yeah. I just assumed that the gifts were things we could use that were specific to us. Shelby is always getting lost and Duke is always on the water and needing it to cooperate."

Maggie nodded. "That makes sense, but I'm not sure why I got rain. It's not like I'm a farmer or something."

"Maybe we're looking too deep into it. Or maybe we'll figure it out in time."

"I still feel bad for Nell."

"I don't think it would just skip over her. Either she didn't need an ability, or it just hasn't shown itself yet."

"I hope so. Here we are all talking about our new gifts, and she's left out. That would be hard. Especially after the year she had last year."

"She's probably still trying to figure out how to be alone."

"She's adjusting well, but I think she's getting a little lonely. Even with all the customers she sees every day."

"Maybe she'll start dating again sometime."

"Speaking of dating, what's going on with you and the hot new guy?" Maggie leaned forward onto her elbows, propping her face in her hands. By now, her chin and cheeks were covered in the white powder.

"Nick." She breathed in. "That's getting complicated."

"How so?"

"I'm getting mixed signals," she said, twisting her mouth. "I thought it was good and we were on the same page, but it appears that we weren't."

"I'm sorry, Willa." She put a hand on her shoulder, adding more flour to her jacket. "If he doesn't like you, though, he's crazy. You're the most creative, beautiful soul ever. And you're patient in a way I never will be."

"I've seen you with some of the tourists you get in the cafe. You're patient and kind. They can be difficult!"

"True, but they're either having a bad day or they're showing off. They don't mean anything bad by it."

It was still an energy Willa didn't want around her. Give her a calm yoga studio or kitchen to do her work in any day. "I couldn't do it."

"It's easy." She cast another glance over her shoulder. "I've been doing it for a long time. I'd like to learn a real skill, something harder."

"I think you underestimate yourself and your skills. You shine a ray of sun on everyone who goes into the cafe. It's half the reason they come in all the time."

"Don't tell Nell that!"

"She's the other half." Willa winked. "I think that friendliness you give everyone is an important contribution. You brighten their day."

Maggie leaned over the small table, hugging Willa. "Thanks, friend. I needed that."

"Me too."

And Nell was right; if Nick didn't like her, it was on him. She wasn't going to freak out or sacrifice who she was.

"Wiggle your toes and your fingers. Start to bring movement back into your body, waking your muscles back up," Willa instructed her class in their post-workout savasana. She'd taken a longer rest than normal, enjoying the cleared headspace. "Roll onto one side and get up slowly. Thank you for joining me today, everyone."

"Thank you," the class murmured as one.

Rising, Willa switched off her diffuser and picked up the mat cleaner sprays and washcloths she kept on a shelf at the front of the room. Spraying her mat down, she handed the sprays and extra cloths to Loris and Izzy, who had joined her for the evening class.

"Good class," Loris said, kneeling to wipe off her mat.

"Thank you." Willa wiped hers and rolled it back up.

"Savasana is my favorite pose." Izzy laughed. "I just have to try not to fall asleep."

The corpse pose, lying flat on your back to let the muscles cool down in an anatomically neutral position, was in reality a hard pose. To do it properly, you were supposed to relax completely and allow the muscles to fully release, but so many people weren't able to achieve full relaxation. Today was an unusual struggle for Willa. Even though she'd let go of the worry about where things were going with Nick, it kept creeping up in her mind.

"How've your knees been, Loris?" Willa bent to pick up a couple of yoga blocks.

"Doing fine!" Loris danced around, lifting her knees high. "I've been feeling great. Getting a lot of walking in and enjoying this spring weather. In fact, that's what I was doing this morning. I walked out to the marina to watch the fishermen bring in their morning haul, then had coffee with Dena."

"I've been enjoying the weather too. I got a little hike in this afternoon." It warmed her heart to help the woman, who had barely been able to bend in between yoga classes. She was a regular and generally made it to morning classes for circulation and mobility for the day. "How often are you using it?"

"Just in the mornings. That seems to be enough."

"I'm glad. Let me know when you need more."

"Will do. Have you seen Mary?"

"Yes, I checked in on her yesterday. She was still doing well."

Loris nodded. "Good. I'll check in on her tomorrow. She'll probably need Tommy to mow her lawn in the next week or so. It's been growing fast."

"So, how'd he like the rug?" Izzy asked, sliding over. She wagged her eyebrows.

Willa pressed her lips together in a polite smile. "Nick was happy to get it. It looked good in his kitchen."

Izzy clapped her hands together happily. "Are you going to come back and get those lamps?"

She had found a pair of beautifully designed wrought iron floor lamps when she perused Izzy's store. They had stained glass shades in green hues with intricate vines and leaves winding around the base and up to the top. They would add some romantic low light in the living room. The shades were whimsical and feminine, but the big, bold iron bases fit in with the masculine cabin feel of the place.

"Um, I'm not sure yet," she said noncommittally. She wasn't sure if she'd be invited back. "He's still remodeling. I'll see if they fit when he's done."

"That's a good idea. Let me know if you want them and I'll set them aside for you."

"Will do." Willa walked over to her desk. "I made a sleep spray for you, Izzy."

"You did?" She hoisted her bright orange and purple yoga mat under her arm and walked over. Taking the little spray bottle, she took the lid off to sniff it. "Ooh, that's nice. How calming. What is it?"

"Lavender and chamomile. They're good for relaxation."

Izzy yawned. "Sorry, must have been a long day."

"Maybe you'd better head home. It was a long class with the meditation." Willa hurried her towards the door. She hadn't thought of that. It would be much more potent now with the ocean magic.

Maybe not magic. Shelby certainly didn't think so...but screw it. Willa liked to think of it as magic and so she would.

"Yeah. Mondays, you know." Izzy raised her shoulder and pushed through the door, stifling another yawn.

"So," an interested Loris appeared at her elbow. "Who's this guy you're buying rugs and lamps for?"

Chuckling, Willa patted her on the shoulders. "Just a friend, Loris. Just a friend."

At least, she thought so.

CHAPTER 13

"Who is he?" Duke leaned across Warner's desk at the station the next morning. He'd heard about the burly guy poking around town asking personal questions. The townspeople were always in each other's business; questions like that were a way of life, but not from outsiders. Especially not from outsiders. It made them nervous.

"It doesn't matter." Chief Warner shook his head, pushing up from his desk to stand. "He's not in the cove anymore and he's not coming back."

Unless he found the information he wanted, he'd be back. "And if he does?"

"We'll escort him out. Again."

"If he's up to no good, that's not going to cut it." Duke shook his head. Warner sounded like he'd been in a small town too long. "He could have been behind the dead body on the beach."

"You think I haven't thought of that?" Warner's jaw clenched. "But that's my problem."

"It's all of our problem if he comes back."

"I'll keep the people of Orca Cove safe. That's my job. Not yours."

"What's his name? I have connections as well. I can help." Duke didn't like the idea of someone threatening his little town. There was a reason he traveled to Seattle to do business. He didn't have to watch his back here.

"I don't need you running off, getting yourself in trouble. We've got it covered, Duke."

Duke slammed his hands on the desk he was leaning on. Warner's nostrils flared in response.

The old man didn't have any clue, but Duke wasn't going to get anything else out of the blinded cop. He probably still saw him as the delinquent youth he used to be. Frustrated, he spun away, slamming out the front door and back out onto the street.

Palmer paced around the hotel he'd found in Liberty Valley, another little boring town just outside Orca Cove. He was still fuming at being kicked out of town by the old Barney Fife wanna-be. He hadn't even done it himself, just sent his little lackey to do it for him.

They wouldn't pull this shit in Seattle. They knew better than to try to tell people what to do or where they could go. This was a free world. Best they remembered that.

He had a powerful boss backing him.

His bravado stalled when he realized he'd have to call in with progress. Sure, Isaac would help, but even Palmer was afraid of the man and what he'd do if he came to town. The man had no morals and zero limitations.

Gulping audibly, he found his contact number and hit the call button.

"Give me good news," Isaac commanded.

"Uh, I've had some heat. The local fuzz was following me around. Kicked me outta town." He forced a chuckle out. "Like they have the power. Anyway, they know who I am and they're going to make it more difficult to find Nick Ryan."

Silence stretched through the phone. "Did you check property records?"

"Duh." It was like the man thought he was incompetent. "I wasn't born yesterday. Nothing's registered in his name. He must be renting."

"Are there many rental properties in the area? Apartment buildings?"

"There's a cabin rental and a building with townhouses on the canal." He ticked off the list he'd compiled. "A couple of other apartment buildings are in the residential area in town, plus several houses here and there, as far as I can tell. But there's no way to know which one he's living in. And if I go door to door, the fuzz'll make things difficult."

"You could at least try," he pushed. "Instead of what, sitting in some hotel room? Trying to figure out your next move?"

Palmer looked around his hotel room in defeat. "I can try the bigger buildings. Maybe the cops won't catch on that I'm back in town until I've at least checked a couple of them."

"You do that. Mr. Dupree is getting impatient. If you fail, I'll come and do the job you're being paid to do," he said forcefully before the line went dead.

Shoving his feet into his boots, he rushed out the door. He really didn't want that to happen. He might get put on Isaac's list as well.

Almost there. Nick ran a hand over the piece of wood he was planing level. Picking up his wood planer, he scraped across the surface of the old barn beam. It would make a beautiful light fixture. A few more scrapes and he checked it again. Perfect.

A notification came through his phone. Glancing at it, he read that he'd sold another couple of charcuterie boards and a cheese grotto he made the week before.

He'd have to get them boxed and to town. Frowning, he considered going to Liberty Valley to mail them out. He could do that, but he'd still need to go into Orca Cove if he wanted paint. He could order it at Gil's Market and Marina; they didn't mix it onsite. He didn't think there was another general store or paint store where he could get it without going all the way to Olympia.

His stomach growled. It was well past lunchtime, and he hadn't eaten anything all day. He'd gotten lost in his work again.

He packed up the sold pieces and took them inside the cabin to grab a quick bite before going into town. He'd go straight to the post office, then to get paint, and get back to the workshop. No side conversations, and most importantly, no Willa.

Washing up in his kitchen sink, he glanced down, seeing the rag rug Willa had bought for him. It was exactly what he would have picked for himself. He exhaled sharply, trying to shake off the guilt that had crept up. He shouldn't have kissed her. That must have been confusing for her.

He poured a full glass of water, gulping it down quickly. She might not be right for him, but that was no excuse for treating her like that.

Throwing a slice of cheese on top of some ham, he squirted on some mustard and rolled it up, eating it as he grabbed his keys.

There wasn't a line at the post office, so he got through quickly and made his way to Gil's. Pulling open the door, he scanned the shop for Emiliano. He was talking to another customer, so Nick walked over to a display next to the cheeses.

He picked up a bamboo cheese board on the table. He flipped it over to see it was made in Vermont. It had rough edges, like it had been batch cut. Probably commercially made. He winced, seeing that they were charging forty bucks for it. He looked around for hand-crafted boards. They had a few plastic cutting boards over by the knives, all made in Japan.

He wasn't opposed to countries making what they were good at, but for something as heavily used as a cutting board, he'd much prefer wood.

"It makes your stomach turn, doesn't it?" Emiliano said, who'd come to stand at his elbow.

He set the cutting board down and tried for a blank face. "It's fine."

Emiliano laughed and gave him a jovial shove. "You're trying so hard to be polite."

Nick's wall fell and he cracked a smile at being called out. He lifted his hands in an apologetic offering.

"Sorry, I just could..." His words trailed off. He didn't want to sound boastful.

"Do much better?" Emiliano's eyebrows raised. "Then do."

He'd offered to let Nick sell his things in the store. Maybe he should take him up on it.

"Yeah, let me think about it." He laughed out loud at the younger man's expression. He'd said that once before already. "Seriously this time. Maybe I'll bring a few things by next week and see what you think."

"I'm sure I'll love them. Bring whatever you'd like to sell."

He was humbled by the man's faith in him. He barely knew him. "Thanks."

"Was there something else you needed? You looked like you were waiting to talk to me earlier."

"I'm fixing the cabin up."

"Yeah, I heard. Willa got you a rug from Izzy's."

He frowned. "You heard that?"

"Small town, my friend. You'll get used to it."

It was another example of why he didn't need to be friendly with the locals. They all probably knew where he lived by now too. His wall went back up. "I need some paint."

Emiliano watched him with a curious expression but didn't say anything. "I'll get the paint swatches. We only sell one brand here. Is that okay?"

"That's fine."

Backtracking, he went behind a counter and ducked down to riffle through something. Shortly, he popped back up, a large fan of paint swatches in his hand. "Here you go. If you want to take this home, you can."

"Nah," Nick said, flicking to the blue-greens. He found a turquoise that fit Willa's vision of his bathroom. It felt funny taking her ideas when he'd shunned her, but he couldn't imagine the bathroom any other way now. "I'll take two gallons of this one."

"Aquastone?" Emiliano took the swatches back to read the name. "Semi-gloss or eggshell?"

"Semi-gloss."

"You got it. It's going to take probably a week to come in."

"That's fi-" Nick answered, his words cutting off. Across the aisle, he saw Willa watching him, a bag of apples in hand, her perfect mouth shaped in a small O.

"I'll get it ordered," Emiliano said, watching their exchange. He backed away, leaving Nick to stare at her like an idiot.

"You got the paint," she said, taking a few steps closer.

He only nodded.

"So maybe you're not that mad at me?" she asked.

When he tried to tell her that he wasn't mad at her, that she hadn't done anything wrong, she rushed forward, placing a hand on his chest. The warm waves of vibration flowed between them. Her eyes flew open in surprise. She'd forgotten. He hadn't.

"I just wanted to clarify something," she said quickly and firmly. "Duke and I are just friends. We've been friends for a long time. That's- not going to change, but I want you to know there's nothing more between us. There won't ever be, either, as far as I could ever imagine, with or without you in the picture."

"Duke." There he was again. The one she ran to after finding Jimmy on the beach.

He couldn't blame her for running to a friend. That wasn't fair. But why would she tell him about Nick and not the local police? Something didn't add up. And if Nick couldn't trust her, he didn't need to be with her.

"I don't care who you're friends with," he said, a little too sharply. Taking a long, steadying breath, he tried again, "I don't have a problem with Duke, at least the Duke that you know. I don't know who the real Duke is yet."

He rolled his eyes in his frustration. He wasn't finding the right words.

"What are you talking about?" She shook her head in confusion.

"I'm a private person, Willa. I probably should have started with that, but it just seemed like you knew me so well already." He blew out an exhausted breath and ran a hand through his hair, standing it on end. "And there he was, asking about me, pretending to be someone he wasn't."

Willa's head slid back, her eyes questioned him. "You know you can trust some people, right?"

"It hasn't served me in the past," he blew out, taking a step backward.

"Didn't you trust Jimmy?" She edged forward, watching him. She raised her hand as though she was going to touch him but stopped short.

"Not entirely. Eventually. At least on the job. Look, you don't know what it's like to be betrayed by someone who isn't who you thought they were. Not to protect themselves." He waved a hand. "But for personal gain."

"Why do you think I'm here?" She watched him carefully.

"I don't know!" He whirled, searching for answers, then coming back to her, he repeated himself more quietly this time, "I don't know."

"You don't believe he's just a friend?" She looked hurt. He ached to comfort her.

He took another step back.

"You can have guy friends. I'm not the jealous sort. At least, I wouldn't be if we were together. Which we're not." He was so bad at this. Just cut her loose quickly, it'll be better. "I just think we're too different. We don't have enough in common, enough to connect on, for anything real."

She studied her hand that probably still held a memory of their touch, the same as his chest did.

Well, there was *that*. A definite connection.

"Beyond that." He waved it away, dismissing it. "You're warm and friendly. I'm a loner. I'd just bring you down."

That would do it. If he made it about himself, it'd hurt her less.

"If that's what you want." Her eyes softened and flicked down. "Good luck with your cabin."

Leaving her apples, she left Gil's, pushing quickly through the door.

Well, shit. That hadn't gone as well as he'd hoped.

Either way, he wasn't ending up getting manipulated by someone who wasn't who they said they were, pretending to have his back, but then running off to tell a friend about him.

He hadn't asked her to keep quiet, a perfect stranger. She hadn't owed him anything. *Why*, then, had she built that sense of security up, claiming to be letting him share his story how he wanted to, only to betray his trust? It didn't make sense.

No. He wasn't going to be naive. Not again.

"Hello?" Palmer walked up to the reception desk at Siren's Song Cabins.

A young woman walked out from the office near the desk, smiling broadly. "Oh, good afternoon! How can I help you?"

"I'm meeting a friend here in Orca Cove to go fishing, but I can't remember where he's staying." He read the logo painted in script across the wall behind the counter. "Siren's Song Cabins. Yeah, I think that was it."

"Who's your friend?" she flipped her guest book open.

"Nick Ryan."

This was going to be easier than he'd thought. He'd fix the situation and Isaac could stay in Seattle.

"Hmmm, I don't see his name here." Her finger traced down the names. "Maybe try The Wild Cafe in town? Most people end up there at one point or another."

"I'll do that," he said, moving away. One down, many to go. He just had to keep out of Barney Fife's and Dudley Do-Right's way. "Thanks."

There was another woman standing at the office door. She hadn't been there a minute ago.

"Who're you looking for?" she asked, smiling sweetly.

"Nick Ryan, you know the guy?"

She cocked a hip; one hand going under her chin as she thought about it.

"I don't think so." She shook her head sadly. "But I'll keep an ear open. Where are you staying? I can let him know if I run into him."

"Just outside of town," he replied vaguely. He didn't need people asking questions. That was *his* job. "We were supposed to meet here. I'll try the cafe. Thanks."

Well, that was a bust, but he could at least mark it off the list. Maybe he'd have better luck at the apartment buildings downtown. He'd looked them up online and one of the units had vacation rentals in it.

That sounded promising.

CHAPTER 14

Willa shut the door to her apartment, sliding down the back of it to sit on her heels. She wrapped her arms around her legs and let out the tears she'd been holding back since she left Gil's Market and Marina.

It wasn't her fault, she knew that. And she wasn't mad at Nick exactly. He was free to feel how he wanted to. To not find the same connection to her that she had to him. Logically, that all made sense. It wasn't personal.

But it sure hurt like hell.

He had some crazy notion that she'd told Duke all sorts of personal things about him. She didn't understand that at all. She'd told him about seeing him on the beach that night; a light bulb went off in her head. Duke probably went to talk to him about that. And Nick probably thought she'd told him the lot of it.

Well, that was on him. As much as it hurt, it was. She'd known people like that before. If they wanted to believe people were out to get them, there was no changing their minds. And she knew how to set boundaries.

It was just that she'd become attached to the idea of them together. The kiss that they'd shared was pure fireworks.

She'd begun to have hope.

And they *had* a connection, more than most! They *literally* had a physical energetic connection, gifted to them by the ocean...or something like that. It was like they were fated to be together. They couldn't touch without electricity traveling through them. If that wasn't a connection, she didn't know what he considered one to be.

Sniffing, she pushed up from the floor. She kicked off her boots and shoved her feet into her fluffy slippers. She needed comfort. She shrugged off her light jacket and pulled on her biggest, fluffiest robe, knotting it tight around her, fortifying herself in its thick folds.

Flicking the electric tea kettle on, she considered her tea collection. Sunny lemon balm or calendula would help perk her up, especially if she used some of her newly distilled ocean water. But she didn't have the energy.

That was sad, she didn't even feel like feeling better. She just wanted to mope. Sniffing, she decided she was allowed to have a bad day and feel like crap. At least for the night. Tomorrow, she'd pull her big girl panties on and forge ahead.

Tonight, she'd let herself wallow.

Setting a jar of herbs back on the shelf, she searched her kitchen. She needed something stronger. Switching off her tea kettle, she went to her fridge. She didn't have any wine or hard liquor, but she did have some kombucha. That'd do. Blackberry lemon kombucha to the rescue.

Pouring it in a tumbler, she wiped her eyes and raised the drink to the ocean. She froze. Three orcas were in the cove again. Two of them were facing her, watching her. But that was impossible. They couldn't see through the sliding glass doors.

Right?

Peering through the window, she took a couple of steps forward and watched them. Cora rose out of the water, diving in, giving the water a slap with her tail. Right in Willa's direction. Was that a coincidence?

She didn't believe in coincidences.

Taking a big swallow of the kombucha, she shook her head. Were Cora and her family more than regular orcas? Were they magical?

Either way, there was something magical in the water. It was the only thing that made any sense. She suspected that when the lightning hit the water, whatever was in there passed to them.

An idea formed in her mind. Maybe Duke would take her diving. She could find the magic.

Taking her drink to her couch, she tucked her feet under her and curled into the corner. The idea of finding the cause of their powers was exciting, but not enough to improve her mood. She still felt like sulking.

She and Nick weren't that different at all. Where'd he get that idea? She took another sip of her kombucha, letting the sweet and vinegary punch excite her taste buds. She made a contented hum. It was a tasty batch.

Nick created art with wood, she created products focused on healing people, plus her yoga. He made things that made people happy, useful things they could use in their homes. That was a way to help them. And he loved the pieces he made. There was no way he wasn't infusing some sort of helpful intentions into the wood while working with it.

He loved trees, like her. He loved helping people. At her core, that was who she was. Some people saw her as a silly, frivolous hippie who frolicked in the woods and didn't conform to social norms. And while that was technically accurate, she wasn't frivolous, she valued everyone's time and the money they donated for their products.

Sure, he charged a set fee for what he created, but he sold it online, which made a price necessary. There probably wasn't enough of a market locally to support him; selling online made sense for his needs.

Once again, their similarities were much greater than their differences.

But what did she really know about him? She'd only recently met him and still didn't know much about his past. Maybe there was much more to him that she didn't know.

She would have liked to find out. She studied the ice cube floating in her glass. It looked lonely. Getting up, she fished another out of her ice tray and added it. Satisfied, she climbed back on the sofa to continue her bad mood.

Was it possible that being different was *good*? Nell and Gary were totally different. He took care of the books and business, and she did what she did best, cooked. She was a chef and a quiet, nurturing caregiver. Gary, however, wasn't like that at all. Well, that wasn't true, he'd been sort of a big brother or father figure to them all, keeping them in line. But he was also the one that would come visit and see how they were doing. He always knew when they needed to talk, or a shoulder to lean on. Definitely the more outgoing of the two, he kept them connected.

It was almost like he had sent them a gift the night of his birthday memorial. It had brought them back together, almost a year later. Could someone send something like that through the veils?

Could *he* have?

It didn't matter anyway, if Nick didn't trust Willa, that was a bigger issue. And out of her control.

Finishing her drink, she huddled on the couch, the empty glass cradled in her hands. She drifted off to sleep, emotionally exhausted.

Willa jerked awake. Someone was pounding on her head. No, her window. Nope, that was her door. Blinking, she set her glass on the coffee table, pushing it to the center, and made her way to her door.

It opened just as she reached it.

"Are you okay?" Shelby asked, charging into the room.

"Yes, of course." Willa took a few small steps back. "Why, what's wrong?"

"Nothing, I just wanted to make sure you were okay." She walked in through her kitchen, taking in the details of the room. Stopping in front of Willa, she wrapped her fingers around the lapels of her robe. "What's wrong?"

Bubbles of laughter erupted out of Willa, then devolved into sobs. Her friend pulled her into a close hug. She held her for a few moments, before pushing her back and repeating her question.

"Nick."

Shelby's eyes narrowed. "What'd that rat bastard do?"

One corner of Willa's mouth rose at the insult. "No, he's not a rat bastard. He just...doesn't want me."

Shelby searched her face, then pulled her in for another hug. "What an idiot. He's a flaming turd of an idiot. Who wouldn't want you?"

"Lots of people." She raised a shoulder and hiccupped, tears trailing down her face.

"Lots of people are idiots," Shelby said sagely. "Especially those with penises."

A bark of laughter escaped Willa's mouth. She covered it with her hand.

"It's not his fault. He's allowed to not want me. It just...doesn't feel good. I had hoped." She waved her hand. "I really liked him."

Shelby walked her friend to the couch where they sat down next to each other. "I'm so sorry, Willa."

"It's okay. I'll be okay."

"What happened?"

Willa told her all about it, including the scorching kiss they'd shared at his cabin.

"Wow."

"Yeah."

"And suddenly you're too different and not trustworthy."

"Exactly."

"Well, that's shitty."

Willa shrugged. "It's better than finding out later he wasn't interested."

Shelby gave her a hard look. "After he kissed you."

"True."

"Still, better to be done with him." Shelby's head tilted, spying her glass. She picked it up. "Did you have a drink?"

"Yeah." She shrugged. "I needed it."

Shelby sniffed the empty glass, her forehead wrinkling. "Is that... Is that kombucha?"

"Well, yeah."

"You get dumped and you drink kombucha?" Shelby's chest started to heave, then laughter rumbled out of her mouth. Willa joined in.

The two women collapsed back against the couch, clutching their stomachs. Tears rolled down their faces.

"It's all I had." Willa gestured at the glass, still giggling.

"Next time," Shelby wiped the tears of laughter from her eyes, "call me. I would have brought something stronger and drank with you."

"You were at work."

"Doesn't matter." Shelby got down in front of her face. "Next time something like this happens, you call one of us."

"Okay." Willa swallowed hard at the emotions rolling over her. It was what she had been missing over the past year. "But you know I don't drink much."

Her eyes lit up. "Wait. I have the perfect thing. Are you okay if I leave you for fifteen minutes?"

"Of course."

Shelby jumped from the couch and flew back out the front door.

Willa sighed, snuggling back into the divot she'd made earlier, trying not to think about Nick. She considered going to get another glass of kombucha. But before she could muster the energy, the door opened back up and Shelby hurried in, holding a bag high in the air.

"Ice cream and cookie dough!" she proclaimed proudly, presenting them to Willa. "Oh, hold on."

Dumping them on the coffee table, she hustled into the kitchen, riffling through drawers and cabinets. Finding what she wanted, she came back with spoons and napkins.

"No bowls?" Willa eyed the gifts in awe.

"Nah, we can take turns. Less dishes that way." Shelby wiggled off the lid of the Ben & Jerry's Half Baked container and dug a spoon into it. It went into her mouth and she sighed in happiness. She shoved it into Willa's hands. "Your turn."

She read the label. "Cookie dough? So, same thing, but in ice cream form?"

"No!" Shelby gasped, ripping open the cookie dough package. "It has fudge brownies in it and both vanilla and chocolate ice cream. It's totally different."

Willa chuckled, digging her spoon into the ice cream and tasting it. Her teeth sank into gooey dough and chewy brownie bits. Chocolate and sugar detonated in her mouth, sending a sugar rush through her system. She moaned.

"It's good, isn't it?" Shelby said, her mouth full of cookie dough.

"Oh, yeah." Her eyes closed in bliss.

They ate in silence for several minutes until they were both moaning. Pushing the half-eaten container of ice cream onto the table, Willa and Shelby fell back onto the couch. Willa rubbed her stomach. She'd need some ginger tea to help digest all that sugar.

"I got a strange visitor at the cabins today," Shelby said, toying with the cookie dough wrapper.

Willa looked at her, curious.

"Some big guy, an outsider. Leather jacket, not an outdoorsman," Shelby went on. "Asking around for Nick."

"My Nick?" Willa caught herself and closed her eyes for a moment. "Nick Ryan?"

"Yup. Claimed he was supposed to meet him there and was asking if he was on the check-in list."

"Why couldn't he have called him?"

"Good question."

"The bigger question was why he didn't share where he was staying. If he really was some bozo who didn't carry a cellphone or who'd lost Nick's number and was trying to find him, he'd have left his name and number or where to reach him." Shelby raised a finger. "I wasn't born yesterday."

"So, you think he was trying to get information about him?" "I do."

"But why?" "Isn't that the question?"

"Do you think I should tell him? Were *you* going to tell him?" Willa asked.

"I came over to tell you. I thought maybe you'd know what was going on, or that you'd want to talk to him yourself. You know him the best. But *that* was more important." Shelby gestured to the sugar fest on the short table in front of them. "Do you want me to tell him?"

"Well..." She drew the word out with uncertainty. "I may not be happy with his decision, but that doesn't mean we shouldn't do the right thing and be helpful."

"Screw that. He's made it clear he doesn't want to be with you. You don't have to be nice to him."

"I try to be kind to everyone."

"And you don't have to."

"No, I don't. I choose to."

"Dammit, Willa. He was an ass. You get to be a little mad about it. Not everyone is kind. Some people, people with penises, are only thinking with their-" She gestured. "Appendages. They're like that. They love you and leave you. Honestly, you're probably better off. Not everyone finds what Nell and Gary had."

It hurt to see her friend still in pain from her lost love, Keane. They'd been together all through high school and for a year or so after before he just took off. She was still bitter. It was her right.

It was also Willa's right not to hold onto that bitterness. "I'll tell Duke. Let him fill Nick in."

Duke seemed to be trying to step in for Gary, touching base with all of them. It would be the first time she took something like that to him for help.

Shelby raised her eyebrows, acknowledging what she was doing. "Good idea."

It was nice to have Shelby on board.

They sat in silence for a while before Willa got up to turn the kettle on for her ginger tea.

"You want me to grab dinner?" Shelby offered. "I can settle in with you this evening. Could even stay the night if you need me to. This couch is comfy."

It was such a sweet offer.

"No, I'm okay. You're probably hungry, though."

"I won't eat for days," Shelby moaned. She threw an arm over her face. "I may never eat again."

"You'll be hungry within an hour." Willa laughed, filling her tea infuser.

"Probably, but not for a while." She rubbed her stomach.

"Honest, I'm good." Willa walked back over to join her, curling up on the sofa. "I feel a lot better now. I cried it out, ate my feelings. Isn't that what we're supposed to do?"

"Definitely."

"I think I'll get this cleaned up and head in for a nice bath with my tea. Then, I'll binge watch something terrible on TV. I might even eat the rest of that ice cream in a few hours."

Shelby leaned forward to give her a high five. "Do it!"

They both got up, and Willa walked her to the door.

"Fill me in on whatever happens with Duke," Shelby said.

"Will do."

"And check in tomorrow." She wagged a finger in her face. "That's an order."

Willa mock saluted her. "Aye, aye, Captain."

Shelby hugged her and headed out.

Closing the door, Willa leaned against it again. But this time, she did feel a little better. Maybe it was for the best.

CHAPTER 15

Nick pounded a dowel rod into a piece of wood in his workshop. It wouldn't fit. He'd used a jig he'd used a thousand times before. It should fit perfectly. Picking up a mallet, he slammed it down on the wood.

Must be sawdust. He tried to pull it back out so he could clean it out, but it was stuck.

The memory of Willa's hurried escape from the market played over and over in Nick's mind. It felt awful, even though he had done what he planned to do, let her know there wasn't a future for them in the most upfront and honest way possible.

So why then did he feel so miserable?

Letting out a growl, he slammed the piece on his workbench and swung the mallet at the little rod, breaking it off completely.

Full-on hulking out at this point, he threw the box he was building into the corner of his shop, along with the mallet, and let out a larger, primordial howl.

Hearing leaves crunch in the grass outside, he drew his weapon, keeping his first finger along the barrel and not on the trigger; he wasn't an idiot. It was getting late in the afternoon, nearly dark. A little late for a visitor, not that he had many. He moved to the corner of his workshop, next to the open door.

"Did I catch you at a bad time?" a familiar voice called out.

Pointing his pistol down, he peered around the entryway, walking out when he saw it was Willa's friend, Duke.

Of course.

Duke's eyes took in the gun at his side. He stiffened. "Looks like it."

"Sorry," Nick said, holstering the weapon.

"Are you expecting trouble?"

"Something like that." Nick glanced down his drive to see an old, beat-up pickup truck. That was great, he'd been so focused on work that he hadn't even heard him pull up.

"Bad day?"

Duke had resumed a relaxed stance, but his core was still engaged. He was ready to move if needed.

"I've had better." Willa's face popped back up in Nick's mind. He swiped his hand over his face, rubbing hard. He took a long, calming breath. "I'm sure that's not why you're here, though."

He paused. Maybe it was. Willa might have run to him after their last interaction. Typical.

"No, but I do need to ask you something. It's personal."

"Personal?" Oh boy, definitely about Willa.

Duke cast a glance around the clearing outside his shop.

"I need to ask you about the visitor. In town." His eyes were back on Nick, taking in details. "I know you know who it is."

He hadn't told Willa about Palmer, but maybe the chief had. He shrugged, "Maybe."

Duke shook his head, "No. You do. He showed up right after the body was found on the beach. You were on the beach that night. I'm not trying to dig into your personal life. Feel free to live however you choose. I'm not one to judge or pry for no reason, but I think that guy's here for no good. And I'm looking after Orca Cove here."

"Chief Warner send you to get more information out of me?"

"No, but Warner is why I'm here." Duke flipped his too-long hair out of his eyes and took a few steps closer. "He wants me to think that guy's outta town and not coming back. You and I both know that's not true. Not a guy like that."

"Not a guy like that," Nick agreed. He struggled to decide what to share with the man. It was hard to trust someone who had already deceived him. "You're not who you pretended to be."

Duke tilted his head and let a playful smirk play on his lips. He shrugged as though it wasn't a big deal. "Yeah, I knew you'd see through that eventually. Sorry about that. I needed to see what kind of guy you were, what with Willa being interested in you and all."

He knew Duke was judging his reactions, but he still didn't like how it had played out. "I don't like lies."

Duke nodded slowly. "I get that. I should have just asked."

"You should have." Although he probably wouldn't have shared as much. Still, it was dishonest. But had he never done that on the job?

"Yeah, but I am now." He gestured at himself. "Being me."

"Now that I know who you are."

"Yeah, I shoulda thought ahead and kept the cover going." He winked saucily. "But I didn't know I'd need more information from you then."

Nick rolled his eyes. It was hard to be mad at the man. Irritated, yes, but he was so honest about his deception. It was weird.

"Yeah, you've got to plan ahead better."

Duke raised a finger. "Facts."

"So, what are you trying to find out? Whether I killed Jimmy?" He stepped forward onto the grass between them, bringing them closer. "You already know I was on the beach that night with him. And you don't have any reason to believe that I wouldn't have killed him. Lord knows why Willa believed me, but she did."

That thought sat like acid in his stomach. She had believed in him. Even when he seemed like the likely suspect.

"Yes, I know Palmer. But he's not a friend of mine. And you're right, he's not going to go away." He continued his monologue, stopping to muster up the courage to say what he needed to. Part of him desperately needed to. "I'll confirm your suspicions, though. He's here to find me."

Duke blinked. "Wow, thank you for your honesty. You're right. I should have asked you outright the first time."

The tension eased; Nick exhaled sharply. "Does that answer your questions, or do you have others?"

"I have so many." Duke studied the leaves providing shelter over them. "Let's start with the important ones. Who is Palmer and why is he looking for you?"

He'd tell him as much as he'd told the chief. He didn't know Duke well, but in this small town, he seemed like a sort of authority figure. People treated him as such.

"Reginald Palmer. I believe he's the one who killed Jimmy." He sat down on the ramp leading up to his workshop, folding his arms over his knees. "Jimmy and I worked together at the SPD."

Duke nodded slowly, finding a discarded cut log to sit down on. "I pegged you for a cop."

"Not anymore." He just shrugged. "We put away his boss."

"I'm afraid to ask."

"Larry Dupree."

He whistled. "That's a bad guy to piss off."

"You have no idea. That raid took years to pull off."

"And Palmer is trying to get back at you."

He hesitated. "I think Palmer was following Jimmy. Somehow, he knew he was meeting me that night. We were being careful about how we met."

"You're hiding here, after you left the force?"

"Sort of." He knocked the heel of a boot against the end of the ramp. He didn't like the sound of that. "Just trying to start fresh. Didn't want my past to haunt me."

"I can respect that."

"My best guess is that he caught up to Jimmy too late, after we parted." It still burned a hole in his gut. If he'd have stayed a little longer, he may have been able to protect his former partner.

"And he's still trying to find you."

He nodded, keeping the why to himself.

"You've spent more time in town lately," he trailed off.

Nick knew what he was thinking, though. If he was laying low, he wouldn't be showing his face around town. And he was spending a lot of time with Willa, putting her in danger.

"I only just found out Palmer was in town a couple of days ago." Nick closed his eyes and set his teeth. "I ended things with Willa after that."

Maybe not as quickly as he should have, but he'd done the right thing.

"I see."

"I was in town today but was trying to avoid her. I didn't mean for the run-in at Gil's to happen. I should have checked Liberty Village for another general store."

Duke studied the ground as though he was trying to decide what to say. A long pause developed between them.

"I can't say I'm comfortable with Palmer poking around town, or the fact that he's here looking for you. But it sounds like you're trying to take precautions. I respect that you're not letting it bleed onto Willa. As her friend, I appreciate that. But he won't stop, will he? He'll eventually find you."

It was true, and something that had plagued him daily. Every sound sent a readiness to fight through him.

"Dupree's got a court date coming up. If I can lie low until then and he's put away for good, I think Palmer will back off."

There wouldn't be anything else for him to want from Nick then, unless he was just trying to get pay-back.

"Are you a witness or something?"

"One of many." That wasn't it.

"Then he wants to use you as leverage?"

"Possibly to discredit me." It was believable.

Duke nodded. "And once Dupree's sentenced, it'll be a done deal. He'll be out of time."

"Exactly." It was what he was counting on. Then his life could get back to its new normal.

"I care about the cove." Duke met his eyes. "I'll be your eyes in town. I'll let you know if I see him or if he's sniffing about. I'll spread the word to keep quiet about you, although that probably won't be a problem. People around here don't like outsiders."

"Don't I know it."

"You lie low here and keep Willa out of it. If he knows she means something to you, he'll target her." At Nick's bland expression, he added, "Obvious, I know. But I had to make sure you knew the stakes."

"I'm well aware."

"Deal?" He rose and extended his hand.

"Deal." Nick stood to shake on it. In some ways, he was glad Duke had stopped by. He was glad Willa had him to lean on. She may not be for him, but he still wanted to protect her. She was innocent in all this mess.

"Now that that's out of the way, I have to set you straight on one thing." Duke broke his chain of thought. "Willa didn't tell me any of that."

He shook his head. "What do you mean? That's why you came to meet me at the post office, to see what I was about."

"To judge your character because she trusted you." Duke shook his head. "Because she bumped into you on the beach coming from the direction she found the body the next morning. Because she liked you. That's all."

Wait. The world stopped, including his heartbeat. His vision tunneled to Duke. "Willa didn't tell you about Jimmy?"

"She did not." Duke cocked his head; his eyes narrowed. "Did you think she told me all your personal details? We're friends, man, but not like that. Especially with a killer out there. Willa may seem sweet and naive to some, but she's no idiot. She's smart."

He felt like he'd been the naive one, ready to assume she was talking about him behind his back, running to Duke with all his dirty laundry. "Shit. I've been an idiot."

"Sounds like it." Duke ran a hand through his hair again, tossing the ends out of his eyes. "You're going to set things straight with her. Make sure she knows that whatever this issue is, it isn't because of her."

"I can't do that and draw attention to her."

"Palmer is out of town right now, right?" Duke asked. "I haven't seen him poking around town since Sunday. And you said it won't be long till Dupree's court case starts. So, you only have to lie low until then.

"You mean, I could wait it out?" Hope sprung up like tenuous little shoots in his chest. Fear kept him from believing it, though. Did he even deserve that?

"Yes, but not if you don't fix things quickly. But if you wait until that's all over to make things right with Willa, it might be too late for her. She's got her own history. I don't know what you said or did, but by the look on your face, you screwed up royally."

He didn't know half of it. "How will I know it's safe?"

"Eyes and ears, my man." Duke clapped him on the back.

"I've got to apologize." All Nick could focus on was the pain in Willa's eyes. If he could just fix that... He couldn't live with himself otherwise.

"Let me get back to town, check things out. I'll let you know if the coast is clear." Duke pulled out his phone to get his contact info. "It's getting late. It's doubtful Palmer would be hanging around town this late, he'd stick out like a sore thumb. He can't ask questions and the cops would certainly catch sight of him."

Encouraged, Nick gave him his number and promised to wait for a call.

Maybe things would work out after all, and he could still find the peace he'd been searching for.

An hour later, Nick's phone rang. It was Duke.

"I drove all around town," Duke said. "No sign of Palmer or anyone else I don't know."

"You know all of the tourists?"

"I can spot a tourist."

"He could be parked somewhere inconspicuous."

"I know all the good spots."

That was interesting.

"You're sure it's okay?"

"The town's quiet. The cafe's even quiet for the evening. I think you're good. Just park at the cafe, or- behind the post office is even better. It's a longer walk, but if he pegs your truck, he won't be looking for you at Willa's."

He'd already planned on parking elsewhere. The post office was a good idea. There were lots of trees behind it for cover.

He pressed his hand against his stomach. He had freaking butterflies. He was anxious to make things right but didn't know how she'd react.

"I'll drive into the residential area first. Make sure no one's following me."

"Good idea."

"Text me when you get parked. I'll sit at the cafe and keep an eye out for Palmer until you let me know you've made it without a tail, then I'll take off. It gets safer the later it gets. He's not going to be out canvassing the area late at night. Just be careful when you leave."

"I'll be careful. And leave by the beach."

"Ten-four." Duke hung up.

He had one shot at this. Hopefully he wouldn't screw it up.

CHAPTER 16

J ust as Willa was drying from her bath, she heard a knock on her door. Pulling her robe back on, she headed towards it.

"I told you I'm fine! You don't have to stay with me tonight." Willa laughed, pulling the door open. She froze, seeing Nick standing in her doorway. He seemed confused, then his eyes traveled down her body, taking in her robe. She pulled it tighter around her. "Yes?"

What in the world could he want?

He dropped his gaze to the toes of his boots, shuffling from foot to foot. Then he looked back up at her, his eyes tight. "Do you think I could come in for just a minute?"

"Sure," she said, ever polite. But should she let him in? She waited just for a beat, then stepped to the side and motioned him in, her brain spinning. She was afraid to have hope; he'd not exactly welcomed her with open arms when she had visited him.

Keep some distance, she told herself, leading the way into her apartment.

"Thank you." He followed her.

"I'll make tea." Walking into her kitchen, she checked her kettle; it was low. Lifting it, she refilled it with water.

"Does tea make everything better?" He let out a half laugh, obviously trying to relieve the tension. He wrung his hands, then wiped them on his jeans.

"Sometimes." She barked in laughter. "Right now, it's giving me something to do."

She was going for honesty. Hopefully it wouldn't bite her in the butt.

Chamomile and lemon. That would do for a difficult late-night conversation. Prepping the cups, she redirected her attention to him, settling back against her countertop.

"I guess that's my cue, huh?" He started for a grin but his face fell. He took a shuffling step towards her. "I talked to Duke."

Her eyebrows went up. "Duke?"

He nodded, dropping his gaze. "I realized I had misjudged you. I'm so sorry about that."

Her heart surged, but it didn't change anything. "You have a hard time trusting people."

He winced. "You're not wrong. I've been betrayed so many times... Well, I'm not like you."

There it was again, their differences.

"I choose to trust people." She made the distinction.

"It's different when you've been betrayed. My last relationship-" He broke off, his face scrunching into a grimace. The corners of his eyes tightened, and he ground his teeth.

He was obviously struggling to talk about it. She may have boundaries, but she understood pain.

"You were wrong about one thing. I do understand what it's like to be betrayed for personal gain." Her tea kettle clicked. Perfect for storytime, she silently snorted at her dark humor. "It's why I'm here, actually."

She poured the hot water over the tea infusers in their mugs.

"I *was* in Seattle, and it was profitable. But my partner Trey, sorry, Guru Uni." She rolled her eyes before continuing. "It means 'contented one.' Ha. He took my business.

Turned it into an investment opportunity for his own personal benefit and left me stranded."

He set his jaw. "What happened?"

"We were in business together. Started up a big yoga studio. It was awesome, actually. We had some great regulars and were able to reach so many. He had some good ideas to make money from it, but I was the one who taught the classes. I'd already gotten my teacher training certifications and had done all the research to teach people safely. You know, to watch them and make sure they wouldn't hurt themselves." She waved a hand in the air and took a sip of her tea. "One day, I went into our studio to work and found it empty. He had taken all our equipment, mats, oils, diffusers, the computer, everything. The place was completely abandoned. I thought we'd been robbed. I called the cops and everything. We'd just started a police report when one of the officers pulled up the LLC information and talked to the building owner. He had put it all in his name. Everything. I didn't have a leg to stand on."

Nick's eyes had grown hard and he shook his head, but he remained quiet, his attention focused on her.

"It was greed, pure and simple. And his own limitations. He didn't believe he could do it on his own from the start.

So he took from me and decided not to trust me, and probably thought I'd do the same to him." It had been a hard lesson, but she didn't want it to harden her. She wanted her heart to stay open, even if she had learned to set better limits in her relationships. "Shortly after, I found a shop that had opened elsewhere in Seattle with the same name. He was claiming to have trained in Tibet, the whole nine yards. He'd taken all my notes, my classes, and reopened. I finally got ahold of him. He told me to leave him alone or he'd sue me and get a restraining order. The funny thing was, I wasn't even trying to get all of that back when I finally found him in that new studio. I was still worried about him."

Nick watched her, his eyes softening. "Even then?"

She nodded. "I couldn't understand why he had done it. I thought something had happened."

"Some people are just bad, Willa."

"I'm not sure I believe that. We don't know what they're dealing with, or what led them to those decisions."

"Couldn't you have reopened? Tried again? You were the brains of the operation, yogically speaking." He screwed up his face. "I'm not sure that's a word."

"I was going to. That was my first idea, but he told me that I had no right to any of it. He'd even trademarked the class schedule and training, plus the name. I was so angry it had all been taken from me. Eventually, I realized we don't have control of things like that in our lives, that they come and go naturally. We have to let go and let things come as they can."

"So, I was wrong. You have been hurt and manipulated by someone."

"Yes."

His eyes found hers. "Were you romantically involved as well?"

She hesitated. "On and off. It wasn't the most fulfilling relationship. We were better as business partners. At least I thought so."

"Why try again?" he questioned her. "Why allow yourself to be hurt?"

"Why not?" She tried to explain. "I've been blessed with the people of Orca Cove. Sure, they have issues, but they've also been so giving. I haven't wanted for anything."

He didn't reply, just quietly studied his tea.

"Sometimes it's hard to accept, but other times it's beautiful." She moved closer to him, wanting him to gain her awareness, but knowing that these things had to be self-realized.

"I don't know if it's worth it." He finally glanced up. She could see the pain and uncertainty in his eyes. "It feels so...destined to fail."

She'd often thought the same thing, at the beginning.

"I've found that largely, people are beautiful. Sure, they mess up." She lifted her shoulder. "Mostly out of fear. That can cause greed."

"How can you let go?"

"When you lose it all, you don't have a choice."

He nodded at that.

"And now I choose to trust," she went on, saying it simply, even though she knew it was anything but that. "Even if it makes me naive on occasion. I'm happy and at peace. For me, at least, it's the right choice."

"Wait." His eyes shot open. His head swiveled to her money jar and then behind him to the front door. "You don't lock your door."

"I do when I go to bed. Just not typically when I leave," she explained. "Mr. Pemberley, who owns the studio I rent downtown and the town's bookstore, insists that I lock the yoga studio when I leave. So, I can't keep product there.

And what if someone needs something? What if I need to leave a new body butter for Izzy or Solomon needs more sunscreen?"

That man went through sunscreen. But then, he needed it with the amount of time he spent on his fishing boat. "Willa," he said, walking to her. He set his mug on her counter and took her arms in his hands. His eyes bored into hers. "You can't do that. You can't leave your door unlocked when you're gone. Someone could be waiting for you when you return."

"But-" The familiar buzzing of energy began again between them, focused on where he held her.

"But nothing," he cut her off, pleading with her. "It's too dangerous."

Terror filled his eyes. It tugged at her heart. She wanted to just promise him she'd be okay. That she'd be safe. She hadn't had anyone this worried about her in a very long time.

She was close to many people, but ultimately, she was alone.

His breath hitched and his eyes flicked down to her lips. Unable to help herself, she moistened them. His nostrils flared.

"I'm so sorry I doubted you. I know I was limiting myself by not trusting you. I was just so afraid." His grip tightened, but not unpleasantly so.

She wanted so badly to believe him, to trust him again after he refused her. Hadn't she made a point to open her heart?

Gazing up at him, the memory of the kiss they'd shared in his bathroom flashed in her mind, unbidden, the emotion and passion from that moment picking up where they'd left off.

She wanted him. There was no doubt about that.

She chose to trust her heart.

Rising on her toes, she met his lips and waves of desire washed over her again, as heavy and full as before.

Nick's fingertips pressed into her skin, urging her closer. His hungry mouth drank from her, and he crushed her against his chest. Heat traveled down her, settling low, blossoming into an aching need.

The pulsing waves of energy that emanated from wherever they touched grew to a raging, tingling beat between their hearts.

Overcome with sensations, she pulled back only to see the naked look in his eyes. In their icy depths, she saw pain and fear, but also hope. Naked, unadulterated hope.

"I want you," she breathed out.

His chest rose and fell. His eyes glassed over, as though he was bewildered and couldn't think straight. He shook his head, leaning his forehead against hers. "I'm not good enough for you."

It was like an arrow to her already trembling heart. She wrapped her arms up around his neck and pulled him close. "You're exactly what I need. Now take me to bed."

He sucked air between his lips, exhaled with a ragged breath and crushed his lips to hers again. Then, he pulled away and nodded.

Turning, she watched his hungry expression over her shoulder and gave him a coquettish smile. Trailing her fingers down his chest and arm, she snagged his hand and led the way to her room.

Thankfully, she'd taken the time to pull her bed together that morning. Piles of fuzzy pillows were at the head of the bed. There were regular pillows too, but these were for comfort, to tuck under a leg or an arm or pull against her chest wherever she liked during sleep.

Her bedside lamp was on; she decided to leave it on so that she could see him better.

She had long since abandoned feelings of discomfort with her shape, having come to terms with it. She was slim, but she'd never have as thin a body as what some considered perfect or ideal from TV or magazines. She had a long, strong, lean frame from years of eating clean and yoga. Most importantly, she was happy with herself.

That was more powerful anyway.

He stopped at the foot of her bed, studying her downy, blush comforter. "I'm not sure-"

She dropped her robe. It pooled in a soft pile at her feet. Stepping away from it, she pressed her hand against his chest. His breath stopped, his eyes taking in all her soft curves.

"Damn," he exhaled finally; his mouth remained partially open. He reached for her.

Lifting to her toes, she pressed her mouth back to his, kissing along his stubbled jaw, nuzzling into him. He caught her against him, his hands spreading against her bare back. Heat and electricity buzzed where they touched her skin.

Her hips pressed into him, tilting of their own accord. She hummed against his mouth. Her hands shoved his thick flannel off his shoulders, her fingers digging into the t-shirt clinging to his warm chest. Stepping back, he twisted to rip his shirt over his head and fling it away.

He was magnificent.

Willa reached forward to run her fingertips down to his stomach, trailing over the light hair there to land on his waistband. She tugged him back towards her, feeling his bare chest against her skin. The buzzing erupted between them again, increasing in pressure to mimic the heat and desire that were building.

She still had her hand wrapped around his waistband. Adding her other hand, she worked the button free and unzipped his jeans. Slowly, she slid them down him, squatting to her heels to untie his boots. He toed them off so that she could edge his jeans off his feet. She looked up at him from her position. He stood there watching her, breath ragged, chest heaving up and down.

With a growl, he pushed off his socks and pulled her up to him, kissing her roughly while walking them both towards the bed. She collided with its bouncy mattress, falling back to her elbows. Giggling, she found his gaze again but he focused on her so intensely, the laughter died in her throat.

Gaze locked with hers, he crawled up her, dropping kisses along her legs, swirling them around her stomach, and up to her breasts. Every kiss, every nibble left tingles on her skin. He took one nipple in his mouth, circling it with his tongue before pulling it inside and gently sucking on it. Her toes curled and she threw her head back, digging her fingers into his shoulders.

The sensation overwhelmed her senses. Her whole body was swirling as though she was in the middle of a cyclone. Waves of need and lust washed over her.

He broke from her breast and moved up her, sliding his stomach against hers to find her mouth again. Her legs wrapped around him, pulling him closer, but he pulled away, reaching down to slide off his boxer briefs. She dipped over the side of the bed to her nightstand, riffling through the drawer for a condom.

Excited, she ripped it open and handed it over.

"Are you sure?" he asked, his eyes taking in every movement.

"About the condom?" she asked, grinning. "In fact, I insist."

"No. I meant about the act." He blushed. It was adorable.

"Absolutely," she said breathlessly, urging him forward. "Nick Ryan, I've wanted you since I ran into you on that beach."

"In the rain." His mouth curled up into a wolfish grin.

He slid the condom into place and moved over her with animalistic moves that sent fire-like heat over her skin. She arched up to meet him, unable to lie still. Her fingers ached for him. Wrapping her legs up and around him, she pulled him down over her with her heels to find home.

They connected like magnets, pulling and moving against each other in a dance. The pressure built between them, like waves gathering, higher and higher. Energy whirled between them to a point and encapsulated them, their bodies writhing in an undulating pulse.

It was like his entire body was vibrating. The pleasure was so intense, she moaned and he responded by moving harder and faster. Her nails dug into his back and her heels pulled him closer, closing any possible gap between them. She ground into him. His stomach slid against hers, moisture building between them in the heat.

Sensations mounted, cresting over and crashing down harder than she'd ever experienced before. She held onto him as the waves died down like gentle laps over the ocean. She lay, entirely wrung out, shattered against her pillows. His body was slick and wet over hers.

They stayed that way, out of breath, for several moments before he struggled to rise, to meet her gaze.

"Are you okay?" he asked her, searching her face for the truth.

Eyes barely able to focus, she gulped for air and nodded. "Yes."

She raised a hand to his cheek, gently caressing it. Nick rained kisses over her face.

"That was incredible," he said, watching her again. "Did you feel that too?"

"Yes." She nodded, her breathing starting to regulate. "Freaking incredible."

He dropped beside her, pulling her to him. He kissed the top of her curly hair, breathing in deeply.

The vibrations had lessened, dropping down to a light tingle just where they touched. But there was a new warmth in her heart that still connected them. She didn't know what it was, but it sure felt like home.

CHAPTER 17

Blinking against the light shining in, Nick took in the gauzy gray sheers surrounding wide opened windows overlooking the cove. Memories tumbled back into his mind, reminding him of how he got here.

Willa lay nestled in the crook of his shoulder. A fluffy pillow was under one knee and another under his elbow. He never slept surrounded by pillows but they were oddly comfortable. Her long, curly hair spread out like a mermaid's on her pillow, shoulder, and onto his chest where her hand rested. And she was making the sweetest cooing sounds in her sleep.

Man, he had it bad. He couldn't remember the last time he felt this strongly for a woman. The emotion he'd had for his last girlfriend, as much as it'd hurt to be betrayed by her, felt like puppy love in comparison. He tightened the arm he held around her, trailing his fingers lightly down her shoulder. She was so precious, so perfect, so pure. And she had the kindest heart he'd ever had the pleasure of being near.

And the passion they'd shared through the night! After getting up for water to quench their thirst, they had begun again. He couldn't resist her soft skin and open playfulness. He felt himself stirring and he pulsed, but there was no way he could go again. He shifted so her hip wasn't lying in such a close spot.

She moaned, stretching like a cat. He felt her toes trace down his legs and her arms rose over her head. Her body went rigid before relaxing limply into his arms. She blinked up at him, green eyes almost glowing in the morning sun.

"Good morning," she whispered against his chest.

"Morning." He pressed a kiss into the mess of curls on her head. He needed a toothbrush and fast.

Wait, he didn't have one here.

She hooked a heel over his leg, sliding her thigh and hip over his.

"I don't know that I have another one in me just yet." He laughed, pulling her close.

"That's okay. I'm just soaking you in. And enjoying the vibration from your skin."

She pressed against him, causing him to move to adjust himself again. Then he pulled her close.

"I think it's your skin that's vibrating." He lifted his head to kiss her shoulder, her skin smelling like their sex.

"I think we share the energy." She smiled up at him. "Do you want breakfast?"

He hadn't intended on staying this long. The reality of their situation fell back onto his shoulders with a thud. Maybe they shouldn't have done this. But last night, he'd been so caught up in the moment, nearly intoxicated by her presence.

"You okay?" she asked.

He realized his fingers had dug into her side. "I'm so sorry. Yes, breakfast sounds great. Can I help?"

He shifted, sitting up. He wanted to take as much advantage of their time together as he could. He shouldn't be here now, but since he already was, he was going to enjoy it to its full extent.

"I'm not much of a cook, Nell has that area on lockdown."

Willa swung her legs out of bed, getting up. She was still stark-naked and didn't even move to cover herself. She was gorgeous and her comfort in her own skin, inspiring.

She left the room, going into the hall. "I have an extra toothbrush you can use."

Maybe she simply was perfect. He could hear her rummaging around in a cabinet before appearing again, bamboo toothbrush held high in triumph.

"Thank you," he said, getting out of bed. He stopped to put his boxer briefs on.

She kissed him in the doorway.

"Me first." She disappeared into the bathroom with a grin.

He took his toothbrush into the kitchen with him, finding the glass he'd used the night before. He filled it at her sink and leaned against it, drinking the entire glass.

Maybe she had juice or something in the fridge. Opening it, he searched for anything resembling that. What he found were mason jars filled with odds and ends. One on the top shelf had a purply brown paste in it. Curious, he lifted it, unscrewing the lid. It smelled amazing. He dipped a finger in it and tasted it. Hmmm. It wasn't exactly good, but it had so many interesting flavors.

"That's my hair wash."

He spun, finding her standing at the doorway to her kitchen, a wide smile on her face.

"I'm sorry." He hurried to put it back where he found it. "I shouldn't have been poking around."

She walked up to him, still nude, and wrapped her arms around his neck. He could smell the minty freshness on her breath. "That's okay. Feel free to poke around, but I'm an herbalist. Best not to eat anything unmarked in my fridge."

"No fair," he complained, raising his head over hers. "I haven't had the time to brush yet."

She laughed, planting kisses along his jawline.

"You make your own hair wash?" he said curiously, heading towards the bathroom. He left the door open and found a jar of powder on the counter that read: Tooth Powder.

"Tooth powder too," she answered, helping him along. "Just wet the brush and dip it in. It's different, but it'll do."

Fair enough. He followed her orders. The powder was weird on his tongue, but peppermint erupted as he brushed. "Wow."

"Glad you like it," he heard from the kitchen.

He finished brushing and spit, rinsing in the sink. He smacked his lips. Odd, but refreshing. He shut the door to use the toilet and washed his hands, splashing water on his face to freshen up as well as he could.

He'd appreciate a shower, but he shouldn't stay long enough for that, unless he could talk her into sharing it with him. No, he'd enjoy breakfast with her and head home. This was a momentary pause in the seriousness of the situation he was in. Once he was home, he'd give her space. It wouldn't be long until the coast was clear.

He'd talk to her about it.

"So, hair wash? What's that?" he asked, emerging from the bathroom.

"Shatavari and yucca, mostly." She shrugged. "I add a few other things."

"Why's it in the fridge?"

"So it lasts longer. No preservatives, remember?"

He kissed the top of her hair, breathing deeply.

"But why does it smell like lavender?" He sniffed. "And rosemary?"

She giggled at his affection. "Mermaid tonic."

Surprised, he held her at arm's length. "I knew you were a mermaid!"

She laughed, shaking her head. "It's just a hair tonic I make. I spritz it on my hair as a conditioner after washing it. I love lavender. It's in my bath salts and body butter."

That explained it. The woodsy, herbal-floral scent was everywhere on her skin. He ran his lips over her arms, smelling and kissing. Intoxicating. "You know, I really did think you were a mermaid when I ran into you on the beach. You came right out of the water and into my arms."

"Really?"

"Well, not for long. I know it's impossible." He paused, thinking about the energy that passed between them. "Improbable at least."

"I wish," she sighed. "That would be amazing. But no, I'm no mermaid. Just a yoga instructor."

"And herbalist." He raised a finger.

"Very true. Let me throw on a robe," she said, heading back down the hall.

"But why?" he said, raising his hands in playful disappointment.

She reappeared, tugging on her robe. She tied it across her waist. "Hot grease."

"Fair enough."

She pulled things out of her fridge and heated a skillet on the stove. Placing a plastic cutting board in front of her, she grabbed a knife and a pile of veggies. He frowned; she'd have a new cutting board before the week was out.

It was peaceful, more so than being in his own cabin. He loved the woods and spending quiet moments out in them, but it was the enigmatic being in front of him that put his soul at peace.

"There are things we should talk about," he finally broke the silence.

She paused sautéing veggies. Lines appeared between her brows. "Do you regret it?"

"God, no." He stood to go to her, holding her arms in his hands. "Definitely not."

She looked at him questioningly, her spatula still in her hand. "Then what is it?"

The skillet sizzled next to him.

"I should have taken more time to explain last night." His eyes dropped to where they were touching, his fingers on her slim, toned arms, trying to find the right words. "I need to go away for a little bit. I have something to take care of."

"Because of Jimmy?"

She probably thought he'd be going to Seattle for his funeral, even though it was the last thing he could do. But it was related. Best to let her think that. With the stakes, the less she knew, the better.

He nodded. "I won't be gone long."

"Promise?" She snuggled in closer, sighing in contentment. The skillet popped again, and she hopped away. "Oops!"

Quickly, she stirred the veggies, scraping them from the bottom, and poured whisked eggs over them.

"You don't mind?" It felt wrong keeping her in the dark, but the danger was just too great. He'd explain everything once the threat had passed. With any luck, he'd be back in a week, and she'd be safe and sound.

"Of course not." She lifted her shoulder, her focus still on the skillet. "You've got things to do. But I will be anxious to see you when you get back. You'll have some time to make up for."

Twisting around from the stove, she smiled flirtatiously at him and winked. His heart skipped a beat.

He watched her finish their eggs and plate them, a tightness wrapped around his heart. He'd take care of Palmer and Dupree and be back before she knew it.

Kissing her one final time, he left using her back porch, claiming to want to walk along the beach for the crisp morning air before finding the truck he'd left in town. He'd make sure he wasn't seen leaving her house. That was the most important thing.

He took in the early light. It played on the water like broken glass blinking back at him. Two dorsal fins he'd begun to recognize as orcas, plus several dolphins moved near the fishing boats. Breathing in the fresh air, he walked along the pebbled beach. Life was feeling good.

Coming up to the road, he scanned the area for any signs of Palmer. He was far enough now from her apartment. If he ran into him, at least he wouldn't be drawing attention to her.

He crossed the street, heading further into the residential area, but at the top of the block, he glanced back down her street, envisioning her at the door waving at him.

But she wasn't there. Palmer was.

He was crossing through the lot and headed straight to her front door.

Nick stumbled on the sidewalk, catching himself before he fell. He checked for bystanders, contemplating drawing his sidearm. He didn't see anyone, but there were houses all around. He cursed. What should he do?

If he ran to her, as every fiber of his being wanted to do, Palmer would know he cared about her. She'd be the perfect leverage. And neither the chief nor he had enough to take Palmer in for good. Not yet.

Fumbling, he pulled his phone out, dialing Duke. "Yes?"

"Where are you?" he growled into the phone.

"What's wrong?" Duke said sharply.

"Palmer is walking towards Willa's door right this minute." He held the phone in both hands, the severity of the situation making everything crystal clear. "If I go, he'll know he can use her against me. It's better if you go, but if you're not close, I'm going anyway."

It would make her a target, but he'd take her and run. Maybe he could hide her somewhere and come back to deal with Palmer.

"I'm walking out of the cafe." He could hear Duke's footsteps crunching on the pavement. "I can be there in moments."

Relief washed over him as the call ended. Duke was close. The cafe was a hundred yards away at most. But danger was only feet from her door.

The brute paused, peeking through her windows first. Nick's blood boiled, his hand forming a fist at his side. The man finally made it to the door, pounding on it.

Down the sidewalk, he could see Duke jogging up, crossing through the parking area in front of the townhouses. Nick had to bite back the howl crawling up his throat.

Willa's door opened and her cheerful face appeared. Luckily, she was properly dressed. Nick dipped behind a row of tall evergreens lining someone's driveway. He was ready to race over and intercept the thug at the first sign of danger.

"Morning, Willa!" Duke hollered, coming to a stop next to the visitor.

Nick couldn't hear what else was said, but Willa's smile only dipped once, tilting as she listened to something Palmer said. Whatever she shared, he was willing to take the consequences. He'd run if he had to, but he wasn't giving up that duffel bag. Jimmy had given his life for it and so would Nick, if need be.

He'd made his decision. Dupree would get it over his dead body.

Lifting his phone again, he dialed the police station.

"This is Nick Ryan. I need the chief," he told the officer on duty.

He heard the officer scramble to get up. "I'll put him on."

Palmer left, heading back down the steps and away from Willa. Duke dipped inside with her and shut the door.

Nick squatted, getting further from view.

"Detective Ryan," Warner said, taking the phone.

"Palmer's back in town. He was just at Willa's place," Nick said, needing any help he could get to protect her.

"Judy, divert to Main Street. Reginald Palmer is back." His voice was directed away from the phone's speaker, as though into his radio. Then, back into the phone, "I have an officer heading that way. I'm coming, too."

The line went dead.

Nick sagged against the branches behind him. Duke was with Willa. Palmer wasn't. And the cops were going to chase Palmer from town yet again.

"Hello?"

He spun around, finally seeing the spritely elderly lady coming down her front steps. Surging to his feet, he checked to make sure Palmer wasn't in sight before meeting her on her sidewalk.

"Hi. Sorry. I was out for a walk this morning and I-" He trailed off, not knowing what to say. "Thought I saw someone but didn't want to seem foolish if they didn't know me."

He closed his eyes so she couldn't see his eyes roll, but they were rolling alright. What a dumb line.

"Oh, I've done that loads of times. If you don't know them, though, just make new friends!" She snapped her fingers high. "Voila, problem solved."

He fought back a grin. "I'll try to remember that trick next time."

"Loris Franklin." She stuck her hand out.

"Nick Ryan." He shook it.

His hand still firmly in her surprisingly strong grasp, she pulled him closer. "Willa's Nick?"

"Well." He cast a glance back towards her place. "I guess so."

She clapped him on the shoulder with her other hand, squealing, finally letting go of his hand. "Then you did see her, silly. That's her place."

He hoped she wasn't this open with everyone, but it seemed like they were friends.

"Oh, good, that's what I thought."

"You should go see her, take her to breakfast." She leaned in, wagging her eyebrows.

Loris didn't know Willa had already made him breakfast. He was a lucky man.

"I'm headed out of town for a little while, so I don't have the time, but it's a great idea. I'll do that when I get back."

"You do that. She loves the cafe, too. She's friends with the owner. She and a few others in town. Thick as thieves. Just don't wait too long, that girl's a catch!"

The woman was full of information.

"We're fairly new." He tried to temper her enthusiasm. "But I'll keep that in mind."

Moving away, he lifted a hand in farewell.

"Well, okay."

"See you around, Loris."

She brightened and waved. "See you, Nick." He watched her disappear into her house.

Breathing a sigh of relief, he rechecked the area and dipped back out to the sidewalk, making his way to his truck.

CHAPTER 18

"I don't understand," Willa told Duke, looking for answers.

"Palmer is a thug, a bad guy." Duke had hold of her shoulders, his face grim.

"But what does he want from Nick?"

She'd immediately disliked the man who had been on her front porch. It was totally unusual for her. He gave her major creeps.

"That's probably best answered by the man himself." Duke peeked out of her curtains, then came back to her.

"He said he'd be away for a while. Out of town, something like that."

Duke raised his head, watching her, but said nothing.

"What's that look for?" She knew that expression. He wasn't happy about something.

"The guy's trying to take care of you. My advice? Let him. Give him some space to figure it out."

Sometimes a little space was a good thing, especially if Nick was going through something. But she cared about him and was worried. If only she could see him and make sure he was okay.

"It was a good call not telling that Palmer guy you knew Nick. He's bad news."

"No one is entirely bad, but he didn't have good intentions. I figured I should tell Nick first."

"Always a good course of action when a stranger like that is looking for someone you know."

Shelby's visitor popped into her head. She forgot to tell Nick last night. He'd surprised her on her doorstep, ready and willing to open up to her. All other thoughts had fled her mind.

"He visited the cabins too. Asking around for Nick." Things clicked in her head. He hadn't been entirely truthful to her.

"Are you sure?"

"Pretty sure." She nodded. "Shelby came over last night and told me the same story. She could tell he wasn't here for the usual reasons. He'd made up some story that he was supposed to meet Nick there."

"Digging for information. And now he's come here. That's not good. I'm assuming Shelby sent him packing."

"Yep, she saw right through him. He has no idea she knows who he is."

He nodded.

"Do you think he's a threat?"

"He's not here to make friends."

"But he does know Nick. He knows his name, at least," she prodded, trying to figure out more of this tangled tale.

"I know a little, but Nick can fill you in." He was being especially vague. Not entirely unlike him, but in this scenario it was. "Be careful, Willa. While he's in town, your best bet is to keep to yourself. Teach yoga, go shopping or to the cafe. But don't be seen with Nick and stay away from Palmer and any other strangers."

"How can I be seen with Nick if he's out of town?" She frowned. Had he lied to her about that too?

"Call him. Let him explain. But listen, just lie low a bit, okay? You don't have to help everybody." He looked her in the eye.

She didn't like hiding, but if it made Duke feel better, she'd be particularly careful, for a little while at least.

"I'll keep to myself and look out for strangers." She rolled her eyes. "Thanks, Dad."

"You've been hanging out with Shelby too much." Duke snorted.

"But I'm calling Nick and finding out what's going on."

"Good idea. Just give him a little time to get home first."

If Duke knew he wasn't home, then he'd spoken to him this morning on the phone or in person. With his well-timed arrival at her apartment, intercepting the big guy at her door, she suspected the former. That meant Nick had called Duke and sent him to her place instead of coming himself.

That didn't make any sense. It didn't feel anything like the passionate, protective man that was here with her the night before. He'd been so worried about her trusting people and leaving her door unlocked.

Thoughts swirled into place. He was worried about her unlocked door because of the stranger. And he hadn't even told her.

She tried not to assume the worst, but with all the false starts between them, it sure didn't feel good.

"Willa." Nick finally answered on her second try. "Is everything okay?"

"I'm genuinely not sure," she said, walking out to her back deck. "You need to be honest with me. What's going on?"

She had so many questions. There was a long pause on the phone.

"Willa, I'm sorry about everything. I never should have gone to your house last night. I put you in danger."

His words cut like a knife. He regretted what they had done?

"Why are you sorry? If something bad followed you from Seattle, that can hardly be your fault."

"If it were only that simple. That man, or rather who he works for, is just pure evil."

"I don't believe that anyone is inherently evil." She shook her head. "People make bad choices, especially if they've been hurt and had their reality twisted. They often act out of fear."

"I disagree. I've seen it, Willa. Some people are just evil."

"I don't know. We're all the same at our core."

"My last relationship, she was dating me to get close to me. Larry Dupree had orchestrated it to get information from me. And I bought it, hook, line, and sinker."

"But why would he do that?" It didn't make sense. What would he want from Nick?

"Because he's wicked, corrupt, whatever you want to call it. I'm serious, Willa, you have to take this seriously. Once I figured out who she was, he pretended she was some sort of sick gift to me and I messed up, I messed up badly, because when I rejected him and the gift, he called one of his guys and had her killed. She-" His breath caught in his throat. "She'd been pregnant at the time. I didn't know it until the coroner's report later, but she had been. I don't know for sure, but I think it was mine."

Willa was stunned. She had no idea what to think. No wonder the guy had trust issues.

"That's awful, Nick. I'm so very sorry. I can't imagine what it was like going through that."

"It still hurt," he said wistfully, caught in the memory. "Even though I knew it had all been fake."

"Surely, she developed feelings for you. It would be hard not to. I think you'd recognize feigned attraction."

"I'd like to think so, but it's just a pretty thought. No, she worked for Dupree. There was no love there."

She would be surprised if that were true, but stayed silent.

"But why was he targeting you?"

"I was trying to take him down, Jimmy and I."

"Take him down?" It still didn't make any sense. "But why?"

"It was my job, Willa."

"How? You're a woodworker." Her mind swirled as quickly as her stomach.

"I wasn't. Not when I lived in Seattle. I was a detective for the Seattle Police Department." He spoke evenly, without emotion. "Following in my dad's footsteps."

"I thought you followed in your grandad's footsteps," she said sadly, almost argumentatively. He'd implied as much.

"I did. Just not at first."

"Is that why you left the job? Your old girlfriend?"

"Fake girlfriend," he scoffed bitterly. "It's only part of the reason I left. But it was the culmination. I'd already gotten tired of all the lying, cheating, and killing. It was hard to watch all of that. I was getting numb to it."

"Is that why you lied to me so easily?" she asked, the words acidic on her tongue. "Because you were numb to it?"

"I wasn't lying to you when I told you that I came out here to find some peace. That was true."

"But it was only part of the truth. You left a lot out." She paced her deck, emotion rolling off her in waves. "That wasn't an accident. You knew what you were implying."

"I did," he said succinctly. "You're absolutely right. I was trying my damnedest to keep you safe. And then I failed."

"Failed?""I was trying to stay away from you. Keep you away from whatever is haunting me. I even pushed you away."

"The market," she said, remembering his explanation about them being different. It hadn't quite made sense, even at the time.

"Yes," he said quietly. "It was so hard to do. You looked so hurt."

"I was."

"And then I talked to Duke. I thought that if I stayed away for a while, after all of it was over, you'd be safe and we might have a chance." He paused for a moment. "But this morning, seeing Palmer at your apartment like that... I realized I'll never know for sure that some criminal isn't going to come after me, trying to get payback for putting them in jail. I don't deserve you anyway."

"What do you mean?" She sat down on her bench on the deck, unable to process everything he was saying. It was just too much.

"You have no idea what I've done." He breathed. "I did what I had to do to keep people safe, but I'm not a good person, Willa. I don't deserve someone as perfect and pure as you."

She shook her head. "I'm not perfect. Far from it. I just try. I always try. I refuse to stop trying to be better."

"That's what makes you so pure though, don't you see? I would mar that."

Standing, she walked back to her railing, leaning on it. She stared off over the water. Pelicans and seagulls dove for breakfast. How could it seem so calm out there and be so upside down and twisted in her gut? Nothing was as it had seemed, and she couldn't sort it out. She pressed the heel of her hand to her forehead, closing her eyes.

"Wait, so what were you doing on the beach with Jimmy? That doesn't make sense. If you left the job, why did he follow you here?"

He fell silent and stayed so for a long time.

"He wanted to update me on the case. We met on the beach to keep my location as quiet as possible," he said finally.

He didn't elaborate. It sounded like more lies. Or at least half truths.

She couldn't tell the difference anymore.

"And Dupree followed you here? He's the one who killed Jimmy?"

"No, we got Dupree. He's in jail awaiting trial. It was one of his guys," he explained. "Dupree's court case is coming up soon and I think they're trying to find anything that could be used against us to throw the case out and set their boss free."

"Why didn't you just tell me you were a cop? Everyone has history. I even shared mine with you."

"I know you did." He paused a long moment. "And I should have told you sooner. I should have trusted you."

It made more sense now why he hadn't, though. Even though she didn't know where the lies ended. Would he ever be fully honest?

"I was trying to put that life behind me," he went on. "I really wanted it to be like it never happened."

"You can't rewrite history. It's a part of you." His protective nature made more sense now too.

"I was also afraid you wouldn't like that part of me." His voice got quieter.

It sounded like the truth. "Me? Judge you? I try very hard not to judge others."

"You're so full of love and light, though. I wasn't, and maybe I'm still not. Hell, I've killed people, Willa."

"And you decided it wasn't the path for you. You're trying to change that."

"I am."

"You're still not being completely honest with me." She just called him out on it.

"No," he admitted. "I'm not. I can't be."

"But why not?" She straightened back up, fingertips pressing into the wood grain of her railing. "I've been honest with you. I've protected you twice now. Does Chief Warner even know the truth?"

"Most of it. He knows I was a police officer and that Palmer, the guy you met, is one of Dupree's guys, digging around."

"But there's more."

"Willa, I can't tell you the rest," he pleaded. "It's too dangerous. You have to trust me."

"How can you ask me to do that? You haven't done the same for me."

"I know. You're entirely right. I'm only asking that you don't tell the chief I'm leaving anything out."

It was a lot to ask. Suddenly, she didn't feel so secure about what she knew. Maybe she was naive to trust people. Maybe Nick was right, some people just couldn't be trusted.

"I'll think about it." It was all she could promise at the moment.

"Do you think Palmer bought your story? Do you think he believes you don't know me?"

"Yes, I think my lie was believable," she let her discontent at her dishonesty slide off her tongue.

She'd believed she was keeping someone she cared very deeply about safe, but only to let him know so that he could handle it himself. He wasn't handling it at all. He was running from it until a court case. Then again, the man in question wanted something from him, possibly to hurt him, she didn't know. And she didn't know because he refused to tell her.

It put her in a state of dissonance, at odds with herself. And she made a point to live her life in harmony.

"I just want to keep you safe, Willa. Palmer won't stop, but I'll stay out of town and away from you."

"When you said you were going out of town, that was a lie too."

"I said I'd be away for a while."

"You implied it." She was tired of searching for truth in his words. Pain wound its way into her heart.

"I did. You're right. I told you I wasn't the man you thought I was. I'm so sorry for that. I should have just stayed away."

Maybe he was right. It went against everything she believed in, but maybe she'd been wrong too.

"Palmer stopped by Shelby's place, Siren's Song Cabins, too. He's pretending to be your friend. Said he was trying to meet up with you but couldn't get a hold of you. Shelby didn't say anything. The townspeople don't share a lot with outsiders."

"I'm grateful for that. But he might still eventually find me."

Fear for him surged in her stomach, even after everything.

"Should you leave town?"

"I don't want to leave in case things get worse. What if more of Dupree's team comes? It's my mess and I'm not leaving Orca Cove high and dry."

"You should call the Seattle Police Department. They could send help."

"He hasn't done anything illegal. They have no recourse."

"Not yet. And if he does?"

"Then they'll provide backup. Until then, the best I can do is lie low, keep danger from town and hope the chief can keep running him out until the court case. In the meantime, please be careful, Willa. Please stay out of his way, and for goodness' sake, lock your door."

It made sense now. She'd misconstrued his concern as caring about her. He was just trying to right a wrong. One he'd brought to town.

"I'll lock the door," she said tightly. And because she couldn't help herself, she added, "You be careful, too."

CHAPTER 19

Nick sat there staring at his phone. He'd genuinely lost her this time, pushed her away once and for all. Even though it was what he meant to do, it still hurt. It hurt bad.

Dupree's face flashed back into his mind.

"I gave her to you, aren't you grateful?" he'd sneered into Nick's face.

"Why should I be grateful? It was all a lie," he'd roared back.

They'd been face-to-face in front of the restaurant where he found Dupree. He'd found out from Rachel's phone that they were working together. They'd just moved in together and he had been helping her unpack her things.

He saw a message from Dupree flash across her screen when she went to the restroom.

He hadn't been trying to read it, but he was worried it was her work. She so often had to run in at odd hours. She'd told him she was a personal nurse, but she'd been running off to meet Dupree.

"Congrats on getting him to ask you to move in. Well done, Rachel. You're earning your place on my team." The message had drilled into his brain. He'd tried to rationalize it so many times. At first, he thought someone was congratulating them on a new stage in their relationship. But the contact name gave him away.

She'd been so sure about his trust that she hadn't even bothered coming up with a code name. It read loud and clear: Dupree.

And then everything else suddenly made sense. All the drug busts that should have gone right, that somehow went wrong. Dupree and his guys knew they were coming. Nick thought they had a mole, but he had no idea it was in his own home.

He knew he should have gone to find Jimmy first. He could have leaned on him, used him as a safe space to crumble. But no, his dad had taught him better than that.

Keep your emotions close and never let anyone know you care. It was one of his first lessons in life after his mom left

.

Jimmy would have tried to talk him out of what he did next. It was probably the main reason Nick hadn't gone to him. Instead, he'd gone straight to the streets, to find Dupree himself. And he did, at a restaurant the man often frequented. Of course, he had friends with him. There was no way Nick could have done anything to stop the man.

"It's always a lie," Dupree had told him. "Every woman is always with a man for one of two reasons, money or protection. That's all."

"Is that why she did it?" he'd asked. "You offered her protection from something."

Dupree laughed in his face. "No, it was for the money."

"You bastard."

"You ungrateful piece of shit," he said an inch from Nick's face. He'd felt droplets of spit from the force of Dupree's words. "She was a gift. Don't you want her?"

It was a game and a threat, and he knew it. But he was too angry to play along anymore. "Why would I want some washed-up prostitute? I've never had to pay for sex before, unlike you apparently."

Dupree snarled at him, then backed up. A sick smile spread across his face. "I gave her to you. I can take her away."

He flicked his phone open and hit a button. The call was answered immediately. "Kill her."

"Wait, what?" The world slowed. His heart beat so loudly that the sound pounded down around him until he could barely hear the people in the street. He knew who Dupree was. What was he thinking? He shouldn't have gone after a man like him. Not without a plan or backup.

All rational thought fled his mind. Even though he knew it was a lie, he was a protector. He ran home as fast as he could.

He'd been too late. His actions had cost a life.

It still haunted him.

He couldn't let it happen again. But he could think more clearly this time, now that he was away from Willa. He couldn't protect her himself, but someone else could.

"Duke," Nick said into his phone. "Are you sure Palmer believes Willa doesn't know me?"

"Yeah, man. You're good," Duke reassured him. "I got there in the nick of time too. Palmer started to press, asking more questions. He played up the story about him trying to meet up with you. I hopped in and pretended Willa and I were together. I said I'd seen a new guy around town, but I had no idea who he was or where he lived."

"Thanks," he said. He didn't like how things had played out, but at least she was safe now.

"No problem. You're one of us now, we keep an eye out for each other."

The acrid knowledge that Duke was wrong sat like a large cast-off piece of wood in his stomach. It couldn't go up. It couldn't go down. It would just sit there forever, making him uncomfortable and wishing for something that couldn't be.

"So, Willa called you, then?" Duke went on.

"Yeah, she had questions."

"You'd better have given her the whole story. I'm not lying to a friend."

"I did." As much as he could anyway.

"It was a dumb move staying overnight."

"I know, I never should have gone."

"I was going to say that you should have had a better escape plan." Duke waited for a beat. "Did you tell Willa that?"

"I did. It just put her more at risk. It never should have happened."

He exhaled loudly. "She's gonna be a mess. Geez, dude."

"She's got all of you."

"It's not the same and you know it." Duke's voice hardened.

"What happened with the chief?" Nick changed subjects.

"He and Palmer had a showdown."

"Shit."

"Warner did everything he could to threaten him, but you know he can't actually keep him out of town."

"I know. I just hoped he would back down."

"He left eventually, but he'll be back. Palmer isn't backing down this time. That's certain. He won't rest until he finds you. You'd better let me know if you need anything. You can't be seen in town."

"I've got plenty of food. I'll just stay here."

"Let me know if you need help. I'll bring Warner and his team.""Thanks, Duke, but I'm done putting the town in jeopardy. I've got this. Keep an eye on Willa for me."

"Are you going to tell her that, man?"

"I tried to. But every time I try, it doesn't go as planned."

"You don't want to."

"Hell no, I don't, but it's the right thing to do. I don't deserve her." He cared about her too much. He'd never felt this way about anyone before, not even Rachel. If he wasn't such a cynical asshole, he'd say he loved her. But that was impossible. He hadn't known her long enough.

It didn't matter anyway. He wouldn't saddle someone like her with someone like him.

"But you said the court case would be soon. You can still make things right."

"If it's not Palmer, it'll be someone else. I left a legacy in Seattle. This isn't the first time someone went after the cop that put them away."

"Maybe not, but you can't predict the future. You can't ensure her safety from everything."

"No, but I can step aside. If she comes to harm, it won't be because of me."

"That may be too late, man. Seems to me that you've already hurt her twice."

Nick ground his teeth. "Well, I'll make sure there isn't a third time."

And he hung up the phone.

"What do you mean, he ran you out of town again?" Isaac seethed in anger.

"He didn't run me out, exactly. He was causing problems, that's all, getting in the way of me interviewing the townspeople. I told him he couldn't make me leave. I left because I had talked to who I needed to on my list." Palmer gripped the phone tightly. He didn't like being treated like a kid. He'd been working for the boss for many years before Isaac came on board, younger and more devious. The guy would kill his own mother if ordered. He was a true sociopath. "I told him I'd be b ack."

"Oh, you told him that? Then I'm sure he's taking you seriously."

Palmer ground down on his teeth, his jaw clicking. "I will find him."

"No, you won't. You're a pathetic excuse for help," Isaac said coldly, almost without emotion. "And it's the bag we need, you idiot."

"I'm looking for Nick so that I can find the bag. He has it," he tried to explain. He could do the job.

"But you haven't yet. You've had more than enough time. I'm tired of waiting. Apparently, I'll have to come and clean up your mess. It sounds like there are several things I need to take care of for Dupree."

"You don't." He struggled to stop him.

"I have one thing to take care of and then I'll be headed that way. Keep an eye out for me."

He didn't like the sound of that. He could be one of those things.

Willa was safe, for now at least, and Warner had made sure Palmer had left town yet again. Duke would have at least a little time without a crisis. He finally had time for food.

After getting a breakfast burrito and a coffee to go at the cafe, he took it down to one of the picnic tables at the marina to eat. As much as he liked catching up to Maggie or Nell, he didn't feel like being around all the townspeople today. There was too much going on with

Warner and the other officers, and people were starting to ask questions.

He hated questions.

Instead, he sat and watched the orcas in the cove. Only two today. They must have a lot of tasty fish in the cove this year. They'd never had this many, this often. The cove might not be large, but the opening was deep and wide, easy for the large dolphins to make their way in. He had to be careful when he left port.

He bit into his burrito, enjoying the crispy potatoes and spicy fresh salsa. Nell probably made the sausage too; it was meaty and spicy. Perfect.

A pelican landed on the other end of the table he sat at, its beady eyes trained on his burrito.

"Nuh-uh, little dude," he warned the bird. "This one's mine. Go into that ocean and find yourself a tasty fish."

The pelican ignored him and spread its wings, flapped them, then waddled forward on his webbed feet.

"Go on." He raised a hand and waved it. "Get."

"Sorry, Duke."

He heard a voice behind him. It was Solomon.

"Hey, Solomon. Taking the day off?" He was normally out on the water at this time of day.

"Just came in with the morning haul. I stopped to get something to eat." Solomon hurried over to him. "Roy was hungry, and apparently still is."

"Roy?" He frowned. Solomon fished alone. "Did you get help?"

"No. Roy!" He pointed to the pelican on Duke's table, still eyeing his breakfast. "He came to me last week."

"You have a pet pelican? That's cool. Kinda like a sailor and his parrot." It *was* cool, even if it was a little weird. Duke didn't mind eccentric people. He kinda preferred them. It was easier to read them. They weren't trying to be anyone but themselves.

It was the ones who seemed normal that you had to watch out for.

"Not a pet. He's my friend." Solomon reached over and stroked the pelican's back. It let him.

That was unusual.

"It's good to have friends," Duke said. He felt bad for the fisherman. He knew the man didn't have many, but thinking a pet pelican was a friend? It was a wild animal. Not the most affectionate pet.

"He wants me to get him whatever you're eating," he laughed, then addressed the pelican. "I saved you fish from this morning. There's more on the boat. And that burrito would be bad for your digestion. Remember the last time you ate human food?"

Solomon wagged a finger at the bird.

"Nope. It's sole. It's too early for Chinook," he went on, calmly addressing the pelican. "I know you prefer trout, but I already caught my limit today on that. No, you'll have to make do with the sole. Or shrimp, there's plenty of that. If you want trout, you'll have to get it yourself."

The bird raised its wings again, flapping them lightly. Solomon laughed.

Okay, it was going past eccentricity. He seriously thought the thing was talking to him.

"You feeling alright, Solomon?"

He blinked, as though surprised to still see Duke sitting there. "Never felt better! Life's more interesting now that I have a partner."

He should check in on the man more often. "Good to hear."

"I'd better get this guy more food. What a hog," Solomon teased, shuffling towards the pier. His knobby knees jutted out at angles as he walked, unused to being on land. He gestured over his shoulder. "Come on, Roy."

Astonishingly enough, the bird flapped his wings and lifted off the picnic table. He tucked his legs up under him and flapped again, banking towards Solomon's boat bobbing in the water.

Duke's jaw dropped.

His amazement quickly ended, however. He saw someone walking along the pier, scanning the crowd intently.

The man was black, as dark as night, his hair cut very close to his head. He had on a loose T-shirt and baggy pants with flip-flops, but the most startling thing about him was the large, angry scar that rose out of the wide neck of his shirt, up his neck, and across one cheek. It had long since healed, showing no signs of redness, but it made the man look scary as hell. What had caused something that terrible? He was lucky he still had the eye

.

Realizing he had stood, Duke put the rest of his burrito back into its wrapper and made his way to the pier. He might be one of Dupree's guys, come to help Palmer since he'd been made. Duke dropped his leftovers in the nearby trashcan, he'd had enough to eat, and lifted the coffee to his lips, his eyes tracking the man's motions.

Keeping his body loose and casual, he strolled along the pier, nodding to a few fishermen he knew. Coming alongside the stranger, he lifted his head in greeting. "Morning."

The man stopped and turned towards him, his eyes flashing wide for a microsecond. It was like he recognized him. He'd never seen him before. He'd remember a scar like that.

"Good morning," he said, his voice rumbling.

"Haven't seen you around, you here to fish?"

A lazy smile spread across his face, gathering the scar at his cheek. "I've been fishing, yes. It's good fishing."

"Yeah, we'll get more fishermen when the season gets going, when the restrictions lift."

The man's face brightened; laughter rolled from his mouth.

Duke fought a frown. He didn't know what was funny.

"I don't worry so much about that," the man said.

"Ah, oyster fisherman?"

"I like oysters, yes."

That made more sense. Clams, mussels, and oysters were open year-round in the Hood Canal.

"I don't think I've seen you around before." he prodded gently, raising his coffee to his lips.

"You could say I'm new to the area."

That was vague. He was definitely hiding something.

"Let me know if I can help you out with anything," he offered, raising a hand. "I'm Duke."

"Percy." He grinned, showing teeth. "It's good to meet you, Duke."

Percy nodded politely and left, walking to shore. Duke tilted his head as he watched the man go up the ramp and towards the cafe. It was strange, but he got the feeling he'd seen those eyes before. How could he forget a face like that, though?

He texted Nick to see if he knew a man named Percy and gave him the stranger's description. Drinking his coffee, he waited for the reply.

"Doesn't sound familiar," his phone read. "Is he asking around for me?"

"No. Just felt like he was looking for something."

"Does he look dangerous?" Nick texted back.

Oh, yeah. Oddly enough, he didn't get the feeling he was up to no good.

"I didn't get a bad feeling about him," he texted back.

"Best to keep an eye out, though."

"Agreed."

He pocketed his phone and went back to his boat. He had a few things to do this afternoon. If he was lucky, he could get them done before a new crisis arose.

CHAPTER 20

"**M**orning, Willa." Maggie leaned in for a hug. "Want to sit outside? It's beautiful out."

"Sure, that sounds good." Willa gave her a tight smile. It was all she could muster.

She'd come to the cafe for lunch, needing to be near her friends. Sure, Shelby would have come over, even though it was the middle of the week. As much as she'd like to see her, she simply didn't want to wallow in her apartment. She needed to clear her head.

"You alright?" Maggie asked, noticing her mood.

"I'm having a rough day," she admitted, following her outside.

"Wanna talk about it?" She visually checked her tables. "I'm not too slammed right now. I have a little time."

"That's sweet, but I'm okay for the moment. Let me get some lunch in me and see if that helps."

"Hey, food'll do it for me," Maggie shined her beacon-of-light smile onto her and tapped her shoulder before heading on to another table.

Willa perused the menu out of habit.

After her phone call with Nick, she had sat at the corner of her bed, her hand trailing over the sheets still wrinkled from their lovemaking. A tight ball wound inside her, but the emotions tumbling around it weren't easy to sort through. It was such a contrast in feelings from mere hours earlier.

Nick had dumped so much information on her during their phone call. He'd been a Seattle cop and never once mentioned it. Although it made sense now why he hadn't trusted her, and she couldn't imagine something like that happening to her, she had shared her story with him. Why had he waited until his past literally stepped onto her porch before telling her? It didn't make sense.

It was obvious that he wanted her. Even when he said he wanted to put distance between them for the sake of her safety, he'd still kept in touch and tried to protect her. But he'd made it very clear he didn't think they had a future. He said they shouldn't.

He'd tried to put space between them twice before, though, and been unable to. Willa wasn't sure his resolve would last, but then again, she wasn't sure what to want. He'd led her on a rollercoaster of emotions, and she'd given him plenty of chances to trust her. She wasn't sure anymore.

There was a lot she wasn't sure about anymore.

"Hey, Willa," Nell stopped by her table, sliding into the seat across from her.

"Maggie tell you to come say hi?"

She nodded. "She said you needed a friend and weren't talking."

"I told her I was okay." Willa sat back in the wrought iron chair. "I had a bad day, but I'm alright."

"Is it that guy, Nick?"

"Yeah," she said, not having any reason to lie. "But it's complicated. Apparently, some danger has followed him from Seattle and he doesn't think we should be together. It's unsafe."

"Sounds like he's trying to shelter you from it."

"I agree."

"But you like him a lot, don't you?"

Willa pressed her lips together. Did she? Oh, hell, she did. Maybe she shouldn't, but she did.

"I do. You're right, but I'm not sure it's the best thing for me. He wasn't entirely truthful to me, until now."

Nell watched her. "You're right."

"What?" She frowned.

"It's complicated."

Willa cracked a smile. "You're a lot of help."

Nell lifted a shoulder. "I'm infinitely helpful. Now I've got to go check on food. You want avocado toast? I have some smoked salmon that would be good on it. It'll make you feel better."

"That sounds good. Oh, and a cup of tea."

"Maggie's already getting it for you." Nell stood up. Maggie appeared at her elbow with the steeping tea on her tray. "Nice timing."

"Here ya go, sweetie." Maggie set it in front of her.

Emotions welled up like a faucet inside her. She'd missed this. "Thanks."

Walking past, Nell stopped at her shoulder. "You take your time deciding what to do. But either way, give him hell for making you feel like crap."

"I will." She grinned at her friend.

After lunch, she sat watching a pair of seagulls fight for some scraps on a table several feet away.

"Hey, shoo!" Nell rushed the scavengers, waving a dish rag. "Go on, get. I swear, people think it's funny to feed them and then they start thinking they can take food whenever they want."

"They gotta eat too," Willa said, intentionally teasing her. Nell shot her a sharp look. She had to bite the inside of her lips to keep from smiling.

Nell was right, her thick-cut sourdough covered in avocado and smoked salmon had made Willa feel better. She still didn't know what to do about Nick, but she felt better about it, less dumb and no longer questioning her life choices.

"Nell." One of the patrons at the table next to her waved at the store owner. "We're heading back home today. Thanks again for feeding us."

It was a table with four men, obviously here to hunt by their camo clothing. They were covered, head to toe.

"Did you get your elk?" Nell asked, cleaning a table nearby.

"Yep, we finally got one early this morning!" one of the other men replied cheerfully.

"Congrats."

"Dinner was great," another one of the men said. "The Wild has never been this fun."

"Yeah, that was a wild night last night," the first man chimed back in. "Wild at The Wild!"

"Well, thanks. I'm always happy to have you guys in town." Nell stood, her hands on her hips, her rag in one hand. "It *was* a good night."

"What happened last night?" Willa asked when Nell came by her table to pick up her plate.

Nell stopped to think. "Well, I got a lot of flounder yesterday. Made a lemon beurre blanc sauce, crusted the flounder in herbed parmesan."

"Sounds good. You've always liked cooking." That wasn't what she meant, but her friend did always think in terms of food.

"Yeah. I guess things are feeling a little more normal again." She gazed down at her shoes. "That doesn't feel right to say, but it's nice to have normal."

"Gary would have wanted you to find a new normal. He'd never want you unhappy."

"I know that," she said quietly. "Last night, it just felt easier than it has in a while."

"I'm glad."

"I guess I am, too."

Maybe it was time for Willa to get back to normal as well. She thought about her new gifts. Maybe a new normal was the way to go. She stood.

"I'm gonna go find Duke. Do you know if he's in?"

"I think he's in the marina. He was here a few hours ago for breakfast."

"Great, thanks."

Paying, she waved goodbye to Maggie, who was helping another customer, and took the outdoor steps off the back deck instead of walking back through the restaurant. Leaving the sidewalk, she walked through the rocky area before the beach, watching the waves play along the shoreline, rising and falling, in and out.

She did feel more normal, more like herself.

Hopping down onto the deck of Duke's boat, she called out. "Ahoy there!"

The door to the enclosed helm opened and Duke peered out, surprised to see her. "Everything okay?"

"Very." She raised her face to the sun, which had made a surprising appearance. "I want to learn to dive."

Stepping out, he shoved his hands into the pockets of his jeans. He tilted his head. "What kind of diving?"

"I don't know." She hadn't thought that far.

"Diving isn't the easiest thing to learn, and you have to have all sorts of equipment. What about snorkeling?"

That sounded fun. She wouldn't be bogged down with an air tank. And she wouldn't have to think about the math part. "Let's do it."

"Now?" He shook his head slowly. "What's going on?"

"Nothing's going on." She raised her arms up. "I just want to figure out more about our cove, and why the orcas like it so much. Maybe I can find out why we all got magic."

"It's not a bad idea." He wandered around the crates and boxes that were stacked up on his deck and over to his benches to sit. "I've thought about it myself. I just haven't had time."

He gestured for her to come over and sit on the other bench. "I know, things have been crazy." She made her way over and sat down gingerly. She leaned back, pulling her feet under her in a crisscross. "And we're supposed to stay out of it, pretend we don't know Nick and let the bad guys just flounder about, unable to find him. Why not go diving- I mean snorkeling."

He pursed his lips, considering. "I wouldn't mind getting into the water to have a look around. Do you have a wetsuit?"

She hadn't thought of that. "No. Can't I rent one, like the tourists do?"

There was a kayak and canoe rental a few miles up the canal that rented them.

"I have a couple of extras." He eyeballed her frame. "I think one will fit you."

"Cool!" She brightened. "Let's do it!"

"Hold your seahorses," he laughed at his pun. "I have one more phone call to make first. And then, we go over safety rules."

"Deal." Satisfied, Willa settled into her seat. She was feeling good and had goals for the day. Funny how things could change in such a short amount of time.

The water felt cool against Willa's hands, but her body was nice and warm inside the wetsuit. Bobbing along beside Duke just off the pier near his boat, she couldn't help but grin from ear to ear. She might be more at ease in the woods than in the water, but being surrounded by all the life so close around her excited her senses.

"You remember what I said, right?" he double-checked. "Stay close to me and let me know if you have any trouble."

"Aye aye, Captain." She raised her arm out of the water to salute him.

"We're already past the waves here so we won't be fighting their natural push towards the shore. But we may get in the wake from another boat or jet ski."

"I'll be careful," she reassured him.

"We're not going anywhere near the orcas," he repeated what he had told her earlier.

"I know."

"I know you're used to seeing them, but they're still wild animals and could be dangerous."

"I still don't think they're that dangerous. It's uncommon for orcas to attack a human."

"I know, but we're not going to give them a chance. They're huge and could easily hurt you without even meaning to."

"I know. I'll do as you say. Promise." She put her snorkel in her mouth, motioning him to head out.

Giving her one final stern look, he fitted his snorkel in his mouth and surged through the water. She had to move quickly to keep up.

As soon as she dropped her face into the water, she stopped breathing. There was a school of fish directly under her, their bright blue and green colors catching the sunlight, flashing like diamonds. Finally remembering to breathe, she treaded water, holding her spot. The fish darted this way and that, making beautiful patterns, then jutted off towards a dark spot under the pier.

Redirecting her attention further into the cove, she saw Duke's figure moving further away. Oops, she'd spaced out, caught up in the fishes' dance.

Duke paused, waiting for her. She hurried over to him. Maybe over time, she'd learn to move as easily in the water as he did. He popped his head out of the water.

A wide smile lit his face. "It works in the water, too."

"What works?" Then it hit her, his ability to move and influence the water. "You can move the water around you?"

"I can't make it propel me forward without swimming." His brows drew together in concentration. "At least I don't think I can, but I can use the underwater currents to help me move through it faster."

"That's so cool."

"I thought we could go to the jetty," he said, his gaze in the direction of the main body of the canal, away from the cove. "It might be a good place to look around."

"Works for me," she said, following.

They made their way past the pier, leaving the marina behind, and swam towards the long, thin jetty made from rocks indigenous to the area. They'd been there as long as she could remember.

When they were all kids, they used to take turns running to the end and jumping off into the cold water. Only in the heat of summer, though. Gary was always trying to talk them into it as kids. It was how his cold swim started. Once he was a teenager, it had to be more challenging, an April dip to show what a tough guy he was.

Under the surface of the water, she could see that the coastline followed the jetty. She didn't know if it was natural or built that way, but it was beautiful and it curved as it dropped down into the water.

The water was colder here; the depths of it got darker and darker below her. Larger fish swam under her. Her heart skipped a beat. Being scared hadn't occurred to her. Reaching out towards Duke, she pumped her legs, moving her swimming fins against the water to drive her forward.

An iridescent light flashed way below, deep in the blue. Tapping Duke on his arm, she pointed.

He looked, treading the water much easier than her. He popped his head above the surface. She followed suit.

"What is that?" she asked.

"Maybe a fish. I'm not sure."

"Can we go deeper?" He had told her how to hold her breath and swim with her snorkel underwater. She just had to blow it out when she resurfaced.

He took in the area around them. "I'm not sure. It looks deep here."

"I'd like to try."

"Okay, but if I signal to go to the surface, you follow my lead."

She nodded.

They dove back under the water, swimming hard to drop deeper. The weight belt Duke had given her helped her stay under without too much effort.

The gleaming light caught her eye again and they pivoted towards it, following the glittering radiance. This close, she could see blues and purples. It was beautiful.

Whatever was ahead of them was further away than she had thought. She was already feeling the burn in her lungs, wanting to take a breath. The surface was a decent swim away. She waved at Duke, who stopped. They both swam straight up.

Emerging from the water, he said, "I think it's too deep. But I can see there's something there. Maybe if I got diving equipment, I could get closer."

"I want to come with you."

"It takes a long time to get certified. You'd need to do that first."

"Can you certify me?"

He shook his head. "I'm not certified to teach. But I can go and tell you what I find."

"Let's go one more time," she urged. She knew they'd come back up because of her inexperienced lung capacity, but she didn't want to miss seeing something interesting. And there appeared to be something down there.

"Okay."

They dove back down and she pushed harder this time, trying to get closer. They were directly above an outcropping. There was a ledge down below, but it was still so far away.

There it was again!

Glitter winked at them. It looked like a long tail. Maybe it was an iridescent fish? Then it was gone again.

Her hands started tingling, like the vibration she felt when her cut was healing or when she touched Nick. She inspected her hands curiously.

Duke waved his hands. There was no way he had run out of breath quicker than her. He pointed. Following his arm, she saw three orcas heading in their direction. He pointed upward firmly and forcibly. She followed.

When they crested the surface and cleared their snorkels, he pointed towards the jetty, waiting for her to get out in front. The orcas were still on their path straight towards them.

As they swam, she could see Cora, her baby, and the larger male orca following them. The lone male orca was out in front. He was gaining on them. For the first time, they didn't bring her comfort. She wasn't sure why they were approaching them, but it didn't feel friendly.

It was hard to keep from panicking. Willa had to concentrate to pull air through the snorkel.

The jetty wasn't far away, and she hurried towards it. Casting a glance behind her, she checked to see how close they were. At this distance, she could see the larger orca clearly. He had a long scar, zig-zagging along his body, practically from his eye to his tail. It was healed, but it was amazing he had lived through an injury that severe. Whatever had gotten him had left its tattered calling card on his flesh forever.

Duke braced in front of her when they hit the boulders at the base of the jetty. She hurried up, exiting the water as quickly as possible with fins on. It would have been comical had she not felt chased. Duke followed, emerging next to her, the waves knocking them against the boulders. They crawled up them backwards to the top rocks of the jetty.

From this side of the water, she saw three black dorsal fins from the orcas and two from Risso's dolphins who had joined them. They continued to approach. She glanced at Duke, not sure what to do.

His eyes were wide.

"What's going on?" she asked feebly.

He shook his head. About fifteen feet from them, all five mammals stopped. Their blunt noses rose from the water, the large one's visible scar making a bold impression.

"I don't think they want us to find out what's under the water," Duke said, not taking his eyes off the one with the scar. He was the closest.

"Maybe that's why they're here," Willa said.

"Like they're friends?" Duke said as though it was impossible.

"We all have actual powers." Willa raised her hands. "From the water. Why is that crazy?"

He watched the orcas. "Maybe they're protecting it."

The male orca dipped his head into the water, then raised it.

"Holy cow." Willa's surprised reaction pierced the air. "I think he just nodded."

"He did." Duke's eyes were wide.

"Woah." All rational thought left her mind. This was the coolest thing ever. Next to healing people with plants, that was.

"We'll leave it be, man," Duke spoke to the orca. "I won't go back there."

"Did you just talk to him?" she asked.

The orca shifted towards her.

"I think he wants you to say the same," Duke instructed.

"I won't go back there again," she said, her hands over her heart. "But for the record, I never would have hurt anything. Like ever. I couldn't hurt any of you."

Emotion welled up inside her and a tear slid down her cheek. She'd never seen anything that majestic and glorious in her entire life. It was overwhelming.

To her delight, Cora, or the one she called Cora, swam closer. She no longer felt threatened. The scarred orca moved towards her, but she pushed in front of him with a flick of her massive tail.

Duke put an arm out in front of Willa, as though he was trying to block the large animal. It rose partly out of the water, focused on her, and winked. The resplendent animal actually winked. Tears fell from both of her eyes now, her face shining with joy.

Cora turned away, and the rest of them followed.

The large orca raised his tail out of the water, like a wave goodbye, and then he disappeared, leaving rings in his wake. Emerging from the water further out, he jumped high, twisted, and then dove back below the surface of the water. His body was visible beneath the water as he swam to catch up with the others.

Duke and Willa both sat stunned.

He opened his mouth. "Well, shit."

CHAPTER 21

"I'm here, boss," Isaac spoke into his cellphone. Dupree had finally gotten use of his phone; he'd better not waste his time. "I'll have this wrapped up in a day or two, you have my word."

"Good. Don't disappoint me, Isaac. You know what the stakes are," Larry Dupree forewarned him.

As if he needed the reminder.

"I've got it handled. Just leave it to me. I have a few ideas, depending on what I find in the bag."

"Just make sure whatever it is gets me out of this hell hole." Dupree ended the call before Isaac could say anything else.

That was okay. He didn't need fluffy, reaffirming praise. He knew his worth and was perfectly capable of handling this little issue.

He'd brought a knife with him that was used in a murder last year. It was tied to a scene they had all been involved in, Dupree's guys and the cops. Things had gone downhill, and several people had been hurt, including a teenager. No one knew exactly how the teenager had gotten into the mix. Had he worked for Dupree? Was he a Confidential Informant? No one knew. All they knew was that he'd been murdered.

And Isaac had the bloody knife.

If the cops found it stashed in former detective Nick Ryan's house, he'd get the heat for the teenager, even without prints on it. Ryan had training, he would have been more careful than that. The knife itself had a specific shape and would tie back to the scene of the crime. Especially with the matching DNA evidence on it.

He smiled, pleased with himself.

He'd find Nick and the bag, but worst-case scenario, he was covered. They had no idea what was in the bag, but that didn't matter. The judge would throw out any evidence Nick had submitted, which had been most of it.

He still needed to find it, though; who knew what they were hiding?

Opening his car door, he scanned the parking lot where he had stopped.

So, this was Orca Cove.

He scoffed at The Wild Cafe, a small diner in front of him. What a hick town. The market to the left was marginally better but still looked too small and limited for his tastes.

Pasting on a phony expression, he headed into the market.

Still no one. Moving away from the opened window Nick had looked out a dozen times that morning, he sighed. Abandoning it, he paced around the little cabin. It was better but he still needed a few things to make it feel like h ome.

Like Willa, he thought briefly before dashing the idea away. The paint would be here soon, but he wouldn't attempt to pick it up until after Dupree's court date.

Would he even be able to stay here once it was all over? Could he live that close to her and not be in her life? He wasn't sure. Maybe he'd just take the longer drive and shop in Liberty Village instead. It would be safer for her.

He tapped his fingers on his kitchen counter, anxious to find something else to do rather than think. Now, all he had to do was wait. He'd built up enough extra products to sell online for a good month and was working on a couple of larger projects. He'd had a lot of time to think and that had kept him in the workshop late into the night the last few days.

Except for last night. Last night he'd refinished all of his hardwood floors and re-sealed them. Even with the opened windows, the polyurethane scent was still strong. But the wood had turned out good, especially against the refinished baseboards. He'd be able to replace the furniture the next day and get his space back. It was currently stacked in the kitchen, porch, and his workshop, wherever it would fit.

It might be safe if he drove out to Liberty Village for a few things. He could stop by that salvage store and get that farmhouse kitchen sink. It would give him something else to work on. Not that Willa would ever see it. Somehow, even though it was pointless, it felt right to finish her vision.

Maybe when this was all over, he'd sell the cabin. He didn't like the feeling of that but it might be the best option.

He considered calling Duke, to make sure there was no new development, but he would have called if there was. And he didn't feel like talking about Willa yet, which Duke was sure to do.

No, it was better if he stayed clear of things for a little longer and kept his head down.

Grabbing his keys, he headed out to the front porch to put his boots on so he wouldn't mar the still-curing floor.

After chatting with a couple of locals, Isaac moved on to another. None of them were readily sharing and he didn't want to send up any red flags. It was easier if he stayed under the radar. He would get more out of them if he came across as a friendly visitor.

"What is the best place to eat around here?" he asked a friendly-looking older lady. "I'm just stopping here for the day and I'm starving. I haven't had breakfast yet."

"Oh." She brightened. "You should try The Wild Cafe. It's just next door. Nell, the owner, is the absolute best cook in town. She and her late husband, Gary, started the place when they were only twenty. It's an amazing story, really, they started as a little sandwich cart on the pier."

Jackpot. A talker.

"Wow, how'd they go from a sandwich cart to that big cafe?" He peered through the window to appraise the log-sided building. From here he could see a large outdoor seating area and bar in the back. It was nicer than the front. "That's impressive. It must be good food."

"The best." She preened. "You have to stop by."

"Say," he pressed a finger to his chin. "I have an old friend that moved here a bit ago. I was hoping to run into him while I was in town. You wouldn't happen to know a Nick Ryan, would you?"

"Nick Ryan." She paused. "That must be Willa's new guy. I just met him yesterday morning!"

"No kidding!" He didn't have to feign his excitement this time. "Any chance you could point me to where he's staying? I don't have a good number for him. It's been years since I've seen him."

She frowned. "Well, he just moved to town last year."

"Friends back home said he'd moved here," he covered his tracks. "I'd love to catch up with him."

"I'm sure he'd love that!" Her smile returned. "He bought the old Hostettler place, just outside town."

"Where's that?"

She directed him to a little cabin just on the outskirts of town. It would only take him five or ten minutes to get there.

Bingo.

When he got Dupree out of this mess and Nick Ryan in his place, he'd get a better seat at the table.

"I'm excited to catch up with him. And he's got a new lady friend here? Willa?"

"Morning, Loris," the store clerk said, joining them.

"Morning, Emiliano," she greeted the newcomer. "I was just telling-" She stopped, realizing she didn't know his n ame.

It was time to go. The clerk had moved in close, and his body language said he didn't like her sharing townsfolks' personal news.

"James," Isaac said, giving her a false name. He doubted they knew who he was, but he wasn't taking the risk. "James Langston."

"James is old friends with Nick," she said, catching him up. "He's trying to reconnect with him here. I was just telling him about Nick and Willa.""High school friends," he offered, hoping that would help. But no, Emiliano's eyes had sharpened, taking in his details. "I'd better go, make the most of my time here. I won't be here long."

Not if he could help it.

"Oh, well, good luck! If you can't find him there, check the cafe."

"Will do." He grinned, backing away.

Oh, he most certainly would.

He'd take care of the bag and the knife. And then he'd take care of Palmer.

Nick knew something was wrong the minute his cabin came into view on his way home. His blood went cold. Not only was the front door of his cabin open, but his workshop doors were open wide and through the door he could see scrap wood lying in the walkway.

He never would have left it like that.

Stopping his truck, he swung out of the cab, drawing his weapon at the same time. He didn't see any movement and there were no other vehicles on the property, but that didn't mean no one was there lying in wait.

Moving quietly, he went straight to the workshop. He had several pieces of furniture there, including his bed while his floors were curing, so the place had already been a mess. But when he stepped into his workshop, anger flooded his senses. Not only were the few pieces of furniture scattered about, but his table saw lay on its side and several of his nicer hand planes lay on the floor, broken and discarded.

His computer had been pulled from the wall and was left lying on the floor of his workshop, a crack in the screen. They had tried to access it. Bastards. He didn't have anything important saved on it.

Finally, his eyes found the piece of paneling he'd stashed the duffel bag behind. It was still intact. Carefully stepping over broken things, he got closer. Some of the scrap lumber he'd kept in that corner had been moved, but a particularly large piece he'd placed in front of the wall was still in place. It didn't appear to have been moved.

Satisfied, he left, his eyes scanning the area. He entered his cabin, silently stepping on the porch. His dresser and desk that he'd stashed there temporarily had been gone through. All the drawers were pulled out and dumped on the floor. The kitchen was the same. Cabinets were open, drawers all unloaded on the counters and floors.

Unconcerned about his boots this time, he cleared the rest of his house. No one there either. He went back into his kitchen and sagged against his counter. He set his pistol down and ran both hands hard over his face. Exhaustion overwhelmed him. Hadn't they done enough? When would he feel like Larry Dupree wasn't hanging over his head, able to take away things that mattered to him?

An ugly scar had been cut through his carefully refinished living room floor. The floor he'd tried to make nice and pretty for Willa. Not for her to live here, of course, but to finish the plan she'd put in motion. For some reason that bothered him more than the broken bedframe or tools in his workshop.

It could be fixed, but it stood out as a reminder of how far Dupree's reach still extended, his ability to violate Nick's safety, even while in jail.

He needed to get out of here. They hadn't found the bag or him, so they'd be back. Retracing his steps to his truck, he still didn't see anyone around, but he couldn't be sure. If they had to, they'd burn the place down. He needed to get the bag and get out of the area, but he couldn't risk being followed.

Leaving, he turned out onto the highway and headed to the park trails down the road. He hadn't seen any sign of anyone following him, so he parked his truck and went back through the trails in the woods. His cabin was only a half a mile or so from the park.

Circling around in a wide path, he came up behind his workshop. He sat there for ten minutes, carefully watching the area. Satisfied that no one was waiting, he entered his workshop and retrieved the bag, putting everything back the way he'd left it.

Before long, he was back in his truck and headed out of town.

He found a motel in Liberty Village, wanting to be close in case of danger to the town. He checked in under a fake name. Bringing the bag into the clean but worn room, he sat down on the faded bedcover. He could go back out later for food and a few supplies.

He dialed Duke's number in his phone. Things had been escalating and he wanted to make sure nothing had happened in Orca Cove.

"I was wondering when you'd call," Duke said blandly. "Someone new's been poking around at the market asking about you. Said you're old friends. James Langston, know the guy?"

"Doesn't sound familiar, but he might not be using his real name."

"Tall guy, dark hair, late thirties, early forties, from what Emiliano said. Apparently not blocky like Palmer. Anyway, I think he got info about you."

"I know. He found my place."

"Man, are you alright?"

"Yeah." He exhaled audibly, leaning back on one arm. "The place is trashed, but luckily, I wasn't home when they came by."

"Thank goodness for little favors."

"No kidding." Had he been there, one of them might not be alive right now. "Look, they're probably pissed they couldn't find me. Especially if Dupree's sent another man. Things could escalate in town. I don't want anyone stuck in the middle of that because of me."

"Did they find it?" Duke asked quietly.

"What do you mean?"

"Dude, don't play dumb. It's not a good look on you. I know you're a private guy. I get that, trust me, I do. Some things you've got to keep to yourself. But if you think I'm going to believe they ransacked your place just to find...clues, you don't think much of me."

He should have thought of that. Why hadn't he thought of that? Because he was more worried about keeping Willa safe.

"So, did they find it?"

"No," he said simply.

"We're all involved now. It'll be easier for us to help if you tell us what you have that they want."

"No." There was no way. It wasn't even really his. "I can't do that."

"I can tell you have trust issues, but we're not the bad guys, Nick."

Oh, he had no idea. His trust issues were legendary, but he'd earned them.

"It's not that," Nick tried to explain. "Jimmy died keeping his secret. I have to honor that."

Duke was quiet.

"Any idea who this guy talked to?" He tried changing the subject. He wasn't sharing.

"Loris," Duke said. "But don't be mad at her, she's a nice lady. Wouldn't hurt a fly. She just can't keep a secret. Not that she knew it was one."

"It's not her fault," Nick said. He snorted at his luck. He'd just met her too, after his life-changing night with Willa. "She's friends with Willa, isn't she?"

"Yeah, I already thought about that. I told her she needs to be careful."

"She needs to be out of town."

"With you?" Duke asked with a sharp questioning note in his voice.

"Of course not. She's not safe with me." Even though that's exactly what he had been thinking. He wanted to keep her safe, but he was afraid of having her near him. "She has to stay with you. You can keep her safe. On the boat, or better yet, in another town. You can get her out o f there."

Duke let out a low laugh. "If you think I can tell Willa to stay anywhere she doesn't want to, you're crazy. Any of those women. They're all good people, but they're headstrong as hell."

"But it's not safe," he continued to argue.

"I know, I'm keeping an eye on her," Duke promised. "We're all meeting up at the cafe later to talk about it. You still staying out of town?""Until the court case."

"Okay. I don't like it, but we'll play it your way. Let me know if something changes. We'd be stronger together. And I have connections that could help."

"I appreciate it, but all I need you to do for me is keep Willa safe."

"I'll do what I can."

He certainly hoped so. He wasn't sure what he'd do if she got hurt.

CHAPTER 22

"**Y**ou actually went *into* the water?" Maggie's eyes were as round as saucers. She squealed.

Willa nodded, glad to finally have them all together to share the news as a team.

Shelby looked oddly impressed.

"Did you find anything?" Nell asked, finally sitting at the table outside.

She had insisted on meeting there again even though she claimed she didn't have many leftovers today. There wasn't a lot of any one dish but she had set out little bowls of fresh veggies and sides that she wouldn't be able to serve the following day. She'd also made up a huge bowl of oyster wild rice to accompany them. There was enough to feed them all and then some.

"Sort of. Now, this is going to sound crazy, so bear with me, but it's all true." She glanced over to Duke for support, but he was distracted.

"I can make it rain," Maggie said drolly, her lips pressed flat. She wiggled her fingers. "We're already talking about magic. It doesn't get wilder than that."

"Science that hasn't been explained yet," Shelby piped up, her finger in the air.

"Whatever," Maggie said.

"We saw something flashy, like a brilliant, iridescent tail. Way down in some sort of a cave near the jetty. It was big and long." She turned to Duke. "Isn't that what it looked like to you?"

He glanced up, a frown on his face. "Hmm? Oh, yeah. A colorful tail. Coulda been an eel or a fish, though."

What was up with him?

"A *big* fish," Willa clarified.

"How'd you know it was a cave? Did you go in?" Shelby asked.

"No, we could see a ledge or something, and the fish thing swam in," Willa said, moving her hand in a wavy motion. "It was too deep to get to with a snorkel."

"Go back with diving gear," Shelby said logically.

"Can't." Willa glanced at Duke. "The orcas chased us off."

"Wait until they leave." Shelby gave her a quizzical eyebrow raise and drew up one shoulder.

"No," Willa tried to explain. "They literally chased us off. They didn't want us there."

Shelby and Nell looked back and forth between her and Duke. Maggie's mouth just dropped open.

"You felt threatened?" Nell asked. "Like they were trying to hurt you?"

"I don't know," Willa said. "But they chased us up onto the jetty. All three orcas and two dolphins joined in."

"Orcas are dolphins," Maggie supplied helpfully.

"That's true," Willa said. "I think they were Risso's dolphins."

"Ooh, I love them. Everyone loves bottle-nosed dolphins because of Flipper, but Risso's are my favorite." Maggie's face lit up.

"Whatever," Shelby waved a hand. "They honestly chased you like that? Do you think they were trying to keep you from that fish thing?"

Willa nodded. "Yes, Duke talked to one of them, a big one with an angry scar."

"Wait." Shelby raised both hands, palms out. "Hold up. Are you telling me that the freaking orca spoke?"

"Not exactly," Willa said. "Duke asked it a question and it sort of nodded."

"It nodded?" Shelby asked, redirecting her question to Duke, who was staring off again. "Good Lord, Duke. What's wrong with you?"

At least someone had asked him.

"I'm sorry." He shook his head, noticing the bowl of rice in front of him. He began loading his plate and shoved a few forkfuls in. "Yes. He nodded. I told him we wouldn't be going back there."

"That's so cool!" Maggie clasped her hands in front of her.

"That's...odd," Nell said finally. "I'm just glad you both are safe. It's probably best not to try that again."

"Huh." Shelby frowned, her arms crossed.

"But that's not all," Duke raised his fork. "Earlier that day I saw someone walking along the pier, some new guy I'd never seen before. This big black guy, calm and powerful, you could tell. Polite and collected. Not someone you'd want to cross."

"Another stranger?" Willa asked. This was the first time he'd mentioned the guy.

"Another?" Nell asked.

"That's not the important part. He had a major scar that ran from here..." His fork traveled from under one eye to his collarbone. "...to here."

Willa's mouth dropped open. She whispered, "The orca."

He nodded. "His name is Percy."

"The orca?" Shelby tilted her head.

"The male orca has the same scar," Willa answered.

"You're not saying," Maggie shook her head.

"Are you absolutely serious about this?" Shelby's eyes narrowed as she inspected Duke's body language.

"One hundred percent," Duke said flatly.

Satisfied, Shelby sat back in her seat and uncrossed her arms.

They all looked towards the cove. The sun had set, but light from the city lit up a little of it. There were no orcas visible.

"I've noticed there've been more orcas in the cove," Shelby said, watching the water as though she could will one to appear.

"I haven't seen the third one since we were in the water," Willa said. "Just Cora and her baby."

"Cora?" Maggie asked.

"Well." Willa shifted shyly in her seat. "That's just what I like to call her. I watched her last year with the baby and this year the baby is nearly as large as her. They might not be the same ones, I know that, but I like to think they are."

"I noticed them too," Nell said. "It's like they're watching us. I figured they were just drawn to all the noise and movement from the cafe. Do you think they have something to do with what happened to you all? The powers from the water?"

"Maybe?" Duke shrugged. "They might at least know what happened."

"And you think it had something to do with that fish thing," Shelby surmised.

"They were trying to keep us from it. It's important to them."

"You're not going to mess around with it, though, right?" Nell asked.

"Not with whatever's down there," he said. "I promised I wouldn't. But that doesn't mean I won't keep asking around."

"Who could you ask?" Willa wondered. "It's not like we know anyone else who turns into an orca."

"What would you call that?" Shelby asked, head tilted. "Would you say were-orcas, like were-wolves?"

"Or orca shifters?" Maggie said.

"I've heard about a group of people in Seattle. I thought it was a story, honestly. Something people said to scare others off." Duke waved a hand, trying to explain. "There's some sort of company there and the talk is that the people there are more than human."

"More than human?" Nell asked.

"How do you know about that?" Shelby asked.

"I do business with people that specialize in things," he said vaguely. "But I thought they might be a good way to get some answers. There's one guy who's at the Seattle Port a lot. Irish guy. Not too bad to work with. I thought about seeing if he might talk to me."

"You be careful," Nell said.

A smile appeared on Duke's face. He winked at her. "I always am."

"One more thing," Willa said, remembering. "My hands tingled when we got close to the sparkly fish thing. Did yours?"

"Yeah. It was sort of a vibration of energy, like I feel when I'm moving the waves," he said.

"Maybe it's a mermaid," Maggie said, her eyes full of excitement and her voice full of awe.

"Maybe," Willa answered. "I have no idea. We may never know."

A wind whipped up around them, adding a chill to the air. Willa shivered.

"Wait," Nell said, twisting towards Duke. "You said another stranger. What's going on?"

Duke glanced at Willa. "Do you want to tell them?"

"I might as well," Willa deflated. She wasn't looking forward to this part. "Nick's got someone from Seattle asking around town for him."

"Someone dangerous?" Nell asked.

"Unfortunately, yes. This guy's bad news. He might be tied to the murder on the beach."

Duke jumped in. "He works for a guy known for criminal activity in Seattle. We need to keep an eye out for him, and all of you need to stay far away."

"How does Nick know him?" Shelby asked. "Is that why he's here? Did he work for him or something?"

"No, it's not like that," Willa began. Then again, she wasn't sure what it was like. She'd believed him, but he still might not have been telling her the truth. She didn't think that was the case, but she wasn't so sure about trusting her own gut these days. "At least I don't think it is."

"No, he was a cop," Duke said. "He and his partner, man Willa found on the beach, put this guy's boss away."

Either Nick or Chief Warner had shared that with Duke. And since the chief of police wasn't much of a sharer, it had to have been Nick.

That was odd. Willa wove the napkin in her lap between her fingers, twisting it this way and that. Why had it been so much easier to tell Duke than her? The idea chafed at her.

"If his boss is in jail, why do they want Nick?" Nell asked.

"He's not been convicted yet. He's still technically a powerful force with several people underneath him. I think they want something from Nick. Something that will get their boss out of jail," he said. "I'm not sure. He's not sharing."

"Why the hell not?" Shelby asked.

"He's trying to handle it on his own."

It sounded like Duke believed in Nick, in his story at least.

"Another guy showed up today," Duke said, and told them that Emiliano had seen a guy at the market that morning. Apparently, he was trying to get information about Nick as well. "This guy knows about you, Willa. It's probably best if you stay with someone for a while. Or if you still have friends in Seattle, go stay with t hem."

"I'm not going to leave you all to deal with this." Willa tossed the napkin she'd been murdering on the table in front of her. Especially if it had been her boyfriend- or ex-boyfriend, or maybe just person-of-interest- that brought it on them all.

And with that thought, she started to understand how Nick felt about bringing his past into town and putting her in danger. She leaned back in her chair, her eyes tracing the lights above them.

"He could come after you," Duke said. "You're better off staying with me or one of us."

"You can stay with me," Nell offered. "I wouldn't mind the company."

"It might not be a bad idea," Willa admitted reluctantly. There were two of them on the loose now. "Does Nick know?"

She saw Duke nod. He'd been communicating a lot with Nick lately.

"That's good. He's going to stay out of town, then?" she asked, not wanting to contact him, but still wanting to know. He'd been clear about his choice regarding her, and she didn't want it to seem like she was trying to influence that.

"Yeah," Duke drew out. "Loris also gave Nick's address to James Langston, so he's already been there. Ransacked the place."

"Wait, what?" Willa jumped from her seat at the table. What did that mean? "Is he okay?"

Duke held up both hands, pressing them forward slowly to calm her down. "Nick wasn't there, he was in Liberty Village. He's safe in a motel, keeping his head down."

"He should get out, like *way* out of town," Willa said, pacing to the deck's railing. She whirled around. "He could drive down the coast into Oregon, or better yet, California. Stay out there until this court date."

"Why isn't the Seattle Police Department putting him under witness protection if he's at risk?" Shelby asked.

"I don't know the whole story," Duke said. "I think there's more to it than that. And he's not working with them on this."

"And you trust him?" she pushed.

"I think I do." One side of his mouth pulled up in a half grimace, as though he himself was surprised. "It fits his personality and his focus. He's trying to keep people safe. I don't know what he has planned, since he refuses to work with anyone else on it. He doesn't want to put anyone in harm's way, so he's keeping it all close to the vest.""That's dumb," Shelby said.

"Maybe, but I understand it," Duke said. "Especially if he's had his trust betrayed on the job."

And he had, Willa knew all too well. On the job and off.

It was good to hear Duke's acceptance of him. Somehow it validated her own feelings.

"Men are weird." Shelby crossed her arms.

Willa walked back to the table and sat. Distracting herself, she picked up a bowl of green beans on the table and dropped some on her plate.

The conversation continued on the other side of the table. Maggie wanted to know more about the orcas.

Shelby, who sat next to her, asked for the veggies. Willa handed them over, but Shelby's eyes stayed on her as though she was trying to figure something out.

Finally, she leaned in and asked, "How come you're all worried about him now? What happened to 'penises can't be trusted; they break our hearts'?"

"That was a few nights ago. A lot's happened since then." Willa picked at the green beans on her plate. "He showed up after you left."

"He did?" Shelby asked.

"Yeah." She kept her voice low. "He apologized. He felt bad for not trusting me, he wanted to try again. At least I thought he did.""You banged him, didn't you?"

"I wouldn't call it that." She rolled her eyes. "It was beautiful, but yeah."

"And then he booked again."

"I don't think it was like that. I honestly don't believe that was his motivation." She thought back to his pain. It was too real. "He's tortured by his past. He absolutely believes that it's too dangerous for me."

She was about seventy percent sure that was all it was, too. Too bad it wasn't one hundred percent.

She hmphed. "Was it at least good?"

Warmth tingled down Willa's back at the recollection. She let herself enjoy it; a secret smile played at her lips. Leaning in, she lowered her voice even further. "Do you remember when I told you about our connection?"

Shelby wiggled her fingers. "You mean the tingly thing?"

Willa nodded. She closed her eyes, settling into the memory. It was glorious, regardless of what had happened since then. "It gets more intense when we kiss. And it spreads. At one point, it was like we were in a capsule together. The energy pulsed with us, through us, wrapping around us."

Shelby's mouth gaped open. A green bean fell out. "Are you telling me his entire body turned into a freaking vibrator?"

Willa's eyebrow flicked up. She nodded.

"Woah." Shelby's eyes opened wide, and she stared off in silence.

"That's another thing I wanted to mention," Duke said, his voice rising over their private conversation. "Has anyone else noticed anything odd about Solomon?"

"He has a pet pelican now," Willa said. "I think he's okay, though. He's just been lonely. It's not surprising. He is alone all the time."

"I don't think that's all of it." Duke sat back, pulling an ankle over his knee. "He's talking to this pelican. Calls him Roy. He honestly believes Roy is answering back."

"Maybe he is." The puzzle pieces clicked together. "Maybe he was out on the water that night with us. Maybe whatever happened to us happened to him!"

"You mean Solomon can talk to animals?" Maggie said in amazement.

"Some people get the coolest gifts," Shelby slumped in her seat. Then, seeing Nell's silent expression, she added, "Sorry, Nell."

"It's not a big deal," Nell said, but no one believed it.

That still didn't make sense. Why would only one of them not have a gift? At this point, though, Willa was hesitant to offer her any positive wishes. What if one didn't emerge?

She'd stay with Nell for a few days; maybe she would notice something her busy friend hadn't. If all else failed, they'd be able to spend some quality time together.

CHAPTER 23

"**N**o," Nick whispered aloud, peering through the blinds at the motel he'd been stuck in all night. It was early, and he was considering leaving to get some food. "No, no, no."

This was bad. Really bad.

Palmer and a new guy, a younger one, were arguing in the parking lot of the motel. Had he picked the very same motel they were staying at? Or were they on his trail?

He cursed his luck.

The younger one pointed across the street, where Nick had left his truck at the gas station. The two of them headed over to investigate. He hadn't been dumb enough to park it in front of his room, but it would still only be a matter of time before they realized that he wasn't in the store and this was the only motel nearby.

They must have pulled his DMV record to find his license plate and matching vehicle. Dupree had long fingers and a lot of resources. He'd have to abandon his truck.

Shoving his feet into his boots, he scraped everything he'd bought at the gas station back into the shopping bag and grabbed the duffel bag stashed behind the sink. Leaning against the wall, he pulled back the blinds again.

They had just crossed the street and were walking toward his truck. Even from here, Nick could see the outlines under their jackets. They were both armed.

Taking the opportunity, he bolted from the door of his second-floor room and ducked, hurrying towards the vending machine room a few doors down. The room went through the entire motel and he banged out the other side. Jogging along the walkway, now shielded by the building, he made it to the end of the row and clambered down the metal stairs.

On the ground level, he tore across the parking lot towards the strip mall next door. He only needed to get behind one before they came to investigate the motel. He wouldn't be able to go back.

And without a truck, he was stuck on foot. It wasn't worth the risk to go back and get it later. They could be waiting and watching for exactly that.

Checking behind him, he didn't see any sign of the two. He ducked behind the buildings, blocking him from view of the motel. He jogged alongside the building to the end and entered a residential area. He finally allowed himself to slow, walking down the sidewalk and putting as much distance between himself and Dupree's goons as possible.

He'd never seen the second guy before, but he didn't look like Palmer; simply hired muscle. He was different. The thought sent dread through Nick. He was average in appearance, like a cleaner someone brought in to get rid of a problem.

Pulling out his phone, he searched for the next nearest motel, but nothing was close. Siren's Song Cabins in Orca Cove popped up, as did a couple motels from the next town over, past Liberty Village. They were a good twenty miles away. His phone estimated it at five hours to walk. Not ideal.

He had a fleeting thought to call someone in Seattle, one of his old friends from the force. But he wasn't sure who he could trust. Dupree had a long reach.

His phone rang. It was Duke.

Boy, did he have bad timing.

"Hello?" he said.

"Just checking in, making sure you're still alive," Duke replied dryly. Nick could practically see the cocky grin on his face. "And maybe I'm hoping you've reconsidered my offer."

"Barely," he let out before he could stop himself.

"What happened?" he asked quickly, all humor gone.

He growled, curling his upper lip. "I'm in a bad position."

"Tell me."

"They found me. Technically, they found my truck," he corrected. "I made it away from the motel, but the next nearest one is hours away on foot."

"I can be out of here in a few minutes." Nick heard him moving around.

This wasn't how he wanted it to play out. "If you could just give me a ride, I'd owe you one. I should be good once I'm there."

"Where are you?"

Nick cast a glance towards the sky and sent a silent thought of thanks upward. Unfortunately, it looked like rain.

"Liberty Village, just past the motel." Walking to the end of the road he was on, he checked the street signs. There was a park a few blocks away. "I'm near a park, off Elm Street."

"I know it," Duke said. "Give me twenty."

"I'll be there, probably in the woods nearby, just to be safe."

"Got it. See you."

"Okay. And thanks, Duke.""No problem."

Sighing, he made his way to the park, finding a tree to lean up against while keeping the park in his sight. He let his head fall back against the bark, peering through the leaves over him. It started to rain, just a light sprinkle, but the leaves sheltered him from it.

The image of Willa spinning under the maple in front of his house sprang to mind. His mouth kicked up into a smile. At that time, even though Dupree's guys had killed Jimmy, he still felt he could escape that life and find peace. It seemed like ages ago.

Now, he felt more alone. The canopy of leaves offered him some shelter and for that he was grateful.

It wasn't long before he saw an old, beat-up gray pickup stop on the street next to the neighborhood park. It was probably Duke. It was hard to see in the drizzle.

The headlights flashed.

Taking the signal, he jogged out, dipping his head from the rain. Double-checking the identity of the driver, he swung open the door and slid in.

"Hey." Duke's gaze was on the rearview mirror. He pulled onto the road and made a left. "Hey." Nick ran a hand over his wet hair, giving it a flick.

"Any sign of them?"

"None." He checked down the sidewalks, worried he'd see them searching on foot. They drove for a minute in silence, but Duke wasn't heading through town. They were heading back toward Orca Cove. "Aren't we going the wrong way?"

"They know you're near and on the run. They're just going to hit all the nearby motels in the area."

"So, we go further."

Duke gave him a look. "Do you honestly want me to take you all the way to Oregon?"

"No." He breathed out. He didn't want to be that far away from Willa if they threatened her.

"Then you're staying with me."

"Isn't that riskier? Going right to the town where they think I live? Where they've been looking for me?"

Duke shrugged. "You've got us to help you now. You can stay below deck on my boat. They wouldn't know to try there."

He'd have to hide from them. But he'd been hiding anyway, just not behind someone. It didn't feel great. He shouldn't be putting anyone else in danger.

"It's my choice," Duke said in answer to what he had been thinking. "Get over it."

"That's annoying," he grunted. Duke just laughed.

They drove in silence for a while before Duke finally spoke. "So, what's in the bag?"

"It's probably safer if you don't know."

"We're working together now, remember? I want to know what's at stake."

"You want to know I'm not crooked," Nick guessed.

"I wouldn't be here if I thought that," Duke shook his head. "I'll take the risk."

He took a deep breath. If he was accepting the threat, he had a right to know. "Evidence."

"Against Dupree?"

He nodded.

"Wasn't that already turned in, though? The man's in jail."

"Yeah, but you know men like Dupree. He's got guys everywhere. There's a chance he could have it removed, conveniently lost, stolen, or thrown out."

"So, it's additional evidence?"

"Correct. Jimmy and I had been trying to gather more after the raid, just in case." Now that he started talking, it came pouring out. "I knew I wanted out. I was done with that life. Jimmy told me to go ahead and go, he'd continue to pursue the lead. It tied Dupree to illegal deals with a state official, but we were having trouble proving it. We'd been able to get him off the streets, though, tying him to some smaller drug charges, so we went with that at first.""As long as it held."

"Exactly. If we could prove the tie, we could put away a rotten official, too."

"What is it?"

"Audio tapes. Pictures of them doing business to-gether. I haven't listened to the tapes, but according to Jimmy, they're enough to put them both away." Nick's gaze was locked on the trees outside. "If we can get the evidence there when they need it, and put Dupree in jail for good, his guys will spread like the wind."

"They'll just find new masters," Duke said.

"True, but they won't be after Willa or Orca Cove. No more immediate threat."

Duke glanced at him, taking his eyes off the road for a moment. "It's better if we can take them down too. Maybe we should loop in Warner."Reluctantly, Nick nodded, "Maybe it's time."

"So, what else don't I know?"

"That's pretty much it. I think you know the rest," Nick replayed the important facts in his mind. "Dupree and a few of his guys who got caught up in the raid are awaiting their court dates. I took off, leaving the force. Jimmy called, wanting to meet. I thought meeting him on the beach would be safer, so he didn't know where I lived. No one would see us that far out on the beach at night."

"You didn't know Willa, then," Duke chuckled.

"Yeah. Palmer had to have been following Jimmy from Seattle. He must have just missed me. Caught up with Jimmy after I left with the bag. Can you imagine if Palmer had been a few minutes earlier? Willa could have been caught up in it." He shuddered, absently pulling his jacket tighter around him. "If it hadn't been for that storm... It masked my tracks, Willa and me trying to talk over the noise, everything."

They pulled up to the parking lot outside Gil's Market and Marina, finding a spot at the end near the marina.

Duke faced him. "Willa's staying at the cafe. Once we get settled, we need to make a plan."

Nick angled to see the upper floor of the cafe, imagining her through the log exterior, happy and warm. He itched to see her, to talk to her himself. Rain traced random paths over the truck window between them. She was secure there. He pushed open the door and nodded.

"Sounds good."

The rain was coming down even harder now. They leaned into it, walking down the stairs to the pier and out across the wooden planks. Duke pointed to the end of the floating dock. This part of the dock was higher than the rest to accommodate larger boats. Duke's fishing boat was bigger than he'd expected. The wind kicked up and when they stepped onto the dock, it bucked in response. Nick had to hold onto the rope stretched along one side to balance himself. Duke kept trudging along, at home on the shifting base. He stepped over the rope to his boat and hopped down the steps to his deck, glancing over his shoulder at Nick.

Bracing himself on the unstable rope railing, Nick stepped up over the edge of the boat and carefully put both feet on the top stair, steadying himself before making it the rest of the way down. The boat pitched heavily beneath his feet. He spread his legs wide to compensate.

"Come on," Duke gestured. "It's less rocky below deck."

Following him to a door, they went down metal stairs to a narrow hallway. Duke took a right and then a left. He pushed through a door at the end of the hall to reveal a finished space. It was a studio apartment with a bed in one corner and a sitting area in the other.

"You can sleep there," Duke pointed to a couch. "It folds out."

"Thanks." He wiped his feet on the rug just inside the door. Finding the couch, he sank down into it, shaking the rain from his hair.

He set his plastic bag on the coffee table in front of him. It was weathered, like it had been through hell. It was unbalanced, too.

He could fix that. After.

Pulling the duffel bag onto his lap, he said, "Do you have a place where I could stash this?"

"I have several." Duke's face split in a grin. He stood. "Come on."

Leaving the room, he led Nick through the hallways in the bowels of his boat. It didn't take long before Nick got lost in the maze of passageways.

Duke stopped at a wall and pressed. The walls were made from sheet metal with rows of rivets securing them together. An entire column of the wall popped out an inch. Pulling it, it slid out on wheels, blocking the hallway. Shelves lined the unit from floor to ceiling. Various boxes sat on different shelves, some cardboard, some built like crates. One small crate was stuffed with straw and the glint of metal caught Nick's attention. Duke saw his eye flick to it and snagged it.

Kneeling, he moved a few items off a shelf below. He casually stacked the crates below other boxes. Then, he reached through the cart to Nick and pointed to the cleared space. "There you go."

Even though he'd asked for the space, he hesitated.

He'd only known the man a short while. Was it possible Dupree had gotten to him? It didn't seem like his business was entirely legit; he easily could have gotten involved with the criminal in Seattle. It wasn't that much of a stretch.

Noticing his delay, Duke straightened. "You asked, dude. If you'd rather, you can keep it with you. I know it's important. You won't offend me."

Taking the risk, he shoved the bag into the space and rolled it closed. He met Duke's eyes. "No. Not everyone is out to get me."

He didn't entirely believe it yet, but he knew it was true.

He'd build on that.

Duke gave a short dip of his head and led them back to the living space. Nick tried to mentally note his steps so he could get back to the bag if needed.

"If something happens to me, can you get it to the SPD in time for the case?" he asked quietly.

Duke stopped and turned, assessing him. He raised a fist and bumped him on the shoulder. "You'll be down here. Nothing's going to happen to you."

"You can't predict that, Duke. Come on, give me peace of mind. This guy needs to be put away for a long time."

Duke shifted on his feet. "Okay. I can do that, but you'd better try your damnedest not to get killed."

He gave him a half grin. "Deal."

They made it back to Duke's living quarters and Duke dropped into a chair. "Now, what do we do? Should we let Willa know you're here?"

"No, I think it's best that she doesn't know where I'm at. Just in case."

"I agree."

Nick sat on the couch he was going to call home for the next several days.

"Do you need anything?" Duke asked, his eyes on the small plastic bag.

Nick had only picked up a few essentials from the gas station, toothpaste, deodorant, a phone charger. He hadn't taken time to grab anything else from home and the store didn't have much to choose from. "I could use a change of clothes."

Duke eyeballed him, sizing him up. "I'll run into the market and get it for you."

Nick reached into his back pocket for his wallet. He'd been carrying cash just in case and still had some.

"Don't worry about it," Duke stopped him, raising a hand. "We can settle up after."

"Thanks." He tucked it away.

Duke propped a booted foot on the edge of his coffee table. "But we need to talk about bringing Warner in. He should know what's happening."

"Agreed." With the Orca Cove Police Department backing them, they might be able to figure something out to keep everyone out of trouble.

CHAPTER 24

Waves bounced against the rented kayak Willa sat in. The rain had finally cleared, but the sky was still gray. She shivered, pulling her cardigan tighter around her. The precipitation had brought cooler temps with it.

She knew she needed to be on the lookout for Dupree's guys, but she'd been feeling cooped up all alone in Nell's apartment over the cafe. The noise from below had her up and pacing early in the morning. She'd canceled her yoga classes this week, but simply couldn't sit inside any longer. At home, she had her back deck. The only deck Nell had was the one below her at the cafe, shared with customers.

The woods weren't safe, there were too many places for people to hide, but the water...how could that be dangerous? Spying Cora and her baby across the cove, she'd had a crazy idea.

Now that she was bobbing along in the kayak, she started to wonder about the sanity of her choice. But here she was, in rain boots and yoga pants because they dry quickly, heading out to see an orca.

What could go wrong?

Eyes trained on the orcas, she could tell they were watching her. Cora shifted in front of her baby and dipped underwater, her dorsal fin tracing a path away from the jetty and towards the other side of the cove.

That was fine, she wasn't trying to get near whatever was under the water. It would remain safe.

There was a rocky outcropping on the other side of the cove and Cora's fin disappeared behind it. Willa followed, much more slowly. The waves kicked up over the side of the kayak, splashing her face. Her curly hair flew into her eyes, but she couldn't move it away without letting go of the oars. Shaking her head, she blew out to clear it away and kept rowing further from the shore.

When she made it around the rocks, she found Cora and her baby bobbing at the surface, watching her with large, dark eyes. She wasn't as nervous as she had been the last time they were this close, but their size still stunned her.

She kept her distance and paused several yards away. They blinked, waiting to see what she was going to do.

"Hi, Cora," she said loudly, giving them a friendly smile, then realized that wasn't her actual name. If she had a human form like Percy, she'd have a human name too. "Sorry. I made that up for you before I knew you were...more than just an orca. It's not like a pet name or a nything."

She blanched. This wasn't going well. But she noticed Cora's eyes tighten in the corners, like she was laughing.

"I don't see Percy anymore." She'd gotten used to seeing all three of them. "Where did he go?"

Silence. Cora blinked, opened her mouth and closed it.

What had she been thinking was going to happen? The orca probably couldn't make human sounds. Unless she was going to shift. She didn't know what to expect.

"Um." Willa thought. Best to stick to yes or no questions. "Is Percy safe?"

Holding onto her oar, she braced against a wave, watching the orca. Slowly, she raised her nose out of the water and nodded. Joy washed over Willa at the same time as another wave hit the side of the kayak. She giggled in happiness.

"Do you know we have powers?" She leaned closer, rocking the kayak, and quickly righted herself.

Cora nodded again.

"Are you why?" Her eyes widened, excited to finally know the truth.

Cora shook her large head.

"Do you know why?"

She nodded.

That was interesting. This would be so much easier if Cora could speak. "Is that why you're watching all of us?"

Again, the orca nodded, but more slowly this time. Maybe she wasn't sure if she should share.

"Is that your baby all grown up?"

Cora nodded, shifting in the water to see her baby, who had swum in beside her. He was nearly the same size as her by now. They bounced up and down together in the water.

"I don't have a name for him. I assume it's a him?" At the orca's nod, she continued. "I've been watching you since last summer when you had him. I'd hoped it was you again. It's been so nice seeing him grow up."

The younger orca jiggled, the water splashing around him making Willa laugh.

"He's beautiful." She admired him. "I bet you're so proud of him. I don't have kids. Well, I don't have a mate."

She thought about Nick. "I thought I found him, but that didn't pan out. Anyway, you probably know all about this, but my gift lets me heal people, maybe animals too. Hey, I never thought of that before. I might be able to help animals! I can heal with plants from the ocean. I'm a healer anyway, an herbalist, so it's kind of perfect for me."

The orcas watched her.

"Maggie can make it rain. Duke can move the water. Shelby, the dark-haired one, can feel the water, she knows where it's at. Like a locator. Nell didn't get a gift, I'm not sure why. But I've been able to help some of the older people in my community." She thought maybe the orcas were worried they would abuse their powers. She wanted Cora to know they were good people. "My friends are good too. They're kind people. Duke's using his powers to help him when he's on the water. He moves cargo."

She pointed towards his boat docked at the marina. An odd tingling sensation bloomed in her chest. That was weird. She wasn't healing anyone. Maybe it was the water. But it made her think of Nick again.

Loss bubbled up within her, filling her eyes with tears. Now that she'd found him, someone to genuinely connect to, it felt like such a gaping loss.

Cora blinked again, almost like she wanted Willa to talk about it. Here, out in the water, she felt like she *could* just talk it out with Cora. She was a very good listener.

"It's Nick, my friend. The one I thought was going to be my partner. These guys followed him from Seattle." She pointed out towards the city. "They're bad men. They're trying to hurt him. I'm scared for him. And now they might come after me, so I can't go home. I just feel really unsettled."

A tear fell from her eye. She sniffed.

"He...he said it wasn't safe for us to be together. He's worried others might come after him and he doesn't want me to get hurt."

Cora kicked her tail, easing toward Willa's tiny kayak. The large orca was close to twice the length of the red plastic hull under her and at least four times as thick. Her blunt nose rose out of the water.

"I'm okay, honest," Willa sniffed again. "At least, I will be. I always end up okay."

And alone.

Cora came closer, reaching towards her. Willa's heart filled with awe. The beautiful being was trying to comfort her. She reached out a hand, trembling with fear and reverence.

It felt like time stopped. The tips of her fingers met the wet nose, gliding up along the broad ridge. It was so soft and yet firm. A shiver ran down her spine.

Then Cora sank under the water, shifting back.

"Thanks, friend," she said when she resurfaced.

There was nothing left to say. She'd let it all out.

"I have to get back. Thank you for the talk. Thank you so much."

Cora's head bobbed. Willa raised her hand then dipped one side of her oar in the water, turning to leave.

It was a moment she'd never forget.

Isaac glared at the imbecile in front of him. Once they found whatever Nick Ryan had, he was getting rid of the worthless meat sack.

"Can you believe he was staying at the same motel as me?" Palmer asked, shaking his head.

He could. The man wouldn't have even spotted the truck if he hadn't pointed it out. "Let's just find him."

They'd been driving around the podunk town for hours with no sign of the man in question. Isaac'd left a nice little surprise in the truck should he decide to go back there.

"But where do we look?"

He ground his teeth. "He's with someone named Willa. If we can't find him, we just need to find her. He'll come running."

Palmer nodded. "I don't like going after women or children, but we can use her as bait."

Isaac had no such qualms but nodded anyway. He'd do what needed to be done.

They left town and drove back into Orca Cove, going straight to the downtown area. It seemed like everyone gathered there. There was apparently nothing else to do in Hicksville.

Parking at the marina, he scanned the crowd. Maybe he could find another loose-lipped local.

Spotting an older fisherman coming in from the docks, he smiled. He was alone and probably had been all day. People like that needed someone to talk to. And he probably knew everyone in town.

Pasting on a congenial smile, Isaac headed down to the docks. He could get him to talk. And if he couldn't, he'd find another way to get it out of him.

Walking back from the kayak rental, Willa traced the shoreline, thinking it'd be safer than walking through the center of town. If someone *was* trying to find her, they'd be focusing on populated places, right?

Coming up the hill to the marina, she saw two guys on the other side of the pier near the water. They had their backs to her, but their shoulders were tight and stiff as though they were angry. One shoved at something in front of him. She saw Solomon fly backward into the shallow water under the pier and all three of them disappeared under it.

She ran towards them, knowing full well it was the last thing Nick or Duke would have wanted her to do. But she couldn't stand by and let them hurt Solomon. He didn't have anything to do with this.

"Hey!" she hollered, running after them.

"No, Willa." Solomon raised his hands. His lip was split, and he was doubled over. He waved wildly, urging her not to come closer. "Run!"

She charged ahead instead, shoving the taller, thinner man away. She stood in front of Solomon, her hands out in front of her to hold them off.

"Leave him alone!" she shouted.

The man smiled in the most devilish, awful way. "You're Willa."

He lunged for her. Jumping back, she and Solomon tried fighting them off. Solomon pulled a knife from his waistband and swiped it out in front of himself.

"Get him," the taller man rolled his eyes at the burly guy and headed to Willa.

She tried to stay with Solomon, but she didn't have a weapon and they were getting backed into a corner under the pier. The larger man grabbed Solomon, twisting his wrist from behind, trapping his arms behind his back.

"Run, Willa, run!" Solomon shouted.

"Help!" she screamed, but the sound of the waves drowned out her cries. She couldn't get past the man approaching her.

"I don't want to hurt you." His expression turned sincere, but she'd already seen the devil in his eyes.

Reaching her, he tried to wrap her up, twisting her arms behind her, but she squirmed, twisted, and dropped to the water splashing at her ankles. Her left arm came up hard behind her, pinching at a bad angle. She stopped moving, afraid he would break it.

"That's a good girl," he said. "I'm not going to hurt you. We just need something your boyfriend has that belongs to our boss. He'll trade it for you and you'll go to him, no worse for wear. Promise. Come on."

He pushed her ahead, her arm still twisted behind her back. She gasped at the pain arcing up her arm. Maybe it was better to have a broken arm than go with them, though. She weighed her odds.

"Roy!" Solomon shouted, wildly contorting to get out of the other man's grip. "Roy, Roy, Roy!"

"What the hell is wrong with him?" The man holding her turned.

"No idea. I think he's looney." The other man struggled to keep the fisherman in his arms.

"Whatever. Get rid of him."

"Knock it off," the big guy shook Solomon. "She's not worth it. We're not gonna kill her, just use her for trade."

Solomon continued to bellow until a pelican swooped in under the pier and dive-bombed the man holding him.

"Christ!" The tall man pulled a gun with his other hand and aimed it at Solomon. "Do I have to do everything myself?"

Roy flapped his wings, hissing and hovering over Willa and her captor, but the shot rang out, hitting Solomon in his chest.

He fell back, hitting the water. Blood poured from the wound. Roy let out a grunting croak and hit the water near him, hissing and flapping his wings.

The other man backed away. "That bird is crazy!"

"Come on. Leave it." the man holding Willa pushed her forward.

The larger man tried to follow, but Roy attacked him. He screamed.

"I said leave it!" the tall, thin man said, shooting the larger man in the head in a fast double tap, then took a shot at the pelican, but it was beating its wings at the air haphazardly.

"Screw it." He resumed his path.

Willa stumbled forward. Tears sprang to her eyes for Solomon. He was such a sweet man.

"You said you weren't going to hurt anyone," she cried.

"I said I wasn't going to hurt you," he corrected her mildly and aimed her towards a boat docked at the smaller pleasure craft dock near the shoreline. "Get in."

She planted her feet, considering her best move. She searched the shoreline for someone, but at this vantage, the hill blocked the view of the cafe.

He stuck the gun into her ribcage. It was still warm.

"I'm not asking twice." He ground the nose of the gun deeper and they reached the dock. "I don't need you alive to use you as bait. He just has to see a photo of you."

Lifting a leg, she stepped into the aluminum jon boat, but before she could get her other leg in, he shoved her, sending her face-first into the bottom of the boat. He stepped in, sitting down on one of the seats. Willa tried to get her feet underneath her, but he pushed her down with the tip of the gun.

She froze, her insides tightened into a hard ball of fear.

The engine roared to life and they moved away from the shore.

He said nothing as they moved through the water.

There was no use trying to talk to the corrupt man. She took stock of herself instead. Moving slowly, she was able to get her arms underneath her. There was pain in the left one, but she didn't think it was broken. It hurt at the shoulder from being pulled out of the socket so roughly. And her face hurt where it had hit the bottom of the boat. She could feel the ache radiating down her neck.

Wait. That wasn't pain, it was more like pins and needles. The prickly sensation spread over her face, and she realized it was the water at the bottom of the boat.

She was healing from it!Rubbing her right hand in the water underneath her, she shimmied to move it up to her left shoulder.

"Lie still," the man commanded, shoving her with his shoe.

It would have to wait.

A few minutes later, they pulled to a stop. He ordered her up.

Gingerly pushing herself up, she grabbed her left shoulder, sliding her hand under her shirt to touch the skin. Pins and needles exploded across her shoulder. It was so intense, she hit her knees.

"Get out of the boat," he spoke louder, motioning her out of the boat with his gun.

Shoving to stand, Willa staggered out of the boat, her rain boots sliding on a muddy shoreline. She held onto a tree that stood nearby. They were all around the coast.

"Smile." He took a picture of her standing there, her face full of pain. "That'll send him running."

Stepping down from the boat, he lunged to grab her. She twisted to run, but the trees were too close together to get far. He pushed her against a tree and ran his hands over her. The fear that had been riding high in her chest shot even higher, sending shockwaves through her system. She cried out, her voice piercing the air, but there was no one to hear her.

His hands stopped at her back pocket, taking her phone and giving her a shove, sending her sprawling to the muddy ground.

He turned and got back into the boat. "I'll be back soon."

Willa jumped to her feet. They were on a small island out in the Hood Canal. It was one of many tiny islands scattered along the center of the fjord. The one they were on appeared to be only a few hundred feet wide and entirely full of trees. There was no building in sight.

"Go ahead." He gestured. "It's uninhabited. And unless you have gills, you can't swim anywhere."

He was right, it was too far to swim to the shoreline visible from here. She could see houses dotting the coast, but even if someone saw her, they wouldn't be able to make out her arms waving around. The distance was just too great.

Shoving the boat away from the muddy bank, he gave her a finger wave and motored back into the waves.

Sinking to her feet, she felt as though she had done everything wrong. And there was nothing she could do now. Or was there?

Anger fueling her, she struggled back up and searched along the tree line. Weaving through them, she scanned for anything to help her, but the brush was so thick she couldn't get more than a few feet in before she cut up her arms. It didn't take long to discover that he was right, there was nothing on the little chunk of land but trees.

Finding a larger spot of open land on the bank, she sat on it. Maybe someone would come by, and she could wave them down. She picked at a plant in the rocky m ud.

The man who took her had killed his partner and Solomon too. Maybe Nick was right, there were truly evil people in the world. He had certainly been a shining example of that. If this guy was just someone who worked for Dupree, how bad did *he* have to be? He had ordered Nick's last girlfriend killed.

For some reason, the pure atrocity of it hadn't sunk in until this moment. He'd sent her to get information from Nick and then killed her when Nick found out. It wasn't even her fault. She was just doing her job. She was on his side!

There was no way he would let Nick live. She was certain of that.

He'd draw him out, trying to get Willa. Nick was an honorable man. He was only staying away from her because he didn't want her in danger. He'd come, and then he'd be killed too. Once Dupree's man had what he wanted, he'd either kill her or leave her here to die.

Either way, she had to get off the island.

Her mind raced, trying to think of an option. Surging to her feet, she splashed into the water, her feet slipping in the mud. Maybe she could swim. Even if she didn't make it, it was better than dying at the hands of that man, or not trying.

Numbing cold spread up her legs. It was much colder without a wet suit. Even with her hands and feet exposed, the neoprene kept her from losing her body heat. She scanned the shoreline, not sure what she was trying to find until she saw it. Melissa officinalis, or lemon balm

.

A small patch was poking up from the sand. It grew wild in the Pacific Northwest, particularly in sandy soil. The brightly scented herb was good for depression and anxiety, but most importantly, it was also commonly used as a diaphoretic. Meaning it raised the body temperature and improved blood circulation.

Normally it wouldn't be able to raise body heat significantly enough to swim in icy water, but with Willa's new abilities enhancing plants' normal qualities, it might just be enough.

Gathering the herb, the tangy smell of lemon hit the air in a citrusy blast, already improving her mood. Taking it to the water, she rinsed it. It wasn't the cleanest water in the world, but with the current stakes and the foul man out there, she'd take the risk. Closing her eyes, she focused on the warming qualities of the herb. Her hands immediately tingled.

Swallowing audibly, she paused, hoping this was a good idea. Not giving herself the chance to change her mind, she shoved the handful in her mouth and chewed.

It started slowly. Heat spread from her heart, circling around her core. Speeding up, it increased her temperature until sweat prickled along her skin. Then it shot down her arms and legs, leaving her comfortable standing half in the water. Sinking in further, she felt the chill of the water, but it was manageable.

Now, all she had to do was keep up enough strength to get to the other side. It seemed so much farther now than it had before, but she had a lot of core strength. Hopefully it would get her there.

Taking a large breath, she plunged into the deep water, mimicking the breaststroke as best as she could remember. Swimming had never been her strong suit.

Duke had warned her not to overuse her energy when they went snorkeling, but she had to get past the waves. Once she was further from the island, it was easier to push forward.

Remembering what else he'd said, she tried to let herself float when she could, and take breaks. Otherwise, she'd tire too quickly.

Stopping to catch her breath, she noticed something in the water with her. The surface of the water was moving in her direction. Tamping down her anxiety, she pressed forward, even deeper into the icy-cold w aves.

She'd nearly made it a quarter of the way when she had to stop again, her strength starting to fade. The water in front of her rippled and she could see a dorsal fin tracing a lazy path towards her.

"Oh, please be Cora. Please be Cora," she chanted, searching the water for a second one, but there was only one. At this angle, she couldn't even tell if it was black. The water was murky under the overcast sky.

There was nothing to be done about it, so she faced it and treaded water the best she could.

The water parted and a great black head rose from the surface. Water sluiced down from the nose of a large orca. A familiar scar ran down from his eye.

"Percy," she breathed out. "I don't know if you're still mad at me, but I need to get back to Orca Cove. Can you help me?"

He dipped his head, swimming in a wide circle around her, and came up next to her. His side bumped into hers. She wrapped both hands around his dorsal fin and he took off

.

CHAPTER 25

"**S**omething's wrong," Nick said, meeting Duke at the door.

"What do you mean?" Duke asked, a brown paper bag from Gil's in his arms.

Nick pushed past him to get topside. "It's Willa."

Duke dropped the bag and followed him up. "Did she call you?"

"No, I just know." Nick took the stairs double-time and vaulted over the rope to the dock. Duke was close behind.

Racing along the dock, he bypassed the pier to get straight to the beach. Stopping, he scanned around him, his chest rising and falling rapidly. He tried to locate anything out of place.

"What happened?" Duke came to a stop next to him.

He pressed a hand to his chest. "It sounds crazy, but it started tingling. It happens when I'm with her. It's been going on for a bit, but just increased. It's almost painful now."

There!

Solomon's damned pelican was hopping around the base of the pier. He lunged forward, wading into the shallow water. Two bodies lay under the pier, close to the supports. But neither of them was Willa.

Spinning around, his eyes searched the shoreline.

Duke splashed down to Solomon, pulling him upright. "He's still alive!"

"But Willa's not here." Nick headed out in search of her.

"He might know where she is," Duke called out.

Stalling, he went back, standing over the other man in the water. He was dead, no question about it. "That's Palmer."

"Solomon, can you hear me?" Duke tapped his face.

"Willa," the older man croaked. "He took her."

"Where?" Nick knelt in the water. "Where'd he take her?"

His cell phone pinged. It was Willa. "Oh, thank God. Are you okay?"

"She will be if you cooperate."

His heart stopped.

The man's voice was sour and slick with malice. It poured into Nick, pooling in his stomach, twisting it into a spiked ball of fear. His vision grew fuzzy around the edges.

"If you touch a hair on her head-" he growled.

"You're in no position to threaten me," the man said. "You know what I want."

If he gave him the bag, Jimmy would have given his life for nothing. But if he could find Willa, or maybe even get the upper hand with this new man and put him away, he could still honor his sacrifice. His resolve swirled within him.

"I'm waiting."

Keeping the bag from Dupree's men and ensuring Dupree was convicted had been his main objective, but now the bag was a bargaining chip for Willa's life. Everything snapped back into focus. His priorities shifted in a single moment. "I have it. I'll meet you at my place in an hour."

At least that would get them out of town and away from any further destruction.

"You come alone, or she dies. Looking forward to meeting you in person, Nick Ryan," the voice said snidely, then clicked off.

His phone pinged. He'd sent an attachment. Opening it, Nick saw a photo of Willa. It had been cropped to remove landmarks, but he could see her dirt-smeared and tear-stained face. One of her hands was gripping her other shoulder tightly, as though in pain.

The ball of fear in his stomach tightened, becoming smaller, spinning. For a minute, he thought he was going to be sick.

"Show me," Duke ordered, taking the phone.

Nick shook his head. "I can't tell where he's holding her."

Nick closed his eyes, trying to find the source of the vibration in his chest, but it had lessened. Was that good? It probably wasn't good. He couldn't find any sort of direction from it.

"I'm going to need to borrow your truck." He pushed out of the water, going to get the bag.

"Hold on a second," Duke stopped him. "Let's talk this out. You said you'd meet him in an hour. We need Warner."

He shook his head. "He'll kill her."

"He might anyway," Duke said, stepping back when Nick growled at him. He lifted both hands, palms out. "This guy is bad news, right? You can't trust him."

It wasn't worth the risk.

"I'll do whatever he says right now. That's all I can do."

Mind made up, he went to get the bag from its hiding spot. He was pretty sure he could locate it.

When he got back to the pier, Duke had carried Solomon out of the water. He was lying on a thick chunk of grass, his flannel pressed into the wound at his chest. Blood was soaked into the shirt, staining the blue plaid.

Duke glanced up, his eyes landing on the bag. "Warner is on his way. Are you sure you want to do this?"

"What choice do I have?" He held out his hand for his keys, needing to get out before the chief arrived. He'd try to stop him.

Duke adjusted so he could get his keys and tossed them to him.

Pivoting, he made a beeline for the parking lot, but a large black man crested the hill and headed in their direction. Drawing the pistol he carried, Nick stood his ground.

"Wait." Duke raised his head. "That's Percy. He doesn't have anything to do with Willa."

"Willa's safe," Percy said, taking two more large strides closer. "Drop your weapon."

He lowered it. "What do you mean?"

"I brought her home. She's at the cafe now, getting warmed up."

Nick holstered his weapon and surged forward, pausing only long enough to snatch up the bag at his feet.

"How'd you find her?" Duke asked.

"Solomon sent Roy to find me," Nick heard Percy answer. He couldn't hear the rest of the exchange, already halfway up the ridge towards the cafe.

He busted through the cafe's back door, finding it empty. It was mid-afternoon. Zeroing in on the kitchen door, he slammed into it, tumbling through the doorway to see Willa sitting on a chair in the center of the room. A towel was wrapped around her, and she had a hot cup of tea in her hand. Nell stood in front of her, shocked at his entrance.

"Nick!" Willa tried to stand.

He dropped to his knees in front of Willa, his hands on her legs. Tears sprang to his eyes. Handing her tea to Nell, she leaned forward, wrapping her arms around him.

"Are you okay?" He stroked her hair, pulling her close. He never wanted to let her go. "Please say you're okay."

"I'm okay." She sniffed. "Honest. I'm going to be just fine."

He leaned away to look at her. "I'm so very sorry, Willa. I should never have put you in harm's way."

"He's a foul man." Willa's eyes hardened. "This was *not* your fault."

He disagreed, but that wasn't important. "How'd you get away?"

"He left me on an island." She pointed out over the water. "I tried to swim back, but it was so far."

"And freezing."

She worried her lip. "It was cold."

"And that man, Percy. He found you?"

"Yes," she said slowly. "He brought me here."

It seemed like she was leaving something out, but right now it didn't matter. He needed to put an end to all of this. If Dupree's man got the bag, he'd probably leave her alone. Probably.

He needed better than that.

"Oh, thank God." Duke came through the door behind him. He leaned against the doorway, giving her a warm smile. "Hey, Flower Child."

Willa stood, pushing past Nick to Duke. "Is that blood?"

He studied his hands. "It's Solomon's. He's in bad shape."

"He's not dead?" Her eyes flew open. She bolted past him and out the door, the blanket trailing behind her like a cape. They all followed behind.

"Wait!" Nick said, worried Dupree's guys could be out there.

Ignoring him, she knelt in the yard, the blanket falling from her shoulders, fluttering down to the lawn. She rummaged through the grass until she found a green weed and then ran to the ocean, working her hands together in front of her.

What the hell was she doing?

She stilled for a moment before hurrying back up the hill where Warner and several other people stood over Solomon, who had passed out. Percy was nowhere to be seen.

"The ambulance is on its way from Olympia," Warner said, hitching up his pants.

"It's just plantain," Willa mumbled, brushing a young officer's hands away from Solomon's chest. Squatting, she pressed the wet, wadded up weed to his wound and closed her eyes. Sighing, she leaned back on her heels. "I didn't take time to get yarrow from home. But it should do "

"Of all the idiotic things," Warner said, shooing her away. "Do you think you can heal a gunshot wound with a weed?"

"Hey," Solomon spoke, blinking. "What's going on?"

"How are you feeling?" She pushed forward, touching his arm.

"Okay." He frowned. "My chest tingles, like it's numb."

"It's going to be okay," she reassured him, patting him.

Nick watched the exchange in awe. She'd told him about her salves and stuff working better than before, but he never imagined it was like this.

She stood, stepping back to Nick and Duke. "Where's Percy?"

"He left," Duke said.

"He saved me. Brought me back to the cove."

"You mean, like..." Duke moved his hand like a fish through water.

Nick frowned, not understanding.

"It's the orcas," she started, glancing at Duke. He shrugged.

"What about the orcas?" Nick asked.

"Percy," she said, like it explained everything.

"I don't understand."

"He's an orca." She nodded. "Like Cora."

"What?" She wasn't making any sense.

"It's how he found me in the water. I held on while he brought me back."

His brain still struggled to follow. "Even if you could, the water would be freezing."

"Lemon balm." She grinned like a kid. "I found some to warm me. It's a diaphoretic."

"You made it stronger? With the vibration?" It started to make sense, but in an impossible, fantastical way.

"Exactly!"

"I had no idea you could do all of that," he said, stunned. "That's incredible."

"Thanks." She shot him a grin that warmed his soul. "But I was still getting too tired. Thankfully Solomon sent Roy and Percy found me."

Roy, the pelican. So, the old fisherman wasn't mentally impaired. He actually *had* been speaking to the pelican.

It sounded crazy, but if a man could be an orca, another man could hear a pelican. Right?

His smile faltered and he rubbed his forehead.

"What'd you say about the orcas?" Warner asked, catching a few of her words.

Willa tilted her head. She smiled sweetly. "I was talking to the orcas."

"The orcas?"

She nodded.

"Whatever." He shook his head and turned back to his officers.

"You're running out of time." Duke nudged Nick.

Shit. He'd nearly forgotten. He checked his watch. "I'd better go."

Willa grabbed him. His heart constricted. He didn't want to leave her, but he had to put an end to it.

"Don't be an idiot, man." Duke stopped him. "We have her. Why not bring Warner into it?"

"What if someone else gets hurt?" His fingers tightened into Willa's side, pulling her even closer.

"Isn't that his choice?"

He considered the chief. The man had a lot more resources than Nick did. If he could put away the creep who had kidnapped Willa, there'd be no chance he'd come back to get her. It might be worth the risk.

But he needed more time. He dialed Willa's number, raising a finger to his lips to keep the other two quiet.

"Hello? Having second thoughts about the girl?"

Never.

"I need another hour," he lied, judging by the sky just beginning to darken. "I had to find a ride to get my truck. The bag is stored somewhere else."

Even if his truck was being watched, the man would let Nick go, knowing he was getting the bag in exchange for Willa. Dupree's man had leverage, or so he thought. And it would give them more time, but more importantly, it would be after dusk with less visibility.

Silence. He glanced at the phone to make sure the man hadn't hung up.

"You'd better hope she lives that long," he said at last. "Don't be late."

The phone went dead.

"We need a plan," he said to Duke and Willa, already forming one in his head. "But we need the chief."

Their heads swiveled as one to find him, but the EMTs chose that moment to pull into the lot. They didn't have much time for waiting. Hopefully this wouldn't take long.

Nick pulled into his driveway a few minutes prior to their meeting time. Duke had given him a ride to go get his truck on the way here. It was his first time back since he'd discovered his new home's violation. The feeling of dread still burned in his mind. Getting out, he slammed the door, the duffel bag firmly in his grasp.

He didn't see anyone, but the man was probably already in place. That was okay, he had his own guy in place too. He didn't look over his shoulder, but he heard the leaves on the tree rub together in the wind and knew it was Duke up in his tree stand.

He'd left Willa at Nell's. She wasn't happy about it, but he couldn't have her be a part of this. If Dupree's man somehow got her back, he'd lose any advantage he had.

He was in love with her. There was nothing else to it.

Not that it changed anything. He remained irredeemable and didn't remotely deserve her. His foot scuffed on the gravel driveway.

A noise at his cabin door caught his attention. It was the same guy he'd seen with Palmer at the motel. He had a handgun trained on him.

The fact that the man had made himself comfortable in Nick's home really chafed.

"Where's Willa?" Nick let his anxiety be heard in his voice, keeping up the act.

"Drop your weapon." The tall man waved his gun. "Slowly."

With easy movements, he reached behind himself and pulled out his handgun. He'd hoped the man wouldn't know he'd come armed. Apparently, he wasn't an idiot.

"Toss it away," the tall man ordered.

Nick tossed it well out of reach.

"Now, where's Willa?" he asked. He only had to stand with the gun trained on him for a little while. Hopefully, they'd get what they needed.

He shook his head and tsked. "That's not how we're going to play this game. You give me that bag you're carrying. Then, and only then, if I'm feeling generous, I'll tell you where she is."

It was a good thing she'd gotten to safety. This man would have never given her up. She'd have been stuck on that island until a search party found her, probably several days later. Without fresh water, it might have been too late.

"I'm assuming your name's not James," Nick started.

He snorted. "It's Isaac. Not that it matters to you."

"You sure Dupree's worth all of this?"

"The money is worth all of this," Isaac clarified. "Dupree is simply a means to that end. Drop the bag and back up."

Nick dropped the bag and backed up, wanting to be as close to Duke as he could. He could feel his heart beat faster. Once Isaac had the bag, he wouldn't have any use for Nick.

Isaac came down the steps, his gun still trained on him. He unzipped the bag and rifled through it. "More evidence? I thought as much. Palmer wasn't sure."

All of this, just because one man had been following the cop who put his boss away and thought he saw something important.

"It's evidence that proves Dupree blackmailed the judge and the jurors on the Harrison case. I bet he paid you to do that."

If he could just get him talking...

He shrugged. "So, what if he did?"

"You're a bastard." He baited him.

Isaac tilted his head, a smile ghosting his lips. "Do you know what Dupree asked me to do?" Nick shook his head. Bingo.

"To threaten them, that's it. Maybe offer them money." His eyes widened slightly, sick madness sinking in. "I took care of it, but I also killed that judge's dog. I couldn't kill his wife, of course. It would have made the papers and they would have guessed he'd been coerced. It was the next best thing."

"You're deranged," Nick said, disgusted.

"And I just bet if they did a little research, they would have found quite a few pets missing from the jurors' homes as well. That didn't make any news either. The families were just happy their children weren't next," Isaac said coldly.

"You did that? I was wrong, you're a monster."

"I'm thorough, that's what I am. You want to call me a monster?" He waved his other hand. "It doesn't bother me. Dupree knows what I'm capable of, and that's why he hired me. I get in and get the job done. Just like that bag there. Palmer was here for weeks and couldn't do it. I've been here mere days."

"Dupree will go down even without that evidence."

"No, we've already ensured the rest of it has been disposed of. And with you and Haddish out of the way, this will be the end of it.""You had no intention of letting me live," Nick said. "You kidnapped Willa, possibly killed her, and killed Jimmy too.""I can't take the credit for Jimmy. Palmer took him down."

"What're you going to do with the bag?" Nick asked, stalling. Any time now, Duke.

"Oh, that's going to be fun. I'm going to burn it in your little cabin you've spent so much time on. Your cabin, your workshop, and you will be erased from this world. It's beautiful, don't you think? No evidence." Isaac raised both eyebrows conspiratorially. He grabbed the handles of the duffel bag and, taking a few steps back, he tossed it up the stairs where it slid onto the porch.

He really was an animal.

"You don't have to do this, Isaac." He tried to shuffle away, to put more space between them.

"You want to know the best part?" He came closer, almost close enough for Nick to try for the gun. "I'm the one who killed Rachel."

Anger exploded within him. Even though she had been on Dupree's payroll, it was still hard to bear. He'd cared for her. And it was his fault, his hotheadedness that had caused her death.

And that of his unborn child.

"Come on, into the house," Isaac directed with his gun. Isaac grabbed Nick's arm, his fingers pinching into his flesh. "This'll all be over soon."

Duke dropped down out of the tree, pointing his shotgun at Isaac.

Nick used Isaac's shock to pull away, just as the criminal tried to use him for cover. In the same motion Isaac whirled, pulling another gun. He now had one pointed towards each of them.

"You idiot, I said no one else," Isaac snarled, then changed tactics. "Do you want your sweet lady friend to die? Willa will starve to death, or maybe freeze, depending on how determined she is."

He had no idea.

"If you drop that gun, I'll tell you where she is," he went on, backing up towards the workshop. And the other tree line.

"Hold on there, big boy." Duke kept the barrel of the shotgun trained on him, taking a few steps to follow.

"I don't think so. Willa is currently at a friend's house, safe and sound," Nick said, smiling.

"You're bluffing. There's no way you were able to find her. And I'm not dumb enough to accidentally give away her location."

"No need," he said calmly.

"That's impossible."

Nick just shrugged. He didn't care if Isaac believed him.

Isaac's eyes searched the area. His eyes landed on Nick's truck in the drive. He grinned, lowering the pistol he'd directed at Nick. His hand slid into his pocket with the gun. Nick glanced behind him. Did he have backup too?

His truck blew up, the explosion knocking him off his feet.

He scrambled to stand. The noise around him sounded buffered. He was dizzy and he watched Isaac take off towards the trees with Duke running after him.

His house exploded next, sending Duke flying. Fire rushed through the house, spreading like Isaac had used an accelerant.

Luckily, Nick had been out of the range of the second kickback. He rushed forward, taking Duke's gun and running after Isaac, but his balance was still off and he floundered, watching the man gain a lead.

Gritting his teeth, he pushed forward, trying to catch up before he disappeared in the woods. Nick might never find him then.

Twisting around, Isaac shot at him. Nick dodged, raising the shotgun even though he was too far away for any accuracy.

Chief Warner and two other officers, Ronnie and Judy, stepped out of the tree line, guns trained on Isaac. "Drop your weapon."

"You can't take me in." Isaac laughed. He drew his other gun and aimed it at the officers, shifting it between the three.

Nick caught up with them, walking around Isaac to stand with the other officers. It was a good thing he hadn't taken a shot earlier. The officers could have gotten caught in friendly fire.

He knew Duke had said he'd fill in the chief after he dropped Nick off, but he'd begun to think backup wasn't coming.

"You'll never put me away for this," Isaac shouted.

"I think we already have." Duke came up from behind the man, pressing Nick's pistol into his back.

The officers moved in. Judy twisted Isaac's arm behind him. She slapped handcuffs on him and read him his rights while Ronnie kept a gun trained on him.

"Dupree will get me out of this," Isaac went on, then finally going still. They pushed him forward and he staggered, losing his footing. "It'll be thrown out, you'll see. The evidence is already up in flames."

He was right, the blaze shot high through Nick's front windows. The house was lost. And so was Jimmy's hard-won evidence. Not all of it, though. He'd stashed a few photos of Dupree and an audio tape up in the tree stand. He'd been counting on Isaac not knowing what all was supposed to be in the bag.

Duke walked back from the tree, having collected the parabolic mic and pictures from the tree stand. "But we have such a great confession, by your own account."

They'd planted it to get evidence on him as well, just in case he got away with the bag.

"Come on, now," Ronnie and Judy led him off to their waiting cop car in the hiking trail's parking lot.

Warner turned to face Nick and Duke, his hands going to his waist. "That nearly got out of hand. Do you have a death wish?"

"It was my mess to clean up." Nick set his jaw. He said to Duke, "Thanks, man."

Duke punched him in the shoulder. "Told ya you were one of us. Have you gotten that into your thick skull yet?"

Nick shifted on his feet. He didn't know what to say.

"Are you two going to be okay?" Warner asked, taking the mic and evidence from Duke. "I'm headed back to the station to call SPD to come and get Isaac and Reginald Palmer's body. I reckon their guns will close out a few cases in Seattle."

Nick's eyes followed the new evidence. It was all they had.

"Don't even think about it," the chief said. "It'll be safe and sound. You can pick it up before Larry Dupree's court hearing. Then, he'll be put away for good. Both of them will. By Isaac's hearing, he won't have anyone who could help him anyway."

Nick nodded, finally allowing someone else to take the burden of the evidence.

Warner disappeared into the trees.

"You gonna call her?" Duke rotated back to him.

Willa. His heart beat faster. Now that Isaac was in custody, Nick needed to hear her voice and make sure she was safe. In the back of his mind, he'd worried Isaac had backup that would get to her in the meantime.

"Dupree could still send someone else."

"Not tonight."

"Hello?" she answered on the first ring. "Did it go well?"

He released the breath he'd been holding. She was still okay. He'd been afraid for so long.

"Yes. They have Isaac, the man who took you, in custody."

"And the bag?"

"The chief has the evidence he needs to put him away." He'd explain the rest later.

"I'm proud of you," she said quietly, acknowledging how hard it must have been for him.

"I guess it's okay to let people help you now and then." He raised his head to see Duke grinning at him. He rolled his eyes. "What are you doing now?"

"Enjoying some of Nell's hot soup and a glass of kombucha."

"Would you like some company?" he asked. He needed to see her.

"I'd like that," she said. "We have some things to talk about."

CHAPTER 26

Willa downed the rest of her kombucha in one gulp, plunking the glass down in front of her resolutely. "I think I need another."

"Kombucha?" Nell asked, the corners of her mouth playing at a smile.

"He's coming over." Willa looked at her head-on. "It's not going to be easy."

"What do you want to happen?" Nell got up from her couch and crossed to her kitchen to refill the drink.

"I'm not even sure." Willa frowned. "There are too many things we need to discuss."

"Is it worth it?"

"Yeah, I think it is."

"Well, then." She handed her drink over. "Need anything else?""No, this'll do. Thanks, Nell."

It had been nice being with Nell again, even if the little studio apartment brought back many memories of Gary. They were happy memories.

She had warm soup in her stomach that made her feel all safe and loved, and the knowledge that she could help heal people. Nick and her town were now safe too. What more could she want in the world?Someone to share it with.

Sure, that'd be ideal, but she wasn't trying to just jump back into it. She needed to be certain he would be in it for real this time. And she was learning she'd been wrong about a few things. That was unsettling.

Before she knew it, there was a knock at the door. Nell opened it, letting in Nick and Duke.

"We'll leave you to it." Nell pushed a confused Duke out into the hall. "We'll be in the cafe if you need us."

Alone, Willa stared at Nick. He had dirt smudged on his face and a red mark on his cheek. She took a step forward. "Are you okay?"

He took a step forward as well. They both stopped.

He nodded, his eyes tracing over her. "I'm okay. Are you?"

She closed her eyes for a moment, fighting the urge to run to him.

"Of course." Self-conscious, she ran a hand over her hair. "I was just sitting here while you were out taking down a criminal."

"Yeah, but I'm used to that." He huffed in light laughter, but she didn't smile.

"You said you didn't want that life anymore."

"I don't. I'm trying to leave it." He took another step, then halted. "I meant about earlier. Are you okay? I just-"

His face crumpled and he rushed to her, taking her in his arms. "I'm so sorry that happened. You never should have been put in that position," he went on pouring, it all out as their familiar vibrations began between them.

"I'm okay, I swear." She loved the feeling of being in his arms and their connection but was still so confused. Was this just for right now? Would he change again?

"When I think of that man, that monstrosity of a human," his lips curled in disgust, "touching you, grabbing you, hurting you. It...breaks my heart."

Her eyebrows drew together, and she searched his face for truth.

"I'm not as frail as you think." She pulled back a few inches but didn't push his arms away. "I healed myself back there. I found a way back."

He gave her a soft smile. "You did. You're amazing."

"But you were right about one thing. Some people can't be trusted." She glanced down between them at her feet, surrounded by his larger ones. "It's not like I'm totally naive. I know there are bad people who do bad things, but I never thought they were completely evil. I thought they'd just had a hard road and needed some understanding. I've been able to distance myself emotionally when I needed to. I still felt guilty about it, but I did it."

She shook her head and continued. "And I could even see how someone like that, that man, could do wrong things if he was mistreated, if he only knew violence. You know, for money. But the look on his face? He enjoyed it. I've never seen that before. That pure malevolence. And if I was wrong about that, what else have I been wrong about?"

She'd been questioning everything.

"Don't do that," Nick gripped harder. "Don't change who you are. You're so perfectly kind and open to everyone. It's your gift."

"But you hate it when I take risks. You hate it that I leave my door unlocked while I'm not home."

"You shouldn't have to lock your door, though. That's the thing. If you and Orca Cove didn't have a threat hanging over your heads, you wouldn't have to." His mouth twisted down. "I brought that to you. And this doubt. You shouldn't have to change."

It was the conversation she'd been playing in her head for days now. But having him in front of her, seeing his distress... Suddenly, it seemed so simple.

"Maybe change isn't a bad thing. Maybe it's growth," she started. "Maybe I can try to understand people, but not feel like I'm giving up on them if I see they're beyond help. Maybe I don't need to feel like I have to fix...everyone. Or carry that guilt when I can't."

She inhaled slowly, letting the thought travel over her. It felt right, like a weight could lift off her if she just let go of it. She'd been in inner turmoil and it was the first right feeling she'd had in days.

"You felt like that?" His fingertips gripped the backs of her arms.

"I have, yes. It's part of my drive to heal people. To figure out what I can do to help."

"That's noble. It's what makes you *you*."

"Yes," she nodded. "But I can learn to direct it where I need to."

"And you don't have to feel like you need to fix me, then," he breathed out, relief in his eyes.

She blinked in confusion. "That's not what I meant. My kidnapping wasn't your fault. That man, and Dupree, are bad men. You're not."

"I disagree with that." He broke their connection, stepping aside. "Some people aren't redeemable. You saw that."

"And that's why you said you couldn't be with me. Because you thought you didn't deserve me."

He gave a tight nod. "I don't."

It made so much more sense now. He'd still been trying to protect her. He'd pretty much said as much, but in her pain, all she'd heard was that she wasn't good enough. That he didn't want her because she was so naive.

"Some people, maybe. Not you." She raised a hand towards him, wanting to touch him.

"Look what I brought to you." He ran his fingers through his hair, standing it on end. Pacing away, he made a circle around the small room.

"You did everything in your power to keep me safe. That shows what kind of person you are inside." She went up to him and placed a hand on his heart. The electricity that passed between them sprung up, more intense than usual. "You are kind, and caring, and you are worthy of love."

His breath caught in his throat and he shuddered, his eyes filling with tears. Blinking hard, he lifted his head, his eyes searching for truth. "But what if I'm not?"

She wrapped her arms around him, raising onto the balls of her feet to press their hearts together. His arms went around her waist, holding her to him. The electricity between them got stronger, spreading warmth through both of them. It was as strong as it had been when they made l ove.

"You are most certainly worth it. Because I love you." She didn't move and just let her heart pour as much love into his as she could. "I know it's early, but it's true."

He tightened his hold on her, his fingers digging in almost painfully. He buried his face in her hair. She could feel his chest heaving. "I love you too, Willa Daniels. But I'm afraid I shouldn't. I don't want to ruin your life."

"You've shown me love. When has love ever ruined anyone's life?"

"More of my past could come back to haunt me. Dupree could arrange to send another person."

"And you'll be there to protect me."

"It's too risky. You're too important." He nosed her hair.

"You don't get to make my decisions for me," she gently scolded. "Don't take that from me."

"Are you sure? Really sure?"

"Absolutely."

They stood there for a long time, holding onto each other. The vibrations started to lessen between them over time.

He pulled back suddenly, realization on his face. "I think that's it."

"What's it?"

"When you ran into me that night on the beach, you still had water and electricity on your skin. Or whatever power was tingling over you."

"Okay." She tried to follow him. "It made a connection between us somehow."

"Yes, but I don't think that's all there is to it. I think you were charged up, and somehow, you started to heal m e."

"Heal you?" She shook her head, still not understanding. He didn't have any health concerns then that she knew o f.

"Heal my heart." He took a deep breath. "I think that's why I was able to trust you at first, even when I thought I shouldn't, even though I eventually convinced myself that I couldn't. I'm still sorry about that."

"Wait, you think that's why you trust me? Do you think that's why you came to my apartment? You said later you shouldn't have, like you regretted it."

It still stung. And if he thought the only reason he trusted her was because of magical healing, it didn't have anything to do with her. Or worse yet, he thought he only loved her because of it.

He closed his eyes tightly. "I never should have said that. I'm so sorry. I didn't regret being with you. I regretted putting you in danger."

"Do you think you only trust me now because of this, though?" She laid her hand on his chest and felt the pleasant tingle between them.

"No!" He covered her hand with his, holding her to him. "That's not what I'm saying. I'm saying that you started to heal me, Willa. You struck a chord within my heart that

told me that I was worth loving. I just fought it for a long t
ime."

She nodded slowly.

"Because?" She needed to hear him say it.

"Because you fit me," he said simply.

"You said we were too different once," she argued, worried that he was in love with the idea of her. The promise
of someone to trust.

"We're not that different after all. And mostly, I was
using that as an excuse to distance myself, for your sake."
He tipped his head to one side. "We both try to take care
of people. I do that by protecting them. You do it by healing them. We both believe in service. You take such care
to keep in touch with others. Like bringing your friends
together on Gary's birthday. And that older lady with the
salve... You simply care for them, all the time. Even though
I'm a woodworker now, I still feel the need to take care of
people and to protect them. Just maybe in a different way
."

It made sense. And it felt right. He did know her.

Sometimes, when it was right, it was just easy. She smiled
up at him, her mind settled. Her heart opened further.
"You know. I think some of my drive to help others, espe-

cially my friends, was to fill a hole. I've been alone for a long time Even with my old partner, I was always the one giving. I didn't see it at the time, but I see it now. It didn't matter, honestly. But I've never really had a true partner, someone to share the load. I've never had anyone try to take care of me like you do."

"I want to, Willa. I want to protect you and give you happiness and all the things you deserve."

"I want that for both of us."

He captured her lips, kissing her gently. Pulling back, he kissed her forehead and pulled her into an embrace.

She could feel the energy zinging between them, still alive under the surface. She asked against his chest, "do you think our connection will stop, then, when you're healed?"

"No, I don't think so. I don't think anyone fully heals from something like that."

"I'm sorry you went through it."

"Me too, but it was worth it if my path brought me to you." He snuggled her into him. "Besides, I kind of like it."

She smiled, remembering how intense it had gotten when they were together at her place. She felt a blush creep up behind her ears. "The pulsing?"

He hummed in agreement.

"It certainly intensified things."

"That it did."

Pulling back, she looked up at him. "We can do this."

"I'm still scared of what may happen, but yes. If you're sure you're willing to take the risk, I think we can. Together. I learned today that I don't have to do everything alone."

"I'm glad you're learning that. And I am too." It was a risk for her heart as much as because of the danger. And she was ready for it. "Are you? In it, I mean. No more changing your mind like the tide."

"Oh, I see. You want a forever kind of promise?" He smiled, nipping her chin.

"Not exactly," she hedged. "But maybe a commitment to be all in, at least for now."

His ice-blue eyes pierced into her soul. "I'm ready for that. I'm ready for you."

It was all she needed to hear. All her questions and doubts and uncertainties...

Pushing up on her toes, she pressed her lips to his, showing him all the love she had.

When they came up for air, she took his hand. "We should probably go downstairs and let Nell come back into her apartment." She didn't want to let go of him though, not for a long time.

When they came through the stairway door, two heads swiveled in their direction. They immediately zeroed in on their intertwined hands. Nell smiled and Duke gave a short nod.

"Well, alright then." Duke stood, handing them a piece of paper.

Willa and Nick took it. It was an address.

"What's this?" Nick asked.

"You said Dupree could still send someone else." Duke shrugged. "And I don't think you're willing to leave Willa alone at this point."

"Not a chance."

Duke pressed his lips together to stifle a grin, but it was still evident. "Willa's place is out. They know who she is. Your place isn't an option."

"Why is your place not an option?" Willa spun to Nick. He'd told her that they found Isaac, but it sounded like there was more to it.

"He blew it up with some of the evidence," Nick answered, running his hand over her arm. "And my truck."

"Oh, no!" She knew how much he'd worked on the cabin. It was his home. "I'm so sorry."

"It's nothing I can't fix."

"Neither my place nor Nell's is large enough for two," Duke went on, ignoring them. He pointed to the paper in Nick's hand. "That's where you're going. You can stay there until the court date next week."

Willa read the paper. "Neah Bay."

"The tip of the world," Duke said. "At least in our little corner of it. "It's a small cottage, but you'll be safe.""Ho w'd you get this?" Willa asked.

"Let's just say someone owed me." Duke winked. "You can take my truck."

"Are you sure?" Nick asked Duke.

"Of course. Believe me, I wouldn't offer if I didn't mean it. I'm not that kinda guy."

"He really isn't." Nell gave him a side eye.

Duke threw Nick his keys. "Now get outta here."

CHAPTER 27

I t took them four hours to drive, non-stop, before
they arrived in Neah Bay, but it had given them
much-needed time to catch up on everything that had
happened. Nick shared more about his life in Seattle,
growing up and in the force. Willa told him all about her
youth and a back injury that had sent her to yoga class in the
first place.

He loved the drive. Over the last half hour, she'd drifted off to sleep, her head on his shoulder and his hand
wrapped in hers in her lap. He loved that even more.

Checking the address, he took a side road. They had to
be close now. He made another right, squinting in the dark
to read the sign on the drive. That was it. Serenity, it said.
Turning in, the cottage became visible in the headlights.

It wasn't on the bay side. Instead, it was tucked into the woods at the edge of the town. Trees surrounded the tiny house with bright yellow shutters.

Parking, he kissed the top of Willa's curly head. He gave her hand a gentle squeeze. "We're here."

Groggy, she blinked to clear her eyes. She peered at the dash. "What time is it?"

"Nearly one in the morning." He patted her leg. "Let's get you to bed."

They'd left right away, only stopping to grab Nick's meager supplies at Duke's boat and a small bag from Willa's. At least Duke had gotten him that change of clothes. Man, it was good to have friends.

The key was where Duke had said it would be. Letting them inside, Nick clicked on the lights. It was a cute little place, leather couches, lots of blankets. One bedroom.

"I'll take the couch." He headed over, setting his bag on the floor.

"Don't be silly." She came up behind him, leaning on his back. "I've seen your goods already."

"That's good." He rotated, taking her in his arms. "I probably would have slept on the floor in your room anyway. I'm not keen on letting you out of my sight."

"Shower first." She blinked again, trying to focus.

He nodded, leading her into the bedroom. He was anxious to wash the dirt and soot off after the fight with Isaac. The shower was a large walk-in with a separate soaker tub like Nick had. Used to have, before the fire. This one was way nicer though, with claw feet. He hoped to put this one to good use while they were there.

Willa peeled off her oversized cardigan, throwing it to the floor, and divested herself of all clothing in moments. She waved a hand. "Come on."

Stunned, he hurried to follow, tripping over his boots.

They quickly soaped up and dried off, only stopping once more to brush their teeth. Then Willa, completely nude, shuffled over to the bed and crawled under the covers, instantly rolling on her side and patting the sheets behind her. "Bed."

Following her orders, Nick slid in behind her. She snuggled into his arms and fell promptly back to sleep. Trying to ignore her butt where it was nestled perfectly into his groin, he buried his face in her hair, breathing in her clean lavender scent.

Peace settled in his heart in a way it hadn't in a long time and sleep overtook him as well.

The morning light played in Willa's hair. Nick was obsessed with how it lit up the copper strands. She rolled over to him, her bright green eyes blinking in the morning light. She tucked into his arm, her head snuggled into his chest.

"Good morning." He wrapped his arm around her.

"Mmm, morning." She laid a peck on his skin.

He'd gotten used to the constant light buzz of her skin. It was a pleasant reminder of their connection.

Her hand grazed over his chest, fingertips playing with the light hair there. He shifted, unable to ignore the nude leg she had thrown over his. Or how she traced her foot up and down his shin. His heartbeat ratcheted up, as did the buzzing from her skin. Did it intensify because she loved him, he thought in wonder?

She nuzzled in, kissing his chest, and ran her arm lower. He was unable to keep his mind off it any longer.

"Willa," he breathed, hoping she was truly awake.

"Yes?" she moved up, planting soft kisses along his jawline. Her hand drifted down.

"I don't have any protection with me." He felt himself jerk at the attention of her soft hands.

"That's okay." She swung up and out of bed, leaning over to grab her bag. She produced a condom. "I do."

He had to grip the sheets to keep from pulling her underneath him at that moment. "Are you sure? Are you ready?"

She nodded, a flirty smile playing about her lips. Slowly, she crawled back over him, kissing him lightly. Halting suddenly, she pulled back. "Sorry, I haven't brushed yet."

"I really don't care." He pulled her back down, crushing his mouth to hers, keeping his closed. She felt so goddamn good in his hands.

Pushing up, she wiggled down his legs and ran her soft fingers over him, rolling the condom on.

It was the most erotic thing he'd ever seen.

She then crawled on all fours back over him, centered herself over him and eased him in. Her face flushed with pleasure as she rocked back and forth, her hands on his chest. The sunlight beamed onto her face, highlighting her glorious naked breasts and her soft pink nipples.

Nope, he'd been wrong. This was the most erotic thing he'd ever seen.

His hands went to her waist, gripping her. His breath came quicker. The vibration intensified, pulsing through them. He'd never get used to that.

Her fingers curled into his chest and she leaned forward, her movements getting faster. She contracted around him, sending him over the edge with her. His entire body jerked in response.

Slowing, she sagged into him, rolling to one side. Her arm trailed boneless over him. "That was wonderful," she whispered.

"I agree." He struggled to catch his breath.

She stretched like a cat, curling back over him, and planting another kiss on his torso. "I need food."

He laughed, his arms wrapping around her. Gently, he swatted her beautiful, perfect butt. "Let's get dressed and I'll find you some."

"Nope, it still needs something," Nell screwed up her face as she thought. "Sun-dried tomatoes!"

Snapping her fingers, she whipped open her fridge in search of the jar. She left some in here last time, she knew it.

Ha, there! Her fingers curled around the required ingredient. She dumped the tomatoes onto her cutting board to chunk them up a bit.

Willa and Nick had gotten in just that morning after several days away. He'd collected a bag from Chief Warner and drove to Seattle for the criminal's court case, but he'd be back soon. Willa was with Duke today, but she was due to arrive within the hour. They all were. Hopefully Nick would make it in time.

Nell would have another dinner on the deck, but she was doing it right this time. She'd closed the restaurant, on a Friday night too. And no leftovers. She was making a giant pasta dish with shrimp and scallops. They were still marinating, but the pasta was nearly ready. She just had to finish the sauce and pop the pasta in.

"Kale," she said aloud, grabbing it from the fridge, along with a bowl and several other ingredients, ticking them off in her mind. "Walnuts, goat cheese, cranberries, and pepitas. You can never have too many nuts."

She massaged the kale with a little olive oil and salt, thinking about the table she was going to lay out on the back patio. The weather was officially hedging into summer territory, even though it wasn't quite here yet. It would be perfect outside and she probably wouldn't have to light the outdoor heaters.

Probably after dinner, she could talk Duke into building a bonfire on the beach, like he and Gary used to do. The thought sent a sliver of pain into her heart.

It still hurt, deeply. Tears bubbled up. She was trying to concentrate on the good memories, though, and sniffed back the tears. It had been a year now since he'd been laid to rest. Wasn't it supposed to get easier?

Washing her hands, she dumped the ingredients into the salad. Maybe that leftover quinoa and butternut squash, too. There was no rule that she couldn't add *any* leftovers. It wasn't the main dish. She gently mixed them in. Balsamic dressing and she was done. She wiped the rim, making it presentable, and left it to finish the sauce.

Tasting it, she considered its flavors. It needed more salt. She added in the sun-dried tomatoes, tasting yet again.

"People are arriving," Maggie said, bursting into the kitchen. "Can I help with anything?" "Cut up some of that sourdough, will you? And maybe butter and garlic it and toss it under the broiler?"

"Sure thing, Nell." She broke off to the other table to cut thick slabs of the bread.

"Hello!" Shelby rolled into the kitchen, her arms raised, a glass of wine in one hand. "The party can start now."

Nell laughed, eyeballing the wine. "I'm guessing Duke and Willa are here and he brought more wine."

"He did! And Nick called, he'll be here in minutes."

"Perfect, I'm just getting ready to add the shellfish." Nell picked it up and slid it in. "Now shoo. Get back outside, socialize, and leave me to the kitchen."

"Are you sure?" Maggie asked, sliding the garlic bread under the broiler. She stood, wiping her hands on a kitchen towel.

"Yep, this will be done at the same time. I'll finish up here and bring it all out on the tray. Go enjoy yourself. You're not working, remember?" She'd forgotten when she ordered her to fix the bread. Dang it, habits.

Maggie's head fell to one side, her hands on her hips. She pursed her lips in a sweet smile. "I'd help you any day. Work or not."

She'd lucked out the day Maggie walked into her life. Maggie probably thought it was the other way around, but it wasn't. Nell had needed her to calm her down when she thought she was in over her head. When Gary was away, anyway. Heck, half the customers were here just for Maggie's kind smile and generosity. She remembered everyone's names and what was going on in their lives, even the regular tourists.

"I'm good, promise." Nell waved her out.

This past year, Maggie had been the only person she could handle on a regular basis. It had been too hard with all of them together, going on as if nothing had changed.

But now things had changed. Their dynamic had.

The rest of the team had powers. She didn't, but she'd had Gary. As short-lived as it had been, she'd take their nineteen years together, sixteen of those years married, over any magical power any day.

Duke had recently taken a larger role within the group, even without Gary's prodding. And Willa was actually standing up for herself more. And they had fresh blood; Nick was joining their little circle.

It filled her with hope. Stirring the scallops in the sauce, she watched them change color. This was perfect. This was right. Gary would have wanted this. Another tear of happiness slid down her cheek.

Blissed out, that was how she felt. It might not last, but for now she'd take it.

Moving her spoon to her left hand, she scrubbed her right palm against her jeans. It was burning again. She'd better get that looked at. It kept burning when she was cooking. Maybe an old scar flaring up. She gave the sauce a final stir.

Perfect.

Heaping the pasta into the sauce, she tossed it with tongs to combine it, then loaded up the tray. Pasta, salad, garlic bread. With newfound joy in her heart, she lifted the tray and pushed through the swinging door.

"I'm sorry I'm so late," Nick said, coming up the outdoor deck steps. He spotted Willa immediately, setting his mind at ease.

Willa raced to him, rising to her toes to plant a kiss on him. "It's been too long."

"It's been one day." He laughed, but he didn't disagree.

"Exactly. How'd it go?"

He held her hands. "I still can't believe it. They used the evidence we gathered. Larry Dupree was put away for a very, very long time and when Isaac's trial happens, he will be to."

"It's over?"

"I believe so." He nodded. It was a great feeling. "I don't know why anyone would come after me now. Dupree's in a maximum-security prison for life. A few lifetimes. His people are probably already scattering."

"Finding new bosses," Duke hmphed.

"Maybe so, but I can't get everyone," Nick said resolutely. "I left that to the SPD."

"That was a good call." Duke slapped him on the shoulder. "You're better off here with us."

Nick grinned from ear to ear. He had new friends.

"So, he's in?" Willa looked back at everyone. They nodded.

"What's going on?" Nick asked curiously.

"Sit down, we have something to tell you," Willa said, pulling up a seat.

Duke poured him a glass of wine and she sat down. She told him more details about how she'd gotten her powers and that they had all gotten powers that night.

"So, you weren't the only one?" Nick said in awe. Here he'd thought it was just because Willa was special. It was amazing, especially the rain one. He would love having that one.

"Nope." Shelby wiggled her fingers mysteriously. "We all have skills."

"What'd I miss?" Nell said, carrying out a large tray full of delicious-smelling food. Nick's mouth watered. "Storytime?"

"Yes." Shelby nodded. "He's one of us now."

"Perfect." She set the tray down on a nearby table and plunked the pasta down in front of him.

"Nell doesn't have a power that we know of," Shelby said pointedly. "But she already has a superpower. She's the best cook in the world."

"You're just excited for the free food." Nell blew out a snort. "But I'll take it anyway. Dig in."

Nick heaped the creamy pasta onto his plate, nabbing a slice of garlic bread. The salad looked good, but it would have to wait; the pasta smelled too divine. Closing his mouth over the first bite, he moaned. "That's delicious."

"It better be." Nell winked. "Superpowers."

They all laughed, digging in.

"I forgot to tell you," Willa said, swallowing another bite. "I talked to Cora."

Duke paused, his fork halfway to his mouth. "You did? So she's like Percy."

She nodded, taking a long drink from her kombucha, then frowned. "Well, I'm not sure if she has a human form. She didn't answer so much, but she understood me. She pretty much confirmed that the thing in the water is what gave us our powers. They're protecting it, I think."

"So, the powers weren't from the orcas?" Maggie asked. "But they've been watching us."

"I think they might have been worried about us misusing the power. I assured her we're good people and she didn't have to worry. She doesn't know why it happened. Or at least, I couldn't ask a yes or no question for that."

"I don't think it was supposed to happen," Duke said. "Percy and I talked after he found us to let us know where you were. I pressed him about it, but he said it wasn't his secret to share. He helped you because Roy asked him to for Solomon and because we are all like them now."

"We don't shift from human to fish bodies." Shelby frowned.

"They're mammals." Maggie smiled. "Dolphins, remember?"

"Whatever." Shelby waved her fork, grabbing the salad.

"I tried to ask about the creature in the water, but he wouldn't talk about it," Duke said.

"When did this happen?" Nick asked. He didn't remember the conversation.

"You tore off to the cafe looking for Willa and I stayed with Solomon," Duke reminded him. "I did push a little to find out whether she, whatever she is, was dangerous. We're in and around the cove all the time. I don't want people getting hurt. Basically, he said that we weren't in any danger as long as we didn't go after her, but no one would like it if she had to defend herself. I get the feeling she's a badass with badass powers, but we're okay if we leave her alone."

"Well said," Shelby said.

"Thank you."

"It's a she," Maggie said in reverence. "Do you think she's a mermaid?"

"I don't think it's that simple," Duke went on. "A few days ago, I was able to catch up to that guy in Seattle."

"The scary guy?" Willa asked.

Nick didn't like the sound of that.

"Kinda." Duke shrugged. "Black leather jacket, Irish accent, Colin something. I saw him going into a pub near downtown Seattle. He was immensely curious when I asked him direct questions about Orca Cove. I didn't tell him about Percy, though. That didn't feel right. I only told him about us, and I didn't give him your names. I was just trying to find answers. As it was, I think he got more out of me than I did out of him."

"That's okay. We need to figure it out," Maggie assured him. "Maybe that's why we get so many orcas in the water. Maybe they're drawn to her or are her friends."

"Or maybe they're protecting her," Nick added, curious.

"Maybe, but why, if she's powerful?" Duke asked.

"It might be out of reverence. She's important to them," Nell said.

"It's possible," Duke went on. "Anyway, when I mentioned the term mermaid, Colin rolled his eyes, as though I didn't know what I was talking about."

"Maybe it's just the term that's wrong." Maggie said.

"I'm not sure, but from what I gathered, whatever's in the water is magical. And it's been there for a while. Colin didn't elaborate. It's possible it's an item, or the cove itself, and not necessarily *her*, whatever she is. But I told you I've heard stories about something unhuman in Seattle, some people doing business there."

"Like the Irish guy," Willa said.

"Yes, Colin definitely isn't normal." Duke shook his head. "After I told him the whole story, we worked out that it had something to do with the lightning. Apparently, sometimes powers can transfer. He didn't seem to know why or how it works, as though it isn't common, just that sometimes it happens."

"But our powers are linked to us. Like I'm a healer already and got healing abilities," Willa wondered.

"I think it supercharged us. Gave us something catered to what we could use."

"Wow," Maggie said.

"Do you think we should be worried about whatever this Colin guy is?" Nick asked. They didn't need another threat coming down on Orca Cove.

"No. I don't think so." Duke shook his head.

"Are you sure, though?" They had to be sure.

"I'm a good judge of character." Duke tilted his head. "I'm sure."

"So, it was only because we were in the water, right at that time, on that day?"

Duke nodded. "I think so."

"It actually is because of Gary, then." Nell's eyes filled with tears. "Not directly, of course. But we were there because of him. And you all got one last gift from him."

"Nell." Maggie reached for her across the table.

"No, I'm not sad." She sniffed. "I'm just so very glad you all did. I have more wonderful memories than anyone could ever hope for."

Nick reached for Willa's hand. He hoped they would have what Nell and Gary had. Just maybe longer to enjoy it. But like Nell, he'd be happy with whatever time they had. He'd cherish it.

Before long, they were all groaning at their full bellies. The conversation had grown lighter, happier.

It had been a great night, just incredible. He was getting to know everyone and felt included in the group, genuinely wanted. And for the first time in a long time, he trusted it

.

Shelby had taken to singing along with the music in the background again. She'd lifted her glass of wine in salute to Gary, dedicating a Green Day song to him. She belted out, "I hope you had the time of your life."

Nell was glassy-eyed, smiling contently at the tribute.

Eventually, they all stood to leave.

"This was wonderful. Everything... It's wonderful," Nick thanked Nell enthusiastically. Maybe he'd had too much to drink, too.

Shelby closed her eyes, smiling. She swayed and then caught herself on Maggie, nearly knocking them down. They collapsed into giggles.

"Maybe you should stay with me tonight," Nell suggested.

"Good idea." Shelby plopped down on a chair.

"We can stay at my place tonight," Willa slid up to Nick.

Even she seemed to be feeling the effects of their drinks. It must have been some strong kombucha. He'd have to get the brand from Nell. The woman he loved smiled up at him, wrapping her arms around him, and planting a soft, gooey kiss on him.

"Ewww. Get a room, you guys!" Shelby hollered, giggling.

"Maggie, are you okay to get home?" Nell asked, her eyes closing in a joyous smile.

Maggie nodded, her grin still plastered on her face from ear to ear. "I can walk."

"What a night. Just like old times, but different," Nell said.

"Yeah," Willa said, leaving him to hug Nell. "I just feel...blissed out."

"Blissed out." Nell opened her eyes and smiled, pleased. "That's the perfect word. I was thinking that earlier. *Blissed out.*"

Chuckling, Willa patted her back and spun to Nick, who was leaning against the wall, watching her happily. His heart soared.

She crossed over to him, taking his hand. But when they waved back at the crew, he noticed that there was only one bottle of empty wine on the table. That was odd, how were they tipsy if they'd all only had one glass? Come to think of it, Willa had only had one glass of kombucha.

He shrugged, unworried about it. Maybe it was a strong bottle. Besides, he had a gorgeous woman tugging him toward her house.

He had Willa, friends, and the knowledge that those who had put them in danger were behind bars. There was nothing more to worry about.

CHAPTER 28

The sound of the bell above the door made Willa look up. This time it was Nick's silhouette in the doorway of her yoga studio. They'd been nearly inseparable for the past month, not that she was complaining.

"Hubba hubba." Loris wagged her eyebrows.

"Hands off," Willa teased her. "This one's mine."

Straightening from the yoga blocks she was stacking, she opened the door and kissed him soundly.

"Still. I have eyes." The older woman sauntered out, giving Nick a wink.

Laughing, Willa pulled him in, moving out of the way for the others to leave. "Did you have a good day?"

"Very." He leaned back, his arms around her waist. "I got the interior stud walls up in the new house today. Duke helped me set them. It's a little bigger this time."

"Really?" she said, impressed. He'd been able to save his table saw, which had only needed to be adjusted, but he'd lost a lot of other things. It had taken him a while to build the workshop back up. "That's a lot for one day."

"I know, it's moving along fast. I'd like to take you over before dinner so you can see it."

"Absolutely!"

They were meeting the group at the cafe later, but they had a little time.

He played with the edge of her leggings. "I was kinda hoping when it's finished, you might want to move in with me. There."

They'd been at her place since they came back from Neah Bay, and she'd been worried about him moving back once his place was finished. A grin split her face. "Are you kidding? Of course, I would."

"It's just, I know you love the water. It's the source of your power. And you love seeing Cora and her baby."

"I do." It was true, but her heart was in the forest. "But I've always wanted to live in a cabin, surrounded by trees."

She'd be right next to her hiking trails and she'd have her guy with her. She reached behind her to intertwine her fingers with his.

He led her out of the studio, waiting for her to lock up. They got in his new truck, waiting by the curb. It wasn't as nice as his last one, but he'd assured her that he loved it, rust and all. They took off towards his land.

"Some parts of the house weren't entirely demolished. We were able to save the bathroom sink, but I'm getting you a new tub, like the one we had in the cottage in the woods."

"Neah Bay?" Her eyes lit up. She'd loved that tub, and the memories of being in it with him during those special days.

"Any word from the salvage shop on those planers?" He'd lost his two favorite ones, but they'd asked the owner to keep an eye out for any that came through.

"Not yet, but the last time I talked to him, he said he expected some to be coming in this week. He asked around. I can't believe he's going to the trouble for me."

"That's living in a small town for you."

"No kidding. No one in Seattle would have done that." He glanced at her. "The bed was in the workshop, but it got broken up pretty bad. I'm already working on a new one. It has a cool headboard I think you'll like. I hope. If you'd rather, we can use yours instead. One of them can go in the spare room."

"I'm sure it'll be wonderful." She tugged his hand into her lap.

"You know, back when I was refinishing the house, I was doing it for you, with you in mind." He kicked up the side of his mouth. "I didn't let myself realize it at the time, but part of me knew."

"That's so sweet." But it broke her heart too, all that work wasted. "I'm so sorry, Nick."

"It's okay." He shook his head. "This is even better. I'm building on that initial idea. You'll have a glorious bathroom, just like you deserve."

It was a good thing she'd gone ahead and gotten those stained glass lamps from Izzy at the boutique. They were beautiful. Wrought iron leaves wound up the base of them and the shades were different colors of greens.

They pulled into the driveway. The cabin stood like a promise for their future. It was in the same spot but he hadn't been kidding when he said that it was bigger. Even so, somehow it still had that cozy feeling, even without walls.

"First, I have something in the workshop I've been working on. It's a surprise."

Pulling herself away from the bones of the house, she followed him inside his shop.

There was a large, five-foot-long mermaid pieced together with driftwood lying on the workbench. He'd cut long strips of copper and overlaid them for hair. Tiny pieces of sea glass were embedded in the tail, catching the light. It resembled her, and it took her breath away.

"I thought it could go in the bathroom, hung over the bathtub. I'm making live-edge shelves for your products. I even ordered little blue glass jars. They'll be here next week. Do you like it?"

"It's stunning!" She could hardly pull her eyes away from it. Everywhere her eyes landed, she saw a new, beautiful detail. "Honestly, it's gorgeous."

"I made it after you, but also the mermaid in the water. Since we don't know what she looks like. Duke doesn't think she's a mermaid, but I know you like the thought."

"I do." She grinned.

"Besides, she brought us together. Literally. On the beach."

"That she did."

"Come on," he headed out, his blue eyes sparkling with excitement. "That's not all."

She hurried after him, crossing the yard to the house. The exterior walls were covered with Tyvek, so she had to step into the front porch to see inside. Thankfully the sun hadn't set yet and there was still light coming in from the windows.

The porch and the kitchen were the same, as was the living area. But when they got back to the bedrooms, he'd added a third one. A large master suite leading into a large private bath.

"This way." He spun back around and headed to one of the spare rooms.

The room was the same size but now had floor-to-ceiling windows all along one wall. She twirled to him. "You added more windows?"

"It's a studio for you to work in," he said, as excited as a little kid. "You can do yoga, or keep your products in here, whatever, and see the woods wherever you are in the room. And look."

He pointed. One of the windows wasn't a window at all, but a door with a little stoop. The door from the hall to the studio had a bolt lock on it. Slowly, it dawned on her. "You made it so I could leave products in here and leave the door to my studio unlocked."

"If you decide that's what you want to do."

It was the sweetest thing anyone had ever done for her. He knew how much she wanted to have things available for others and had even planned for it, but in a way that still kept her safe.

"It's beautiful. Thank you so much." She twirled around to kiss him, wrapping herself up in his arms.

"I love you, Willa Daniels."

He kissed her blindly, sending tingles from the tops of her ears to her toes. As wonderful as the new house was, *he* was her home, not the building. And as long as she was with him, she was right where she wanted to be.

From the Author

Thank you so much for your support. I hope you enjoyed Willa and Nick's story as much as I did. I've had Willa's story in my heart for a long time and am thrilled to finally being able to give life to it.

If you liked it, the nicest thing you can do is leave me a good review on Amazon, Bookbub, Goodreads, or wherever you review books.

Connect with me online:

Website: **jenflanaganbooks.com**

Follow me on Amazon

Facebook: **@jenflanaganbooks**

Instagram: **@jenflanagan_author**

Bookbub: **@jen_flanagan**

Join my reader group on Facebook: **Flanagan's Fanatics**

Please visit my website and subscribe to my newsletter at **jenflanaganbooks.com** for upcoming books, events, and free content.

About the Author

Jen Flanagan is a #1 Amazon best-selling author of enchanting magical romance and cozy mysteries, set in the mystical Olympic Peninsula. Her stories weave adventure, intriguing locations, and a touch of magic into tales of love and mystery, featuring richly drawn characters. A lover of travel, history, and culture, Jen offers readers a delightful escape into worlds where magic feels real.

Author of the Orca Cove and Detective Malone series, she also writes non-fiction as Willa Daniels. When not writing, she enjoys culinary magic, surrounded by good food, friends, coffee, and her beloved pups.

Connect with her at her website, Facebook group, or newsletter:

jenflanaganbooks.com

JEN FLANAGAN

WHAT'S NEXT?

Looking for more Orca Cove? Can't wait to find out what happens next? Turn the page for the first chapter of *Uncharted Waters*!

If I've piqued your interest in herbalism, look up *An Introduction to Herbalism,* by none other than Willa Daniels, my non-fiction penname. I've got several more non-fiction books in the works as part of The Natural Path series.

If mystery is more your thing, check out *The Detective Malone Series*, a non-paranormal, cozy detective mystery series.

UNCHARTED WATERS

CHAPTER 1

"Whadya say?" The fisherman scratched his balding head, weathered brown from decades of sun and wind. He pulled a handkerchief from his back pocket, wiped his nose, and then returned it. Its worn, dark blue ends stuck out and waved in the crisp morning air. "It's a fair price."

Emiliano shrugged, his eyes scanning the geoducks stacked in two old milk crates. It was a large haul, white ones, no less. They were the tastiest. Tourists were starting to make their way to their little cove off the Hood Canal due to the warming spring and the fact that it was Friday. He'd probably sell them all by dinner.

But they were overpriced.

He checked the time. Seven fifteen a.m. "Throw in the bucket of oysters, and you've got a deal."

The older man's eyes squinted, elongating the crow's feet at his eyes with the motion. He leaned back on his heels, his fists firmly set on his narrow waist. "How do you know I have oysters?"

"Come on, Solomon. You've always got oysters. Let's get on with it." It was an old game. They would go back and forth before Solomon would offer up oysters or mussels, but it was getting late. He had to get the rest of the fish he'd purchased iced and ready for the day's sale. Especially if he was going to stop over at the café first. He ran a hand over his dark, closely cropped, wavy hair, feeling his heartbeat quicken in anticipation.

Solomon huffed. "You're in a mood today. I was going to give the oysters to Roy. Had to help me fight off the harbor seals for the geoducks, you know? He's earned a few "

Roy, he'd come to find out, was the fisherman's pet pelican. Emiliano bit back the sigh on his lips. He was being a jerk. It was just nerves; he should get over it. "How about this? I'll split the oysters with Roy for his service, and tomorrow morning, you give me first dibs on your haul."

Solomon narrowed his eyes. "I always give you first dibs."

"No, you don't."

"Yeah, I do. I don't go up the canal until after I stop here. Same's every morning."

Emiliano tilted his head. "I've seen you give that pelican the biggest, brightest fish in your net."

"Aw." He kicked at a pebble that had made its way onto the dock. "Roy's my partner. I've gotta give him his fair share."

He almost felt bad for the guy...but it was an animal. He'd seen the ungainly bird pick up old, discarded burritos in the park. It would eat anything resembling food, and unfortunately, the uptick in tourists left out quite a bit. "I bet you can set aside another large fish for him. But I get the biggest."

"Whatever the catch is?"

He nodded.

The fisherman leaned in conspiratorially. "I'll stash a few in the hold so he doesn't see them."

"Works for me." He didn't care about the fish, but he had to give him an out for the light bucket of oysters, or else the other fisherfolk would start shorting him on their hauls.

A pelican landed on a post a few yards down the dock and let out a hiss. Solomon jumped, his eyes wide, then let out a cackle of laughter. He slapped his knee. "You drive a hard bargain, Mr. Gil. It's a deal. I'll be back with your oysters."

Turning, he made his way down the dock to his boat, his knees jutting out as he walked down the pier. He whistled, and the pelican flew after him. "Come on, Roy. You can pick out your half. Don't you worry. No, sir. He's not taking your fish."

Shaking his head, Emiliano hefted the containers of giant clams and headed through the back doors of Gil's Market and Marina. It was his dad's business and their second home, but he'd helped run it for as long as he could remember; a little boy standing on a stool to man the cash register. He'd been barely strong enough to press the lever on the old drawer. That feeling of pride, helping his pop with the store, was one of two things he knew with complete clarity.

This is what he was meant to do, provide for the townspeople of Orca Cove.

"Do you want me to set these out?" Tommy, one of their newest hires and the youngest on the crew, met him near the fish market. His apron was still clean, with no tears in the fabric, his name freshly embroidered in bright blue lettering.

"Not yet." Emiliano set the crate down and pushed it under the counter. "Nell's been wanting geoducks for her menu. I'm going to see how many she wants first. Throw some ice on them, though."

Tommy nodded, disappearing.

Wiping his hands on his own worn apron, Emiliano's eyes flashed to The Wild Café across the picnic area separating their businesses. He paused, lifting his hands, and headed to the bathroom.

What had he been thinking? He'd been handling fish all morning. No way was he showing up with fish scales and muck on them. Using the brush that sat in a wire basket on the counter, he scrubbed his nails. Rinsing them, he blew out the breath he'd been holding, letting the stainless-steel rim take his weight.

He looked in the mirror, searching his dark-brown eyes for the courage to say what he wanted to say.

Was it too soon? What would she think? His brow drew together in worry.

It was her birthday, and she'd probably be in a good mood. The fact gave him courage because it was another thing he knew without a doubt. He'd been in love with Nell Fitzgibbons since he could remember.

Humming, Nell swayed happily as she stirred a large stain-less-steel bowl in her commercial kitchen at The Wild Café. The food was prepped for the day, and she had enough time to make a batch of cookies. She would put them on the dessert menu, and they'd sell well to the brunch crowd, but they were really for later, after the dinner crowd left and she opened the back deck for her f riends.

Her friends.

They were still in a strange place. Nearly inseparable, the six of them used to share everything, but things had changed when they'd lost one person and gained another. It still hurt.

Things were starting to feel more like old times, but in some ways, they would never be the same. Maybe they were finding a new normal. Either way, it was complicated, and this wasn't how she'd imagined spending the day.

And to top it off, she was worried about a customer who'd fallen ill after last night's meal. She'd always been fastidious about cleanliness, but now even more so. She'd scrubbed everything down in the kitchen with bleach, just in case.

It was all weighing on her mind, but she was trying to make the best of it. It was her birthday, after all, and cookies were hands down her favorite dessert. She'd made them just for herself.

Cake was fine, but it was fussy and not worth the extra effort today. *Flavor*, however, was *always* worth the time.

Flowers.

Her mind pinged through things yet to be done for the night's celebration, carefully avoiding anything business-related. Bills, marketing, and general office work had no place on a day like today.

She barely knew what she was doing in that realm, anyway. It made her feel lacking. No, she didn't need any more of that. Not today.

She'd ask Willa if she could gather some wild rhododendrons for the night's festivities. Her herbalist friend would be happy to wander the woods to find some. Maggie, her best waitress and friend, could put them in milk jugs for the table. Simple and pretty.

Her mind drifted to ingredients, eyes unfocusing as she created the recipe in her head. Black sesame paste. Setting her bowl down, she retrieved a jar from the cooler. After giving the bowl a playful spin, she drizzled the paste into the dough, watching it draw a spiral out from the center. Heat blossomed in her hand. It had been doing that. It was probably nerve damage from an old burn acting up. She'd certainly earned enough of them over the years.

"Are you playing with your food?"

Nell squealed, jumping in the air, and the bowl tipped, whirling haphazardly in wide circles. She fumbled the jar, finally catching it between both hands, but the dark paste spilled onto her fingers. A strong arm reached around her to steady the bowl, and a low chuckle rumbled within his chest.

"Emiliano! You scared the bejeezus out of me." She sat the jar down and wiped her hands on a nearby towel.

"Sorry, I didn't mean to startle you. You were zoned out." His eyes crinkled at the corners in amusement. "Again."

"I was tasting through the flavors." She lifted her shoulders as though that explained it all.

"In your head?"

She nodded, then stopped, realizing how it sounded. "That's weird, isn't it?"

"Not at all." His head gave a sharp shake. "That's what makes you an amazing chef. We're lucky to have you in town. You bring in half our returning tourists."

"Aw, thanks, Emiliano." The sentiment seeped into her heart, warming it. "Although it's most likely the weather, the view, the amenities, and possibly even the o rcas."

Visitors had the unusual perk of viewing the graceful marine animals in their little cove off the fjord nearly year-round. It added a little magic to the air.

Then again, it wasn't the only thing that did.

"Oh, them, they're just an attraction. You're the main course."

A laugh bubbled up and out of her unexpectedly. She lifted a hand to cover it. The younger man wasn't typically this playful. And she'd known him since he was a toddler.

"You know it." She smirked and did a little jazzy wiggle, playing along. "Eat your heart out, Jamie Oliver."

He leaned against the countertop in a relaxed pose, watching her.

"What brings you in this morning?" she went on, wiping up the spilled paste.

"Just got a crate of white geoducks. Want any?"

The perfect addition to her birthday meal. Her eyes opened wide. "I love geoducks."

"I remember. How many do you want?"

"I'll take ten to twelve. The weather is bringing in the tourists. I'll throw them on the menu tonight." She'd leave some as sashimi; the rest would be sautéed and added to a pasta dish with fresh chanterelles.

"You got it."

"Just give me a little while to finish up here, figure out what else I'll need, and I'll be over to pick them up."

Even though she had regular deliveries from Seattle, most of her local produce and meats were from Gil's Market and Marina.

He nodded, then pointed to the bowl. "What is it?"

"Cookies." She lifted her head proudly.

"Birthday cookies?"

She nodded. "How'd you know it was my birthday?"

"Good memory." He tapped his temple. "What's in them? No way they're just regular ol' chocolate."

"It's not chocolate at all; it's rye flour. Half rye, half wheat."

"No chocolate?" His eyebrows went up. "No way."

"Well, of course, there's going to be chocolate." She rolled her eyes. "I'm adding dark-chocolate chunks later."

"What's that?" He reached out a finger towards the spilled paste. "It looks like chocolate sauce."

"Black sesame paste. I'll sprinkle on black sesame seeds just before I bake them."

"That sounds interesting." Reaching out, he took a tasting spoon from the container on her counter and hovered over the bowl. "May I?"

She nodded.

After running the tip through the dough and unmixed black paste, Emiliano lifted it to his mouth and closed his lips over it. His eyes closed as well, his unfairly long eyelashes lying against his perfect skin, and his brows drew together in thought.

Nell knew exactly what it would taste like. It would be rich from the eggs and butter, the rye would impart a spicy, earthy note, and the black tahini paste would pack a mellow, nutty punch with an exotic element. She could see his mouth working over the food, tasting all the ingredients with fervor.

Without meaning to, she leaned forward as though a magnet was pulling her towards the man so fully appreciating her cooking. A stirring she hadn't felt in a while bloomed within her.

That was new.

She hadn't noticed how close he was until that moment, and heat spread across her cheeks.

"That's delicious," he said, opening his eyes wide with admiration.

Nell's gaze met his, ratcheting the rising emotions even higher when he flicked his tongue out to capture dough from his lower lip.

"And." Her eyes unfocused again. "Nori. Shredded, dried nori sprinkled on at the end to balance the sweetness. Instead of flake salt."

"Seaweed on cookies?" He narrowed his eyes in thought. The dark pupils were still connected with hers, and he bent forward, shortening the space between them. When her breath caught in her throat and her heart raced, he asked, "Are you sure?"

Metal clinked against metal, jarring her out of her stupor, and her head whipped to see he had disposed of his spoon into the used-tasting-spoon container on her counter. She glanced back up at him and took an unsteady step back.

"No." She shook her head. "I mean, yes. I won't use too much. It'll be good. Trust me."

The words came out in a rush alongside her emotions. By the time she had composed herself, he was standing at the door.

"I always have." His hand rested against the doorjamb. "Thanks for the taste."

"No problem," she breathed out. What was wrong with her? Was it because she'd had a yearlong dry spell? She'd better get a hold of herself. "See you later."

He inclined his head and turned to go, but stopped short.

"Happy birthday, Nell." His words were soft, like peach fuzz.

"Thanks." She tried to smile, but her thoughts were still unfocused.

After he left, she grabbed her towel and scrubbed her face, trying to wipe the fog away.

It was all in her head. Emiliano hadn't been coming on to her. Heat bloomed across her again, but this time, it was out of embarrassment. He didn't need her swooning over him. He was a sweet kid, giving her a compliment. Well, technically, a man now. Barely so.

When had that happened?

She sighed dramatically. Here she was, newly thirty-five, and he was only twenty-eight.

Seven years. It was a large gap.

She still remembered him in middle school, when she was dating Gary. She shuddered. Yeah, no. What did she think she was, some sort of creepy cougar? They had enough of them in the mountain side of town—the four-legged kind. She shook her head. Not gonna happen.

It had just been a while. Too long. She'd get herself together and shake it off.

Throwing the towel in the laundry bin, she picked up the bowl and stirred the black paste into the batter. Smooth, sure strokes to barely blend it in. It would be streaky and leave a chewy bite of oily nut butter.

Yes, this was better. Her brain was back on cooking.

Standing on tiptoe, she reached the Ghirardelli dark-chocolate chunks with one hand and a pinch of sea salt in the other. Shaking a generous amount of the rich bits into the bowl and releasing the spice, the burning sensation in her palm returned. She flexed her hand to ease the feeling, pausing to taste the dough. Perfect. Exactly as she had imagined. She smiled, watching her spoon clink in the jar next to Emiliano's. It wasn't crazy that she was reacting to a man. Maybe she was ready to start thinking about dating again.

Her hand stopped as Gary's face popped back, so fresh, into her mind. Younger Gary, the one she'd fallen in love with in middle school. Tears sprung to her eyes.

She'd loved him since he told her that her backpack was unzipped, spilling pencils, erasers, and snacks all over the sidewalk in front of Orca Cove Middle School. He had knelt and helped her gather her things when the other kids giggled at her misfortune.

She smiled at the memory, then at the million more that zipped through her mind. The two of them opening the shop together, just a booth on the beach before they had enough money to buy the old storefront. And later, when they got married out on the beach and then again when they renovated and made the space above the shop their permanent home.

It didn't seem so permanent now.

Bittersweet. The word was true on all fronts. Bitter and sweet on the tongue and the heart. Bitter from the pain and lost dreams. Sweet from the beauty that had thrived within those dreams. She didn't regret any of it, but still...it stung like a freshly wounded sore, seeping and throbbing.

Nell kept her hands busy, finding her large cookie scoop and sheet pans. With a practiced hand, she scooped ball after ball of beautifully hued dough onto the oiled stainless steel.

Her plans for the future had been demolished. Was she allowed to think about another path now? Could she ever find love again? Did she even deserve it? She'd had better than most. And it had come so easily. Part of it, anyway.

Nell reached for the black sesame seeds, scattering them over the beautiful, rich mahogany-black streaked mounds. Next was the nori, as her hands lightly crushed the bright green shredded strands.

Oddly enough, it was the camaraderie she missed the most. Someone to run through the daily plans and problems with. A partner to share her life. Her friends were helping, but it wasn't the same.

And she missed the look from a man. The one that stirred her deep inside. So much so that she was manufacturing it from the shop kid next door. The thought lurched in her stomach.

Maybe it wasn't the end of love for her. She was only thirty-five, after all. It wasn't ancient. Ignoring the spikes of burning that now sprang into her palms, she scattered slivers of nori across the top of the cookies. The green and black were vibrant against the varying chestnut shades.

Perfect.

She glanced up at the clock. It was still early. She'd have time to take a small box of them over to Emiliano when she went to pick up the geoducks. They'd be to thank him for thinking of her and remembering her birthday. Nothing more, she told herself.

He'd agree the nori was a good touch.

Smiling in satisfaction and hope for the future, she finished garnishing the cookies and slid them into the oven to bake.

Jen Flanagan Fiction Books
Orca Cove Series:

Saltwater Cures

Uncharted Waters

Star Crossed

Red Skies (coming 2026)

Rogue Wave (coming 2026)

Books in the Detective Malone Series:

Bad Company

Here I Go Again

Under Pressure

Willa Daniels Non-Fiction Books
Stand-alone books:

The Art of Living Seasonally

The Natural Path Series:

An Introduction to Herbalism

An Introduction to Soap Making

An Introduction to Sourdough (coming 2025)

Home and Cleaning Solutions (coming 2026)

Body and Skincare Solutions (coming 2027)

Made in the USA
Columbia, SC
03 May 2025

57363375R10267